SOMETHING BORROWED, SOMETHING BLUE

Elaine Barbieri
"Something Old"

"Elaine Barbieri charms! Her characters will steal your heart!"

—*Literary Times* on *Dangerous Virtues: Honesty*

Constance O'Banyon
"Something New"

"Constance O'Banyon is dynamic. Wonderful characters. One of the best writers of romantic adventure."

—*Romantic Times* on *Desert Song*

Evelyn Rogers
"Something Borrowed"

"Best selling author Evelyn Rogers proves once again that her talent, creativity, and love of romance will always produce great keepers for readers!"

—*Reader to Reader* on *Golden Man*

Bobbi Smith
"Something Blue"

"Ms. Smith is an author of many talents. . . . She creates characters that one will remember for some time to come."

—*Romantic Times* on *Outlaw's Lady*

Other anthologies from *Leisure* and *Love Spell*:

SOMETHING BORROWED, SOMETHING BLUE

Elaine Barbieri,
Constance O'Banyon,
Evelyn Rogers,
Bobbi Smith

LEISURE BOOKS   NEW YORK CITY

A LEISURE BOOK®

June 2000

Published by

Dorchester Publishing Co., Inc.
276 Fifth Avenue
New York, NY 10001

ISBN 0-8439-4725-X

The name "Leisure Books" and the stylized "L" with design are trademarks of Dorchester Publishing Co., Inc.

Printed in the United States of America.

SOMETHING OLD

Elaine Barbieri

To my dear friends,
Constance O'Banyon, Evelyn Rogers and Bobbi Smith,
and to the adventures we share.

Chapter One

"Marcy! Wait a minute! I have something to tell you!"

Marcy Tanner turned toward the sound of the shouted summons. She frowned at the sight of the flushed young woman running toward her across Harper's rutted main street. Hannah Worth was a gossip. Judging from the shrill tone of her voice and the excitement flushing her round face, Hannah had some news to impart that didn't bode well for someone. From the barely concealed glee in Hannah's eyes, Marcy suspected that she was that someone.

Breathless, Hannah halted beside her and gasped, "Tierney Walsh is back in town! You remember him, don't you, Marcy?"

The early-morning traffic on the narrow, sunlit thoroughfare seemed to freeze into motionlessness as Hannah's question rebounded in Marcy's mind.

Did she remember Tierney?

Marcy struggled against emotion as Tierney's image assaulted her senses as clearly as if he were standing before her. His hair was the color of sunshine, and his eyes were the color of molten silver. She remembered that, despite his youth, he was so tall and his shoulders so broad that he had somehow managed to block everything from view when she was in his arms. And when he said he loved her, the words were all the more precious because she knew that the gentleness in his deep voice was reserved for her alone.

How she had loved him!

Marcy strained for composure as the image in her mind changed. She saw Tierney's eyes glaring with hatred. She heard his voice vibrating with rage. Accompanying the altered image was the anguished memory of Tierney standing over Josh's motionless form, his gun still smoking while blood drained from the wound in her brother's chest.

She had loved Tierney with all the fervor of her young heart—but, in the end, love was not enough.

Tierney had had no reason to stay in town when she told him it was over between them. When he left, he did not even bother to say good-bye.

Did she remember Tierney?

Hannah was waiting with avid anticipation for her answer.

Marcy responded succinctly. "Tierney *who*?"

Hannah was still standing open-mouthed behind her when Marcy continued on down the street.

The mocking laughter and the rush of shuffling feet sounded all too familiar as Tierney approached the entrance to the Last Stand Saloon. Forewarned by the sounds, he stepped back in time to avoid being struck by the fellow who careened out through the swinging doors to land on the dusty street with a heavy thud.

Harper, Texas—where nothing had really changed in seven years.

Stepping down onto the street, Tierney helped the ill-kempt, unshaven bag of bones that had once been a robust wrangler back up onto the boardwalk. He noted the fellow's surprise at the courtesy. He saw the moment when surprise turned to shock.

"Say, you're Tierney Walsh! What brings you back to Harper after all these years, boy?"

Tierney perused the face of the old man standing in front of him. Sandy Malone's smile was genuine, unlike the few others offered to him since his return. It didn't miss his notice that Sandy had planted his feet squarely in an attempt to control his swaying, but the effort was useless. Sandy was drunk, just like he always was. He had been thrown out of the Last Stand, just as he would probably be thrown out of the Watering Hole or the Silver Slipper at some point later in the day. That much hadn't changed in the seven years since Tierney left, either. He wondered who Sandy spent the nights drinking with, now that Pa was dead.

Tierney extended his hand. "Hello, Sandy. Good to see you again."

Sandy's pleasure as he accepted and shook his hand was obvious, and a familiar ache stirred inside Tierney. Drunks weren't accustomed to common courtesy in Harper. Neither were their sons.

Sandy's rheumy eyes watered unexpectedly as he released Tierney's hand. "Your pa was a good man, Tierney."

"Yeah."

"It wasn't his fault he lost the ranch after your ma died, you know. He kind of lost track of things when everythin' started fallin' apart. But you was a good son to him, takin' care of him like you did and sendin' him money all them years you was away. He was proud of you."

"Yeah."

"It ain't been the same around here since your pa died. I miss him."

Tierney did not reply.

Appearing confused by Tierney's silence, Sandy paused a moment, then shrugged his bony shoulders. "Well, I guess I'll be goin'." He added with a spark of hopefulness, "You know where my shack is. Stop by for a drink if you ain't got nothin' to do. We'll talk about old times." Not waiting for a response, Sandy lifted a hand in shaky farewell.

Watching Sandy's unsteady progress down

the street, Tierney felt a familiar knot twist tightly inside him. Old times. He couldn't count the times his pa had walked home with that same swaying gait. Nor could he count the times his pa hadn't made it to their front door and ended up sleeping in the street.

The town drunk was the town joke, but Tierney had made sure no one laughed at his pa when he was around. Skinned knuckles and bloody noses had been a way of life for him while he was growing up. Sometimes he won, and sometimes he lost, but that hadn't stopped him from wading in with fists swinging, with a ferocious anger, and with a need to hurt someone—anyone—the way he had been hurt.

Tierney paused at that thought. There was only one person he hadn't wanted to hurt . . . and he had ended up hurting her worst of all.

Tierney's broad shoulders twitched as he forced old memories away and unconsciously drew himself up to his full height. The past was dead and gone, like his pa. The past might temporarily serve him well while he was back in Harper, but he was done with lamenting it.

Tierney scanned his surroundings with a practiced eye. The unpaved main street was coming to life with the business of morning and a familiarity the years had not eroded. He saw Joe Carter, his white apron wrapped around a middle that looked twenty pounds heavier, as he swept the walk in front of the general store. He turned toward Ben Parkins's dairy wagon when it rumbled loudly into view on its way to the cafe on the corner. His lips twisted into a tight smile at the sight of Penelope Jarrett walking briskly toward the bank with her no-nonsense stride. The old witch's schedule of weekly deposits hadn't changed. Nor had her sour expression.

Tierney eyed the several unidentifiable figures moving between the peeling, false-fronted, establishments that comprised Harper's business district. He glanced at a woman softly scolding a child as they made their way down the street. He briefly studied the two indifferent cowpokes sauntering toward the livery stable. His gaze lingered for a moment on the well-dressed fellow who emerged from the town's only restaurant and turned toward the barbershop.

Tierney's assessing gaze halted abruptly on the sheriff's office. He remembered it well.

Tierney smiled grimly. No, nothing much had changed in Harper in the seven years he had been away.

But that didn't mean nothing ever would.

"You look beautiful, Marcy."

Her encounter with Hannah Worth a few minutes earlier still vivid in her mind, Marcy was hardly aware of the dressmaker's earnest comment as she stared distractedly at her reflection in the dress-shop mirror. The gown was simple. The bodice was high-necked and long-sleeved, the skirt was cut in a graceful bell shape, and the white lace appeared even more pristine in contrast with her dark hair and heavily lashed dark eyes. The wedding gown suited her taste, but somehow . . .

Marcy unconsciously shook her head.

"What's the matter?" Jessica Hale's lined face drooped with disappointment. "Don't tell me you don't like it. Except for adjustments in the waist and length, the gown looks as if it was made for you."

"Something doesn't look right." Marcy frowned at the older woman's expression of dismay and added defensively, "This gown wasn't my idea. I don't even know where Josh got the catalog he ordered it from. If I had known about it, I would've stopped him."

"That's probably why he asked me not to tell you."

"He shouldn't have done it."

"You amaze me, Marcy. Any other woman would be grateful to have her brother do something so thoughtful."

"So *wasteful* would be more accurate."

"You don't mean that."

"We can't afford this dress, not the way things are at the ranch. Our stock was hit just as hard by that late-season blizzard as all the other ranches in the area. We're still not sure how many of the cattle we have left will survive after that prairie fire ate up most of the grazin' land."

"You don't have to worry about any of that now. Mr. Barnes will take care of everything."

Marcy's lips tightened, and Jessica's face flushed a hot red.

"I didn't mean—" Jessica stopped abruptly, then started again. "I wasn't trying to say that you were marrying Mr. Barnes because he runs the bank and can see to it that your loan on the ranch is renewed."

Sure.

"Mr. Barnes is a handsome man—the best catch in the county. Besides, everybody knows you wouldn't do something like that."

Right.

"Everybody thinks it's fine that you're marrying him and—"

Marcy's limited forbearance snapped. "First of all, his name's not *Mr.* Barnes. It's Willis."

"Well, it's Willis to you maybe, but not to the rest of the people in town. Not that everybody doesn't think he's a real nice gentleman—friendly and all. It's just that—"

"And, second, I don't really care what anybody thinks about me marryin' him."

"Marcy—"

"And third, I don't like the way the town's makin' *my* business *its* business!"

"Nobody's doing that." Jessica shrugged. "Well, not everybody. You can't blame some of us for getting into the spirit of what's going to be the biggest wedding in these parts in years."

Wasteful.

"Anyway, the fact is, whether you wanted Josh to order this gown for you or not, it's here and it's paid for, so you might as well enjoy it."

Right.

"What is it about this gown that seems wrong to you?"

It was impossible.
"You're going to have to help me here, dear."
Especially now.
"Marcy?"
Now that Tierney was back.

"Bold as brass, ain't you?"
"Yes, I guess you can say I am."

Tierney didn't bother to smile as he returned Sheriff Efram Dawson's squint-eyed gaze. Sheriff Dawson had often set him shaking with that look when he was a boy. Now it left him cold. The sheriff's badge was as big and shiny as it always was, but the man behind it was gray-haired, pot-bellied, half Tierney size, and without a leg to stand on if he intended to run him out of town.

Resting his hand casually on the gun belt slung low on his hips, Tierney glanced around the small office. The same scarred desk . . . the same battered chairs . . . the same two cells that shared the limited space of the single-room structure. His pa had spent more time in those cells than Tierney liked to remember, and he himself had been threatened with the same more times than he could manage to forget.

"Lookin' for trouble, are you?"

Tierney's attention snapped back to Sheriff Dawson's bearded face. "What makes you say that, Sheriff?"

"You always was the kind who looked for trouble, and it don't look to me like you've changed much."

Tierney almost laughed. "You can tell that just by lookin' at me, is that right?"

"That's right."

Tierney's smile was little more than a grimace. "That just goes to show you how wrong you are, Sheriff."

"That so? So, why did you come to my office?"

"I thought I'd save you the trouble of lookin' for me—and I thought you'd be the best person to talk to about straightenin' out my pa's affairs."

"Your pa didn't have no affairs. All he left behind was that old shack at the edge of town where he lived, and that mare he treated better than he treated himself. The shack's still out there just like he left it, his grave's up on the hill, and if you're lookin' to claim his horse, you'll have to settle up with Harry Frances at the livery stable for boardin' the animal." Dawson sneered. "Now, is that all?"

"No." Discarding all semblance of cordiality, Tierney continued, "I figured since I was back in town, I'd let you know I found out a while after I left Harper seven years ago that there were witnesses to my gunfight with Josh Tanner— witnesses who said *he* drew first."

"So?"

"You knew it. You knew it all along, but you made sure I heard that you had witnesses who would swear *I* drew first and that you were comin' after me."

Dawson did not reply.

"So I'm back now, for as long as I choose to stay."

"You're back for as long as you stay out of trouble, you mean!"

"I said—"

"I don't care what you said! I'm tellin' you now, if you're thinkin' to stir up some trouble with Willis Barnes, you got another think comin'."

Tierney went momentarily still. Willis Barnes. Dawson couldn't possibly know that he—

"That's right. You ain't foolin' me, and just so's I'm clear, I'll say it right out. Mr. Barnes is an important man in this town. He's got everybody in this town's respect, includin' mine, and I ain't goin' to let you spoil things for him."

"What's he got to do with me?"

"Don't play dumb!"

"I said, what's he got to do with me?"

"All right." Dawson's color grew florid. "I can play that game, too."

"I don't know what you're talkin' about."

"Don't you? You just remember, then. I know you from way back. You're a troublemaker, and there's no way you can tell me you came back here after all these years just to claim your pa's horse. So as long as you mind your business, everythin' will be fine. But the minute you step out of line, I'll be on your tail."

Tierney eyed the older man. It occurred to him that Dawson had forgotten that he was a head shorter than the man he was addressing and that he was long past a prime that had never been truly impressive, while, in sharp contrast, the years had filled out Tierney's own broad frame with hard-earned muscle and sinew that were not often matched. Aside from that, Dawson seemed to forget that he was no longer talking to a boy who could be bluffed by the power of a sheriff's star.

Dawson continued, "And you can be sure that as soon as you walk out that door, I'll be lookin' through my Wanted posters for your picture."

For the second time, Tierney was tempted to laugh. But he had more important things to do.

Tierney turned toward the door, only to snap back briefly toward Sheriff Dawson when the lawman grated, "You'll stay away from *her*, too, if you're smart."

Tierney was closing the door behind him when he heard Dawson add, "But you never was too smart, was you?"

His jaw rigid, Tierney was proceeding down the street when a big woman stepped out in front of him.

"Hello, Tierney. Remember me?"

Tierney hesitated. Could it be the schoolmarm's daughter, Hannah Worth, seven years older and forty pounds heavier?

"It's Hannah Worth."

Hannah Worth, speaking to him in a civil tone for the first time in her life.

"I thought I'd say hello and welcome you back to town."

Yeah.

"I'd be happy to walk along with you and bring you up to date on the happenings in Harper, if you like."

He had a feeling he couldn't stop her if he tried.

Startled, Willis Barnes stared at the leering man who had walked unexpectedly into his office. In stark contrast to the meticulous grooming and tailored perfection on which Willis prided himself, this fellow was bearded and dressed in garments that had doubtless seen weeks of wear without a visit to the laundress's tub.

Standing up without speaking a word, Barnes rounded his desk and scanned the bank's outer office briefly before closing the door behind him. He turned and spat, "Are you crazy, McNeil? What are you doing here?"

"We had an appointment."

"We had an appointment *last night*, outside town, where no one would see us together!"

"I had somethin' else to do."

"You had something else to do?" Willis Barnes took a moment to draw his flaring temper under control. Larry McNeil was a primitive ass who had served his purpose and who was now proving his stupidity. Barnes grated, "Do you realize how dangerous it is for you to come here?"

"Dangerous for who?"

"For both of us, damn it!" Barnes took an aggressive step. "If anyone should associate the two of us—"

McNeil's leer widened. "Yeah, the respectable town banker and a man who's wanted by the law in three states. Who would've thunk?"

"You're not amusing, McNeil!"

McNeil's leer fell into a sneer. "Maybe that's because I'm not tryin' to be *amusin'*. I ain't as dumb as you think I am, Barnes. You did nothin' but string the boys and me along while you were busy courtin' that ladyfriend of yours. Well, maybe you're plannin' your future with a nice, fat pile of money you got put away in your safe outside, but me and the boys are runnin' low on funds."

"That's your fault, not mine!"

"Maybe it is and maybe it ain't, but it's a fact we're growin' real uncomfortable with. The boys and me are tired of excuses."

Willis Barnes raised his aristocratic chin. He was thirty-four years old, healthy, good-looking, and a member of one of the most respected banking families in the east. He was well known and admired throughout the financial community. But if he wasn't careful, this glowering degenerate standing in front of him was going to bring everything down around his ears.

"This is neither the time nor the place to discuss this."

"I'm thinkin' it is."

"I'm the one who does the thinking here, not you!" Barnes's control was slipping. "This didn't all 'just happen,' you know! I didn't 'just happen' to run into you two years ago in Wichita. I didn't make my proposition to you on a whim. An associate of mine pointed you out to me on the street and related your reputation in detail. I followed up on that and decided you were the man I was looking for."

"For the robberies you had in mind."

"McNeil . . ."

McNeil snickered. "What's the matter? You don't like me sayin' it out loud? Afraid somebody will hear me?"

Revolted, Barnes stared at McNeil. He momentarily questioned how he could have become involved with such a man, but the answer was simple. Desperation. A lifetime of advantage and ease had not prepared him for the reality that the family fortune he had inherited was running out. The vices of a rich man's son were deeply ingrained. His gambling bills began to mount. When the threats mounted, too, he took the easy way out.

He remembered how clever he had felt when he came up with his plan. Privy to information regarding the timing of cash shipments to various banks, he was able to determine a strategy for robberies that appeared random, robberies McNeil was able to accomplish without complication. Where debt ended, however, greed began. It wasn't until he realized he was losing control of the situation that he felt the first pang of regret. Now, standing face-to-face with his mistake, he was again *desperate*.

"The situation has changed, McNeil."

"Yeah?"

"My position has changed. When Montgomery Banking, Ltd., sent me here a year ago to expand their operations, I no longer had the

23

same information available to me that I did in the past. Reports of cash shipments reach me only sporadically now."

"That so?"

"It's too easy to track the robberies back to me."

"That didn't stop you when you first got here. We done all right for a while."

"Three robberies of important shipments in the past eight months put the main office on edge. A fourth now might cause suspicion."

"So, what are you sayin'?"

"I'm saying that I went to meet you last night so I could tell you that our association isn't feasible anymore."

"You ain't foolin' me! The only reason you're backin' out of our deal is because you got some money put away and a woman you're lookin' to settle with. That puts me and the boys on the outside. Well, it ain't goin' to work that way. Not yet, anyway."

"Isn't it?"

McNeil's sneer deepened into open hostility. "Seems to me you wasn't talkin' so high-and-mighty when we first met up. You was in big trouble, and you needed us then. Now you're ready to walk away. But you got trouble again, because *we* ain't ready."

"Do you really expect there's anything you can do about it?"

"Think about it. It wouldn't be no problem at all for me to let them highbrows back at Montgomery Banking, Ltd., know that Willis Barnes ain't the man they think he is."

"You'd implicate yourself if you did that."

"Hell, me and the boys are already wanted in three states! It don't make no difference if I make it four!"

Barnes stiffened. "You don't need my help to get by. You did all right before I met you, and there are any number of banks where you and the boys could get some cash."

"Cash, yeah, but nothin' like we'd get from one of them shipments you've been turnin' us on to."

"Another robbery would be a mistake. The board of directors back East won't sit still for it."

"One more. A *big* one." McNeil's small eyes pinned him. "Then me and the boys will head west and disappear."

"I can't."

"It ain't so pleasant behind bars, *Mr.* Barnes. I know. I've been there."

"You wouldn't be so stupid!"

"Stupid?" McNeil's voice dropped to a growl. "Some might think, the way things turned out, that *you* was the stupid one." McNeil paused for silent emphasis, then continued, "You know how to get in touch with me. The boys and me will wait a week. If we don't hear from you by then . . ."

Standing silent and still as the door closed behind McNeil, Barnes came to startling realization. The ignorant bastard was right. McNeil had him where he wanted him. How had he allowed that to happen?

Tierney stood just inside the bank doorway. He looked at the man exiting Willis Barnes's office.

He turned his back as the fellow crossed the small bank lobby, passing within three feet of him before walking out onto the street. Another glance over his shoulder, and his identification was confirmed. The man was Larry McNeil.

His stomach tight, Tierney turned back out onto the street.

"Hello there, Josh!"

It was Hannah Worth. He couldn't miss that voice.

Josh Tanner turned slowly as the flushed young woman walked swiftly past the livery stalls toward him. Of medium height and slim, Josh was acutely aware that Hannah outweighed him by at least twenty pounds, and when she reached his side, she effectively eliminated his retreat with her impressive bulk by backing him up against his horse's flank.

Josh managed a stiff smile. It had been a damned aggravating day. Marcy had been angry when he had thought she would be pleased about the wedding gown he had ordered for her. She had argued with him all the way into town, telling him what he already knew, that they couldn't afford the expense. His horse had thrown a shoe just before they hit the town limits, and he had spent the major part of the time since trying to locate the spot where the blacksmith was fishing so he could get him to fix it. He was irritable and tired, and his chest was aching so bad that he could barely think.

"Well . . . Hannah." Josh paused at her eager expression. "I didn't expect to run into you in the livery stable."

"I was looking for you."

"Is that right?"

"I passed Penelope Jarrett on the street, and she said she saw you come in here."

The old crow.

"I figured you'd be interested in knowing that an old friend of yours is back in town."

"Who's that?"

"Tierney Walsh."

Josh went still.

Hannah's eyes were suddenly bright. "I knew you'd want to know. I talked to Marcy, but she didn't seem to remember him. As a matter of fact, she—"

Hardly aware of his actions, Josh heard Hannah's harsh grunt of protest as he pushed her aside. Rage shuddered through him, numbing his pain, drowning out all but the drumming in his ears that grew louder with every hard step he took toward the door. He reached spontaneously toward his gun when the pounding sound attained the volume of a shout, bringing back the past with a vividness that set him to shaking.

One name on his lips, one thought in his mind, Josh turned out onto the street.

"Now, is that better?"

A strand of gray hair had worked loose from

Jessica's tight bun, and perspiration beaded her lined forehead as she looked up from the hem of Marcy's gown.

Suffering overwhelming pangs of guilt as the woman waited with unfailing patience for her reply, Marcy stared silently at her reflection. Jessica was right. The gown was beautiful.

Tierney Walsh is back in town.

Maybe it wasn't true. Maybe Hannah had mistaken someone else for Tierney.

As if that were possible.

Marcy's eyes flickered briefly closed. So many years had passed since she last saw him. She had been sixteen years old then. In the years since she had spent more time in the saddle than she had in a dress—at first replacing Josh on the range while he recuperated from a chest wound that had never fully healed, and then working side by side with her brother as the ranch slipped further and further into debt. She couldn't remember the last time Josh and she had discussed Tierney—and that was good. Josh had put the past behind him, and she was glad, because there was a time when she had believed her brother's hatred for Tierney would consume him.

As for herself, the ever-mounting problems at the ranch had been almost a saving grace at first. They had filled the aching void inside her after Tierney left. Other men had come calling in the time since, but she'd discouraged them. She hadn't been so successful with Willis. She remembered how amazed she was that he'd bothered to seek her out after their initial meeting, since she had been fresh off the roundup and smelling like a horse.

The truth was that she hadn't liked Willis much at first. His "eastern" attitude had annoyed her, and she remembered thinking his devotion to grooming and style amusing, especially since she paid no heed to style at all. She wasn't sure when her attitude toward him had begun to change. Possibly it was the night he'd said he loved her.

It was incomprehensible to her when Willis spoke those words. It was even more incomprehensible when he asked her to marry him, considering that every eligible woman in the county had had her eye on him from the first day he arrived in Harper, and she had done nothing but try to avoid him.

How had Willis finally worn her down? She was uncertain. She supposed it was because she had begun to grow tired of the sameness of things, weary of thinking the best part of her life was past. There was her concern that Josh wouldn't look for a permanent woman of his own until her life was settled. Then there was the simple fact that she was lonely.

When had Willis worn her down? That was simple as well. He wore her down when he finally convinced her that he meant what he said. He really loved her.

Marcy's frown tightened. And if there was also some truth in Jessica's inference that she might've been influenced into marrying Willis because with him came the unspoken assurance that the Rocking T would be secure . . . well, she owed Josh that much for the physical pain he endured every day of his life because of her.

"Marcy?"

Marcy snapped back to the present.

"How does the gown look to you now?"

Suddenly ashamed of her thoughtlessness, Marcy muttered, "I'm sorry, Jessica. It's fine."

"You don't sound like it's fine."

"Really, it is."

Jessica's glance flashed her disbelief, and Marcy's sense of guilt deepened. What was wrong with her? The gown *was* beautiful. Jessica had labored over the waistline until it fit exactly, and now the length was perfect.

"I know what's wrong!" As if responding to her unspoken question, Jessica stood up stiffly, then reached for the length of fine white lace lying on a chair nearby. "The gown doesn't look finished without a veil."

Adjusting it on Marcy's head even as she protested, Jessica stepped back to view the completed picture. Her eyes suddenly moist and her lips quivering, she whispered, "Marcy, you're the most beautiful bride I've ever seen."

The bell on the entrance door jingled opportunely, eliminating Marcy's need for a reply. Jessica turned toward the male outline etched in dark relief against the bright, sunlit street beyond. She blurted, "It's bad luck for the groom to see the bride in her gown before the wed—"

Marcy turned toward the doorway at the same moment Jessica's expression froze.

Marcy stared into dove-gray eyes that could belong to no other.

It was Tierney.

She was the most beautiful bride he had ever seen.

Marcy—*another man's* bride.

Marcy—who had once said he was the only man she'd ever love.

A latent jealousy flushed hotly through Tierney as he entered the dress shop. He had promised himself he wouldn't seek Marcy out. He had told himself that Marcy had no part in his reason for returning to Harper. He had reminded himself that everything was finished between them the day he mounted his horse and left Harper behind him.

Tierney's jaw was tight. Yes . . . that was what he had told himself.

There was no welcome in Marcy's eyes as she said, "Why did you come back, Tierney?"

Tierney did not respond.

"I asked why you came back."

"I came back for a visit . . . to see some old friends. *You're* an old friend, Marcy."

Marcy pulled the veil from her head and tossed it onto the chair beside her. "We're old acquaintances, but we're not old *friends*. We said everything we had to say to each other seven years ago. I don't have anything to add."

Tierney scrutinized her silently. Marcy was a

woman now. She was taller, slimmer, her features more tightly sculpted. But her hair was the same gleaming ebony that was the texture of silk, and her eyes were still so deep and black that he felt he could get lost in them.

He moved closer. He had to—to see if her skin was still so fine and clear up close that it was almost translucent . . . to see if her lashes were still so long and thick that they almost tangled.

It was. They were.

He saw something else, too. Marcy was trembling.

"What do you want, Tierney?"

"I want to talk to you, Marcy. It's important."

"How important can it be after seven years?"

"Important enough."

Marcy's lips tightened. "I don't know why you came back, but I do know it was a mistake. You left too much hardship behind to expect a welcome."

"The past is over and done, Marcy."

"In some ways . . . but not in others."

Tierney glanced at the older woman, who remained silent beside them. He chanced a smile.

"Hello, Jessica. I'd like to speak to Marcy in private, if you could give us a minute."

"Stay where you are, Jessica! Tierney and I have nothing to talk about."

Tierney turned sharply toward Marcy. "What are you afraid of, Marcy?"

"I'm not afraid of anything, much less you!" Marcy was so close that he could see the angry sparks in her eyes and the color heating her cheeks as she rasped, "I don't want any trouble, and trouble follows you, Tierney. It took me a long time to recognize that. Things are just starting to straighten out at the Rockin' T, and I don't want everything spoiled because you were struck with a sudden whim to renew old acquaintances."

"I'm sorry about your pa, Tierney." Jessica interrupted their exchange unexpectedly. Turning toward the soft-spoken dressmaker, Tierney was surprised to see that her expression was sincere as she continued, "I remember him when he first came to Harper with your ma. Your pa was a different man then."

Tierney nodded, grateful for the first good word he could remember hearing any of the townsfolk speak about his father.

Tierney turned back toward Marcy to see her face flush. Her expression twitched, and she swallowed visibly as she said, "I'm sorry about your pa, too."

In that unguarded moment, Tierney glimpsed the person who was once so much a part of him that he had believed he'd never be truly whole without her.

Memories flooded back, and Tierney reached for Marcy spontaneously. He heard her intake of breath when his hands closed on her shoulders. He wanted to hold her, so he could make her listen when he told her that he—

"Take your hands off my sister!"

The shouted command reverberated in the small shop, sounding simultaneously with the harsh crack of the street door as it banged open against the wall. Turning, Tierney saw that Josh Tanner's face was bloodless as he hissed, "If you know what's good for you, you'll get out of this town now, before the trouble starts!"

"If there's trouble, I won't be the one to start it, Tanner."

"You're startin' it just by bein' in the same room with my sister and me."

"Your sister and I are old friends."

"Bastard!"

"She and I have some things to discuss."

"No, you don't!"

"Look . . ." Tierney paused for a breath. It was happening again, the same spontaneous clash between Josh Tanner and him that once neither of them had been able to avoid. But he was no longer the young, frustrated fellow who allowed emotion to overwhelm reason. He hadn't come back to Harper for this.

Tierney tried again. "I'm not here to make trouble. I came back to settle my pa's affairs."

"Your pa didn't have any affairs."

"You're wrong."

"So it's a coincidence that you're back in Harper now, three weeks before Marcy's wedding?"

Three weeks.

"I asked you a question."

"Yes, it is."

"Liar!" Josh took an aggressive step. "It still eats at you, doesn't it? You thought you had my sister wrapped around your little finger all those years ago. You figured you'd talk her into

34

marryin' you so's you'd get your hands on the part of the ranch my pa left to her, because it was one of the most successful spreads in the county."

"That isn't true."

"It looked real easy, didn't it? Marcy protected you. She defended you no matter what you did, even though your pa was a drunk and you was good for nothin' but stirrin' up—"

"Josh!"

"—stirrin' up trouble!" Ignoring Marcy, Josh continued, "You had nothin' to lose. But when it came down to the line, Marcy chose family over you. She sent you packin' and watched when the law went chasin' after you."

"Yeah . . . the law."

Josh's eyes glowed with hatred. "Now you heard Marcy's marryin' an important man, and you're lookin' to see what you can get out of it. So I'm tellin' you now, you got off the best shot last time, but that won't happen again."

"I didn't come back to trade bullets with you, Tanner."

"Maybe not, but that's what you're goin' to end up doin' if you come near my sister again."

"Josh, please!"

"Marcy's gettin' married to a man who can take care of her like you never would or could."

"You think so?"

"That's right!" Josh took a step closer, his hand hovering near the gun on his hip. "If you got somethin' to say about that, let's settle it here and now."

"Josh!" Marcy stepped between them, her face pale. "I don't want this!"

Josh's chest was heaving. "*He* does."

Turning toward Tierney, Marcy rasped, "Get out of here, Tierney. Don't try to see me or talk to me again. We're not old acquaintances or old friends or anythin' like that. Just finish your business in town, and go back where you came from. It'll be better that way, for everybody."

"Will it?"

"Go away, Tierney, and don't come back."

"You heard her!"

Tierney stared at Marcy's white face. Yes, he heard her. The words slashed deeply as he walked out the door.

Chapter Two

The sun was setting, and the temperature was dropping, but the small shack held the heat in a way Tierney remembered well.

Tierney glanced around him at the run-down structure where his father had spent the last years of his life. One room, sparsely furnished, it had been abandoned for years when they first moved into it. It had been in worse condition a few hours earlier, but it was clean now. He had put it in order. He had done the same with his life after leaving Harper seven years ago, but it was easy to see that there wasn't a person in town ready to believe it.

The past was over and done. Wasn't that what Marcy had said? With that thought in mind, he had left the dress shop earlier that afternoon and walked directly to the telegraph office, where he sent the wire he had been dreading. He then visited two graves on the hill that were sorely neglected, picked up his pa's mare, and bought some supplies before returning to this shack he had once called home.

Appearing unexpectedly before Tierney's mind was the memory of his pa's face when the sheriff posted the foreclosure sign on their ranch-house door and nailed it shut. He had been nine years old then, but he knew he'd never forget his father's expression. His pa did his best to comfort him by saying it was only temporary, that he'd find a way to get the ranch back, but the years passed, and his pa never seemed to have much more in his pocket than it took to put food on the table and keep a bottle beside the bed.

Tierney frowned. That was when his war with Harper had begun. He was a one-man army until the day he lay bloodied and bruised in the street and looked up to see Marcy Tanner standing over him. She was ten years old and mad as a hornet at the fellows walking away, because the fight had been three against one. He told her then that he didn't need or want her hanging around him. She was sixteen years old when he discovered how wrong he could be.

Tierney ran a callused hand through his hair. He remembered that final year. Marcy was heaven in his arms. She was all that made his life bearable. He couldn't seem to get enough of her. She was the only stable stepping stone on his path to the future, and when he held her sweet flesh pressed close to his, he wanted never to let her go. Pa's thinking was muddled, but even he recognized the danger there. Josh hated Tierney almost as much as Marcy loved him. When the smoke finally cleared, it was Josh lying on the ground with a bullet in his chest, but Tierney was the loser—because he lost Marcy.

Marcy's adult image abruptly thrust the younger Marcy from his mind, and Tierney felt a rush of heat. She was still beautiful—more beautiful—but she was angry that he was back. He wanted to tell her that she had nothing to do with his return, because she hadn't. He wanted to promise her that as soon as he got what he came for, he'd leave, because that was what he had intended. He wanted to say it was a coincidence that he had returned when she was supposed to marry Willis Barnes in three weeks, because it was.

Willis Barnes, who was—

Footsteps.

His attention suddenly acute, Tierney snatched his gun from the belt lying on the chair beside him. Silent and still, he listened. He hadn't heard a horse approach, but someone was outside. His finger on the trigger, he watched as the rear door of the cabin pushed slowly open.

A flash of dark hair. A startled gasp.

Marcy!

"I didn't come here for a gunfight, Tierney." Clad in comfortable riding clothes that were a far cry from the bridal gown she'd worn earlier, Marcy stood in the doorway. She was no less beautiful, but her expression was cold and her chest was heaving. He had frightened her, but she'd be damned before she'd show it. Tierney almost smiled. That much hadn't changed.

Tierney dropped his gun back into its holster. "You shouldn't have come sneakin' up on the cabin."

"I didn't sneak up."

"I didn't hear a horse."

"I tied him up a ways from here."

"You didn't want anyone to know you were here."

No answer. He didn't need one.

"I've got some things I want to say."

"Does that mean I'm supposed to listen?"

"Same old Tierney."

"No, I'm not."

"I'm glad." Marcy approached him boldly, but her expression was strained. "I'm not the same old Marcy, either. I'm an adult now, and I've learned to consider the consequences of my actions." She walked closer, her lips tight. "I came here to plead with you to leave Harper before there's trouble."

"I didn't come here to make trouble for you, Marcy."

"Tierney . . ." Marcy's eyes softened unexpectedly. "I never thought you did. You never wanted to make trouble for me, but it happened anyway, and things haven't changed." Marcy paused. Her lips twitched. "I *am* sorry about your pa, Tierney. I know how hard you tried to help him. I never could understand why people in this town wouldn't just leave him be, like he wanted. He never hurt anybody but himself."

Tierney did not reply.

"If it makes you feel any better, he didn't die in the street. He had pneumonia. Doc Whittiker was takin' care of him. Doc put him in the spare room behind his office where he could keep an eye on him. That's where he died."

Tierney nodded.

Marcy took a breath, then continued. "I came here to ask a favor of you, Tierney. You owe me one."

"I owe you a favor?"

"Josh almost died, you know."

"He drew on me first."

"Your bullet hit his lung. He looks fine on the outside, but he's never been the same."

"It was his choice."

"He hates you, Tierney." Marcy took another step closer. "I spent the last three hours arguin' with him. He wanted to come here and finish what was started seven years ago."

"It *is* finished."

"Not for him! It'll never be finished for him!" Marcy's voice dropped a note lower. "Tierney, please . . . please leave Harper. I don't want to see the same thing happen again."

"I didn't come back to fight Josh, Marcy."

"If you stay, you won't be able to avoid it! Tierney . . . you said you loved me, once. If there was any truth in what you said—"

"Did you ever doubt there was?"

"Tierney . . ."

Marcy was close . . . so close. The familiar fragrance of her skin tantalized him. He longed to taste the flush on her cheeks with his lips.

But she was begging him to leave.

Tierney fought to retain his composure as jealousy again rankled. "Is it really Josh you're worried about, Marcy? Or are you worried what Willis Barnes will think?"

"Willis?" Marcy took a backward step. "He has no part in this."

"Doesn't he? He's the man you're goin' to marry."

Marcy's jaw locked tight.

"Well, isn't he?"

"I want you to leave Harper, Tierney. I want you to go away and never come back."

"Do you, Marcy?"

The last of his composure spent, Tierney raised a hand to Marcy's cheek. He felt her shudder as he slid his fingers into her hair and wound them in the heavy strands. He whispered, "You shuddered like this the first time I touched you, Marcy. You were almost sixteen. I had just gotten out of jail. The sheriff had put me behind bars for two days to even off things because Barry Lister couldn't get out of bed for two days after we fought. You said the sheriff shouldn't have done that. You said it was a fair fight, and the only reason the sheriff got involved was because I won. You said you were tired of everybody pickin' on me. You wanted to make it up to me. You kissed me, Marcy."

Tierney's voice deepened as a trembling rose

in him as well. "I was older than you, Marcy. I was supposed to know better. But you tasted so good. I told myself I'd only let myself hold you for a little while. I told myself I wouldn't let it all run away with me, but your arms were around my neck, and I was kissin' you back. Do you remember, Marcy?"

Marcy's shuddering intensified as Tierney continued, "I remember every bit of it. I relived it every night of my life for more years than I want to recollect." His gaze dropped to her lips. "Do you still taste as sweet, Marcy?" He took a ragged breath. "I have to know."

Marcy was in his arms then. He was crushing her close, his mouth devouring hers. Unconscious of the moment when Marcy's arms slipped around his neck, Tierney felt only the warm heat of her as she came alive under his kiss, as she leaned into his embrace. The years slipped away, and she was *his* Marcy again—his friend, his confidante, his love. He reveled in the renewed wonder as his kiss deepened, and the beauty of the moment infused him with joy.

Lips melding . . . hunger surging . . . bodies yielding . . . There was no past, only the present. There were no impediments between them except the frail clothing that soon succumbed to his anxious hands. And when Marcy's naked flesh lay under his at last, the moment was all he had dreamed, and more.

Oh, yes, she remembered!
How could she forget the sensation of being

in Tierney's arms? The elation was the same, but all the stronger for the years of deprivation in between.

Breathless wonder reigned as Tierney's naked flesh pressed tightly against hers. His kiss deepened, and Marcy parted her lips to savor it fully. His mouth consumed her, and she raised herself to meet it. His hands stroked her intimately, and Marcy clutched him close. She rejoiced in the muscled expanse that rippled beneath her palm as she smoothed her hand against his back, clutching him closer still. She tangled her fingers in the tawny gold of his hair to hold him her captive, as she was his.

Enraptured, Marcy returned kiss for kiss, caress for caress. Enthralled, she murmured her bliss as Tierney tasted her womanly core and explored it passionately. Enslaved, she remained motionless, gasping her jubilation as he slid himself up upon her once more to recapture her mouth.

Hard against her, Tierney slid himself inside her at last, and Marcy caught her breath. She heard his ragged whisper.

"Open your eyes, Marcy."

A flush of loving warmth filled her as she opened her eyes to see Tierney's face above her. The dove gray of his eyes held hers intently as he grated, "Say my name."

"Tierney."

"Say it again, Marcy."

"Tierney."

He was moving inside her, stroking her with growing heat, his impetus growing.

"Say it again."

"Tierney." His name escaped her lips in a fervent cry, and Marcy closed her eyes as passion swelled.

"Tierney . . . Tierney . . . Tierney!"

Tierney's soft groan of culmination shuddered within her. It carried her with him on a rapturous wave as she quaked to fulfillment, gasping with the ecstasy of their joining.

The glowing aftermath remained as Tierney's sweat-moistened length lay warm against her—Tierney, the mature, handsome version of the boy who had so stirred her youthful passions. Her affinity for him had been spontaneous those many years ago, immediate the first time she saw him. She had *hated* those boys who left him bleeding in the street. She had run screaming after them, wanting to hurt them the way they had hurt Tierney. Tierney had tried to push her away. He didn't understand her need to stand with him against the others. In truth, neither did she. It came to her gradually, almost belatedly, that she wasn't defending Tierney—not really. She was defending herself, because every blow that struck Tierney struck her as well. When it took too long for Tierney to come to that realization, when the torment of waiting became too great, she took matters into her own hands.

How she had loved him!

Marcy's throat tightened. She muttered an

unconscious protest when Tierney stirred. He lifted himself slightly from her, and she opened her eyes to see him looking down at her soberly, in the same way he had when they first made love. That look had been there with each lovemaking. She had never truly understood it. She wondered—

Tierney interrupted Marcy's mental meanderings with an unexpected whisper. *"I'm an adult now, and I've learned to consider the consequences of my actions."*

Marcy's blood went cold.

"That's what you said, isn't it, Marcy?"

The cold slap of reality sent Marcy momentarily reeling.

Oh, God. What had she done?

As if reading her mind, Tierney withdrew from her abruptly. He stood up and reached for his clothes. Fully dressed, he turned back toward her as her trembling fingers worked unsuccessfully at the buttons on her shirt.

Tierney's tone was harsh as he swept away her shaky hands. "I'll do it."

His knuckles moved warmly against her breasts as he snapped, "I'm waitin'. Say it. You got carried away. Or, this was just for old times." His knuckles brushed the soft mounds more intimately, and Marcy caught her breath. Tierney's smile was just short of a grimace. "I'm waitin', Marcy."

Marcy pulled back from Tierney's touch, her heart pounding. "All right, I'll say it. You're right. I made a mistake comin' here. Too many memories . . ."

Her voice failing, Marcy began again. "I . . . I wish I could say that what just happened changes things, but it doesn't. Too much time has passed. Too many things have happened in between. I don't even know *how* it happened—just like I don't really know *you* anymore . . . who you are now . . . how you live." An almost debilitating thought suddenly widened her eyes. "You could be married . . . with a family."

"I could be, couldn't I?"

Oh, God.

Tierney's eyes were cold. "You don't really know me anymore . . . but you *do* know Willis Barnes."

Marcy took a shaky breath. She didn't want to talk about Willis. She didn't want to explain to Tierney that the hardships of the last seven years had taken their toll. She didn't want to tell him that Josh's harsh rasping for breath sometimes still cut her so deeply that she could not escape its echo. She didn't want to say that she had come to a compromise with life, that she had settled for the peace the many reassurances of Willis's love would bring.

She didn't want to say those things. She *couldn't* say them.

"Do you love Barnes?"

Tierney was waiting for an answer.

Marcy stared at him a moment longer. He was the same Tierney and more—big, with a rugged, blond handsomeness that tore at her heart—but it was too late.

"I'm goin' to marry Willis."

Tierney's eyes turned to ice.

Marcy reached unsteadily for her hat. When she turned back to him, her voice was as frigid as his gaze.

"Go away, Tierney. Harper was never good for you. It never will be."

She was gone.

Tierney stood staring at the door that had closed behind Marcy. The silence of the shack was deafening, as overwhelming as the muted echoes of passion that had resounded there only minutes earlier.

Tierney turned away, his smile bitter.

"I made a mistake coming here."

She had.

"Too many memories."

But she had cast them aside.

All semblance of a smile dropped from Tierney's lips. Marcy had made a mistake, all right. With the click of the door closing behind her, she had dispelled the last of his remaining doubts.

He knew what he had to do.

"What are you doin' here, Willis?"

Willis did not immediately reply. Marcy had finally come home. Darkness surrounded her where she paused in the yard of the Tanner ranch house. If any other woman had asked him that question after he had spent so much time waiting for her to return, he would have walked past her and out of her life. But Marcy wasn't any other woman.

Willis responded with a spontaneous lie. "I was on my way back from delivering some loan papers to the Parker ranch, and I stopped by."

Marcy glanced at Josh, who stood a few feet away from Willis. The tension between brother and sister was obvious, prompting Willis to say, "I can see I picked a bad time."

Marcy approached Willis with that same deliberate stride that had caught his eye the first time she entered his bank. He remembered being amused at seeing a woman dressed in pants and a shirt similar to those worn by the wranglers accompanying her, but his amusement hadn't lasted long. Marcy had put him in his place with a few short words—something no woman had ever done to him before. When her heavily lashed dark eyes then swept over him assessingly and appeared to find him wanting, he'd been infuriated.

Determined to make her crawl, he'd pursued her when she didn't want to be pursued. He'd courted her when she didn't want to be courted. He'd used every ploy he knew to win her over so he might then humiliate her by casting her aside. But he had outsmarted himself. His anger had gradually become reluctant admiration when he realized that under Marcy's glossy dark mane was an intelligence earned, rather than learned, and beneath those outlandish clothes was a woman capable of meeting him on his own level in every way.

He was uncertain when admiration had become love. He was almost as stunned as

Marcy had been when he spoke that word. He was a novice at the emotion. He was still struggling with it, but there was one thing of which he was sure. He wanted Marcy, and he always got what he wanted, one way or another.

Obviously agitated, Marcy halted her advance a few feet from him. Her reply was unexpected.

"That's right. You picked a bad time." Staring at him a moment, she added with peculiar emphasis, "I'm very sorry, Willis."

With a depth of feeling that still amazed him, Willis reached for her hand. "Are you all right, Marcy?"

"I'm all right." Marcy withdrew her hand from his.

Controlling a flash of temper, which he sensed would only aggravate a situation he was not in a position to control, Willis nodded. "I have some work that needs to be done at the bank. Tonight's probably a good time to do it." He forced a smile. "Walk me to my horse?"

Marcy was still silent when Willis reached his mount. Obviously troubled, she began hesitantly, "We've always been honest with each other, Willis. I know I've prided myself on that, and I think you have, too. I don't know how else to say what I'm goin' to say except . . ." Marcy paused, momentarily at a loss for words. "What I'm tryin' to say is—"

"Marcy!"

Marcy's head snapped around as Josh stepped out of the shadows. Willis restrained an instinctive protest as Josh approached. He had no patience for Josh's proprietary manner toward his sister. He would see that it stopped after Marcy and he were married.

His expression impassive, Josh stated, "I need your help inside."

"I'm busy, Josh."

"I need your help now, Marcy."

Marcy stared at her brother. "I said—"

"I heard what you said."

Marcy stiffened, then turned back to Willis. "I can see Josh won't be satisfied until he says what he has to say. I hope you'll excuse us."

Marcy stalked back toward the house without waiting for Willis's reply. Josh followed close behind her, and Willis seethed. He was mounted and on his way before they reached the door.

"I'm warnin' you, Josh." Not waiting until her brother closed the door behind him, Marcy growled, "Don't ever do that again!"

His face flushed, Josh snapped, "I'll do what I think is best for you, like I've always done."

"I don't need a guardian. I'm a grown woman."

"You're a grown woman, all right, but there are some things you haven't grown out of."

"Meanin'?"

"Meanin' I know where you were tonight. You went to meet Tierney Walsh!"

"That's my business!"

"Not when the man you're goin' to marry shows up here and I have to lie through my teeth when he asks me where you went."

"You didn't have to lie. If you hadn't inter-rupted, I would've told him."

"You're doin' it again, Marcy! You're lettin' that bastard Walsh wrap you around his finger, just like he always did."

"No, I'm not."

"You don't really believe what he said, do you? It's not a coincidence that he's here three weeks before you're set to marry Willis. He's schemin', again."

"Again?" Marcy stared at her brother. "How many times do I have to tell you that Tierney's 'schemes' were all in your mind? He never made me do anythin' I didn't want to do."

"You were too young to realize what you were doin'. He wasn't."

"I wasn't too young then, and I'm not too young now. *And* I don't have to make any expla-nations to you!"

"Stop it, Marcy!" Josh's face flushed. "You always were hard-headed! You never would lis-ten to my warnings."

"That's because you were no better than the rest of the town, unwilling to give Tierney a chance."

"I don't want to go over all that again." Josh's expression grew pained. "I don't care where you were or what you did while you were gone tonight. It doesn't matter. What does matter is that if you break off with Willis because of it, you'll regret it for the rest of your life."

"No, I—"

"Listen to me, Marcy. Walsh came back for a reason, and it wasn't to get his pa's mare."

"Whatever Tierney's reason for coming back, it didn't have anything to do with wanting to hurt me!"

"Why can't you see the truth about him?"

"I do see the truth!"

"You're playin' into his hands!"

"No, he—"

"Did you know he went to Willis's bank *before* he came to the dress shop to see you?"

"What's that supposed to mean? He probably had some business to take care of."

"He didn't even go up to the teller's window! He stayed only long enough to get a glimpse of Willis when he opened the door of the office to let some fella out."

"Who told you that? Hannah?"

"Jeremy saw him from his teller's booth."

"Jeremy's hated Tierney since the time Tierney broke his brother's nose in a fight."

"Open your eyes, Marcy! Jeremy doesn't hate Walsh enough to lie about him. Walsh went to the bank to get a look at Willis because he knew you were marryin' him—pure and simple. He's mad as hell that you're marryin' well while he's still a drifter, and he's goin' to do his best to get in the way of the weddin', just for the spite of it. Then he'll run off, just like he did the last time."

"Tierney's not like that!"

"Isn't he? You were about to call things off between Willis and you because of somethin' that happened tonight, weren't you?"

Marcy could not respond.

"Don't do it, Marcy! Don't let Walsh win!

Willis is your chance for a good life. He's a good man, an important man. He'll take care of you."

"I don't need takin' care of!"

"Marcy . . ." Josh was starting to wheeze. His face touched with a pain that was growing physical, he rasped, "I'll make a deal with you. You know how I feel about Walsh. You know there's nothin' I want more than to finish what we started seven years ago. But I'll stay away from him as long as he stays away from me. I'll make that promise to you, but you have to promise me something, too." Josh's gaze grew more earnest. "You have to promise you won't make any snap decisions to give up Willis until you've had time to think things over."

"The wedding is set for three weeks from tomorrow!"

"Walsh will be gone by then."

Marcy blinked, then took a breath. "Maybe. But that won't change what happened tonight, and I—"

"I don't want to know what happened tonight, and Willis doesn't have to know, either. You'll see that I'm right when Walsh is gone and things go back to normal. It'll be like he never came back. You'll thank me, then."

"I have to be honest with Willis."

"I'm tellin' you, Marcy . . ." Josh's eyes grew suddenly wild. "If you let Walsh mess things up for you, I'll see to it that he pays!"

"Josh—"

"I mean it! I won't let him get away with it,

like he did the last time." Josh strained for control. "I swear I'll—"

"All right!" Marcy was suddenly shuddering so hard that she could barely hold herself erect. "I promise!"

"You won't be sorry, Marcy."

"It's too late." Marcy turned toward the door to her room, her lips tight. "I'm already sorry."

The moon was full, lighting a silver path along the trail that Willis traveled, but he was unmindful of the night's beauty. Still seething, he cursed under his breath and kicked his mount to a faster pace.

It had been a difficult day. He hadn't planned on seeing Marcy that night, but he had somehow needed to hold her. He had spent the day damning his own stupidity in allowing McNeil the power to manipulate him. He had needed to see Marcy, so he might be able to look past the difficulties McNeil was sure to cause, to a time when he would again be in full control. Instead, his brief, aborted visit had only increased his agitation by forcing him to realize that he was even more subservient to his feelings for Marcy than he wanted to accept. Most unsettling of all was the feeling, still remaining, that his future with Marcy was at greater risk than he had expected.

Scanning the heavy foliage ahead, Willis grunted when he caught sight of a cabin almost hidden in a stand of trees. His abbreviated visit with Marcy had accomplished one thing, at least. It had given him a glimpse of what it might be like to lose her—and he didn't like it. As distasteful as it was to submit to McNeil's threats, he'd do what he had to do to get what he wanted. That was his way.

A shadow moved past the lighted window of the cabin as Willis dismounted and threw his reins over a branch. He sneered when the door opened and McNeil stepped out onto the sagging porch. The three men behind him paused. Johnson, Brooks, and Porter—as scurvy a threesome as Willis had ever known.

McNeil sauntered toward him. Despising the man, Willis addressed him without preamble. "All right. You win. One more job. A big one. You'll hear from me soon."

Unwilling to suffer the man's reply, Willis remounted and turned his horse back onto the trail before McNeil had time to speak a word.

Chapter Three

Tierney strode down Harper's main street, his brow furrowed. He was tired of waiting. Three days had passed since the night Marcy walked out of his cabin. He hadn't seen her since.

Tierney mentally paused at that thought. No, that wasn't totally true. He had seen Marcy nightly in his dreams, her lips parted, her eyelids heavy with passion. He had awakened each time with the taste of her on his lips—and to the realization that, however intense his feelings were for her, he was unlikely ever to hold her in his arms again.

A sudden uneasiness turned Tierney to scan the boardwalk behind him. He supposed, under other circumstances, he might have been amused to see the sheriff standing by his office, openly following his progress down the

Elaine Barbieri

street. It didn't miss his notice that Joe Carter jumped back into the general store rather than be caught watching him, almost knocking down Hannah Worth behind him. The two made a fine pair. He knew they were partially responsible for making his return the talk of the town, that they had everyone speculating about what would happen before he left, and that they were certain he'd do something to prove he was still the wild youth he had once been.

To spur bogus speculation, he had spent time riding out to the property that had once been the family ranch, and to fulfill their expectations of him, he had made a point of passing some hours in the Last Stand Saloon—all a part of his private agenda.

The most important part of that agenda was the secret time he had spent watching Barnes's house each night until the lights went out and he was sure the man was secure for the night. Tierney knew he could not afford to surrender that task until the situation permitted, and time was passing too quickly for him to be satisfied with his progress. The waiting was more difficult than he had imagined it could possibly be.

His attention caught by the bearded horseman who rode into view at the far end of town, Tierney concealed a flash of gratification. He slowed his step. Taking his first satisfied breath in days, he paused, then leaned back against a post, his indolence carefully conceived while he watched Harper's morning traffic move past.

Marcy pulled her hat low on her forehead to shield her eyes against the brilliant morning glare as Harper's main thoroughfare came into view. She drew back on her mount's reins, feigning a leisurely pace that contrasted sharply with her inner agitation. She was tired of waiting. Three days had passed since the evening at Tierney's cabin. She hadn't seen Tierney or Willis since, and she had awakened that morning uncertain whether she could stand another day of her torturous limbo. She and Josh had carefully avoided any mention of her situation since that night when they made their mutual promises, and she supposed she should be satisfied that he appeared to be keeping their bargain. But she was sick of doing nothing. Instead, she had taken the first excuse presented—medicine needed for a sick gelding—to go to town.

She needed to clear her head. She needed to see Willis. She needed to test her feelings for him, and his for her. Tierney aside, she needed to settle in her mind whether there was any chance of a future between Willis and her now, so she might be fair to him.

Yes, she needed to see Willis, and if she happened to see Tierney along the way . . .

Annoyed at her straying thoughts, Marcy pulled the brim of her hat lower still as she scanned the street surreptitiously.

Penelope Jarrett looked up from sweeping the walk in front of her hat shop as Marcy passed. The old witch looked very much at home with a broom.

Joe Carter raised a hand in a feeble wave from the doorway of the general store. Her smile in return was just as weak.

Sheriff Dawson frowned openly at her when she passed. She favored him with the same.

Marcy withheld a snort. Surely Hannah had to be lurking behind a window somewhere nearby.

She saw him then—Tierney, leaning casually against a pole in front of the barbershop. He looked tall, strong, handsome—appealing in a way only Tierney could be—and he looked relaxed without a care in the world.

Marcy's heart leaped when Tierney saw her. It then dropped to the toes of her scuffed boots when he tipped his hat with an offhanded smile and looked away.

Willis moved restlessly. He glanced out his office window at the sunlit street. It had been three days since his unsatisfactory parting with Marcy and his meeting with McNeil. The encounters had left him discomfited. He despised the lack of control they represented. He had made a temporary mental truce with his situation with McNeil by telling himself that McNeil and his cohorts would be out of his life as soon as the next shipment was in their hands. Like them, he had heard that California was a great place for men with the kind of money they would have, especially men who were trying to avoid the law.

His situation with Marcy, however, was another matter.

Willis's irritation mounted. The more he thought about Marcy's dismissal of him three nights previously, the more angry he became. She had treated him poorly. She had put her brother before him. She had turned her back on him coldly, as if he were a stranger, and walked away from him without a second thought.

She hadn't even let him *touch* her.

The mental image of Marcy snatching back her hand returned to rankle, and Willis's anger flared anew. He had already decided to teach her a lesson. He hadn't attempted to see or contact her in three days, and he was determined to wait as long as it took for her to come to him. For a woman with as much pride as Marcy, that would be enough for now. She'd remember it in the future. He'd wait until after they were married to put further rules in place—and to make sure she followed them.

Willis toyed with his pen. The question was, how long would it take for her to come to him? Marcy could be a haughty witch when she chose to be, and he was tired of waiting. He supposed it was possible that the situation didn't eat at her the way it ate at him, but he continued to avoid the thought.

Damn! Willis slapped his pen onto the desk

with an angry grunt. He'd make her pay for these hours of torment after they were married! He had already made a mental note to—

Willis's angry thoughts stopped dead. A smile creased his well-tended cheeks when he recognized the slender rider who came into view on the street beyond his window. It was Marcy. She had come to town to patch things up with him!

Following Marcy's figure until she slipped from view, Willis pulled open his drawer and withdrew a mirror. He checked his reflection quickly. Satisfied that his appearance was faultless, he turned, faced the door, and waited.

"It took you long enough to get here."

Pausing, Tierney briefly scanned the livery stable again before turning back toward the tall, reed-thin, bearded fellow with the unlikely name of Clarence Cobb. He continued with unconcealed annoyance, "Three days. The plan was for you to come as soon as I sent the wire."

The older man shrugged, but the casual gesture belied the keen, assessing gaze that made him one of the Pinkerton Detective Agency's most effective operatives. He responded, "I got tied up on another case. Billie Bob Ryan escaped from that jail I put him in, and the boss was fit to be tied when he heard about it. The local sheriff wasn't worth the price of his badge, and since the agency didn't stand a chance of collectin' from our clients if Ryan was on the loose again, he said to give Ryan priority over everythin' else. That's what I did.

It shouldn't have taken so much time to get that fella back where he belonged, though." Cobb shrugged again. "I must be gettin' old."

Tierney knew that nothing could be more untrue. He had worked with Clarence before. He knew Cobb was as sharp and quick as a man half his age. He also knew Cobb was a former lawman who had tired of the constraints of the law, but whose devotion to justice had turned him on to the agency.

As for himself, Tierney had recognized immediately that Alan Pinkerton was a hard-nosed fanatic with regard to his work when fate had thrust them into a chance encounter six years earlier. That fanaticism had appealed to the aimless, angry fellow Tierney was then, but it was Pinkerton's intelligence and talent for almost faultless logical deduction that he came to respect the most. He would never truly understand what had prompted Pinkerton to take a chance on him, but the alliance had proved profitable for both men, while providing Tierney with the sense of purpose and satisfaction he had unconsciously been seeking. He had found his direction, and he had not deviated from it in the time since. But never had he believed that that direction would eventually lead him home.

Cobb scrutinized him more intently. "What's the rush anyway, Walsh? Harper's your old hometown, ain't it? You said you wanted this case. You ain't regrettin' it now, are you?"

Ignoring Cobb's question, Tierney retorted, "I got lucky. I saw McNeil comin' out of

Barnes's office the first day I got here. We knew McNeil and his gang were responsible for the robberies, even if the law couldn't seem to catch them. What Montgomery Bankin' wanted the agency to find out was if there was somebody on the inside who was in on the robberies with McNeil. Seein' them together confirmed it, as far as I was concerned, so I sent that wire."

"And the boss was right again." Smiling, Cobb shook his head. "I gotta give Pinkerton credit. He had it figured that way from the first day Montgomery Bankin' called him in on them robberies. Them bankers was suspicious how McNeil seemed to know every time a heavy shipment went out. The boss put his finger on Barnes right off, but there wasn't a man on that board of directors who believed Barnes had anythin' to do with it, because his pedigree goes way back."

"His pedigree." Tierney's laugh was caustic. "I got one of them, too. Ask anybody in Harper. They'll tell you."

Cobb's expression sobered. "That's why the boss let you take the case. He figured you had a personal stake in the operation. It didn't hurt none that he figured your reputation in town would keep Barnes off guard."

"What're you sayin'?" Tierney's realization was slow in coming. "Are you tellin' me the boss knew about me and Marcy years ago, and how Marcy's intendin' to marry Barnes in three weeks?"

"Tierney, there ain't nothin' that gets past the boss, and you know it."

"So he figured to use it all to his advantage."

"You got it right."

"Damn that 'eye that never sleeps'!"

"One thing the boss didn't expect was that everythin' would move so fast. They ain't quite ready for it all back East."

"What do you mean?"

"They're gettin' the money together for another big shipment, just like the boss wants, but it's goin' to take a while."

"They don't have to send a *real* shipment. A dummy will do. All they have to do is send Barnes notification that the money's on its way, so he can set things up with McNeil, and we can catch them in the act."

"The boss don't want to take a chance that Barnes might see through it. If Barnes gets suspicious, we'll miss out on this chance to get him, and we sure won't get another one."

Unable to dispute his logic, Tierney nodded. "How long is it goin' to take to get that money together?"

"Two weeks. Maybe three."

"No good."

"You're thinkin' about the woman, ain't you? You know you can't take a chance of tellin' her about Barnes."

No response.

"Tierney . . ."

"Wire the office. Tell them I'll give them two weeks to get that shipment here."

"If they can't?"

"Do I have to spell it out for you?"

Silent for a moment while he studied Tierney's adamant expression, Cobb said abruptly, "All right."

"In the meantime, we'd better keep an eye on Barnes. He's tied to that bank durin' the day. Any further contact with McNeil would have to be at night."

"That's fine with me, but I ain't watchin' him tonight. I'm sleepin' in. I've been on the road for a day and a half, and my old bones are cryin' for a nice, soft mattress."

"All right. Tonight's mine."

About to turn away, Tierney felt Cobb's hand on his arm. When he looked back, the older man questioned softly, "Are you all right with this, boy? The boss still has time to send somebody else out to finish up on things if you ain't."

"I'm fine."

Withdrawing his arm, Tierney strode toward the stable door.

"Is that all you want, Marcy?"

"That's all I need."

The medicinal smell of Doc Whittiker's office was familiar. It stirred sad memories, which she was anxious to avoid as the gray-haired physician reached for a bottle on the table behind him and placed it on the desk in front of her.

Remembered echoes of an old man's labored

breathing sounded again in her mind, and Marcy struggled against welling emotions. No one but Doc Whittiker knew about the hours she had spent with Tierney's pa while he lay dying in the doc's rear room, and she intended that no one ever would. She supposed part of the reason was because too many questions would be asked that she didn't want to answer, when the truth simply was that, through Tierney, she came to know the part of his pa that Tierney loved—the part that had survived a weakness for the bottle and remained a truly good man. And part of that reason was because she—

"Marcy? Are you all right, dear?"

Doc Whittiker's stubbled face creased with concern. She wanted to respond truthfully, to tell him she wasn't all right. But would he understand if she told him she was suddenly empty inside because she had just seen Tierney Walsh, and Tierney had looked at her as if she were a stranger?

Marcy picked up the tonic Doc Whittiker had prepared. In the absence of a town veterinarian, he treated man and beast to the best of his ability. Another good man.

Marcy forced a smile. "I'm fine."

"Goin' to visit with Willis now, are you?"

Marcy's smile faded.

"The man will be disappointed if you don't stop by."

She couldn't go.

"He'll be real disappointed."

Especially now.

Doc Whittiker was still talking when she walked out the door.

Willis drummed his fingers impatiently on the gleaming surface of his desk. His eye ticked spasmodically, increasing his aggravation.

Where was she, damn it?

Surrendering at last, Willis stood up stiffly and walked to his office door. He opened it a crack and surveyed the outer office. She wasn't there.

Exercising more control than he believed he possessed, Willis closed his office door quietly and walked back to his desk. Fuming, he sat and allowed a familiar litany to roll again across his mind.

He *would not* go out on the street looking for Marcy.

He *would not* allow her to know that he was waiting for her.

He *would not* let her see how easily she could control him.

He . . . would . . . not!

His jaw as hard as granite, Willis turned his chair toward the window in self-disgust. His eyes widening, he stood up abruptly. Standing with his hands against the pane, he stared incredulously at the sight of Marcy riding back up the main street, leaving Harper—and him— behind her.

He had a bad feeling . . .

Tierney squinted into his spyglass. Hiding in

a wooded glade at the far side of town, directly across from the stately clapboard house Willis Barnes had bought shortly after arriving in Harper, he shifted uncomfortably. His first impression of the house had been that its excessive gingerbread trim and towering cupola were pretentious, just like its owner. His second impression, conceived this night, was that it was strongly built—the sounds he heard of slamming doors and windows might have shaken a lesser structure.

It was obvious that something was bothering Barnes and that his patience was at a low ebb. If he intended traveling anywhere that evening, he would doubtless make his move soon, before the roads darkened enough to slow his progress.

As if verifying Tierney's thoughts, Barnes stepped out onto the porch and slammed the door behind him. Tierney watched as he stomped to the hitching post and mounted his horse.

Mounting as well, Tierney allowed a reasonable distance between them before he followed.

"I told you, I'm all right."

Marcy faced Josh, her expression rigid. He had been watching her since he came back from the range that afternoon, his gaze scrutinizing. She had tried to ignore him, but it didn't work. The resulting tension had sent their three remaining ranch hands off to town immediately after supper and had dispatched their aging cook, mumbling, to his room. She didn't expect to see any of those men again before morning—but she hadn't been so lucky with Josh. He had followed her into the barn when she went to check on the ailing gelding, and the confrontation had been immediate.

"Don't lie to me, Marcy. I know somethin's wrong. You were all right when you went to town this mornin'. What happened there to change things?" He paused. "Did you have a fight with Willis?"

"I didn't see Willis."

"You went to town, but you didn't stop by the bank?"

"That's right."

"Did you see Walsh?"

"What is this?" Marcy's temper flared. "What makes you think you've got the right to question me?"

"Answer me, Marcy."

"I won't!"

"All right, if that's the way you want it. I'll find out for myself!" Josh turned angrily toward the door.

"Josh!" Marcy called after him. "All right! No, I didn't stop by the bank. I didn't feel like it. Yes, I saw Tierney, but we didn't even exchange a word. I went directly to Doc Whittiker's office, got the medicine for Whistler, and came back here to dose him with it. Is that what you want to know?"

Josh stared at her. "Are you tellin' me the truth?"

"Damn it, Josh!"

Josh's gaze softened unexpectedly. "I don't

like this any better than you do, Marcy. I'm
tryin' to look out for you. I just want the best
for you, that's all."

"Yes. I know." Marcy stared back at him. She
didn't like it, either. She was sick to death of
it . . . and she was sick at heart. She needed to
be alone. Her voice became brusque. "Now, if
you don't mind, I'm busy."

Josh's gaze went cold. "I'm goin' to town."

Good.

"I'll be back late."

Better yet.

"Marcy . . ."

"Goodbye."

Turning toward Whistler's stall, Marcy
refused to look back when Josh walked away.
Despite herself, she listened intently and
breathed a sigh of relief when the sound of
Josh's departing mount faded into the distance.

Willis waited, his unconscious smile almost a
sneer. Josh Tanner rode past him ,where he had
pulled his horse into the foliage in order to
avoid being seen. He remained hidden in the
shadows until Josh turned out of sight, then
directed his mount back onto the trail.

Willis pushed his sorrel to a faster pace.
Avoiding Josh had been instinctive. The truth
be known, he had never liked the fellow. He
wanted to talk to Marcy alone tonight, in any
case, and he had no desire for Josh's intrusive
presence.

Willis hesitated when he rode into the Rocking T yard minutes later. It was silent and

empty, and the house appeared almost dark. Where was everybody?

A sound from the barn answered his silent question, and Willis dismounted. Yes, he remembered. Marcy had come into town for medication for a sick horse—or so Penelope Jarrett had informed him as soon as he stepped foot out onto the street. Penelope went on to inform him about several other things as well.

His blood again boiling, Willis strode into the barn.

"Willis . . ." Her stomach tight, Marcy watched as Willis approached her. The timing of his visit never poorer, she asked, "What are you doin' here?"

"That's the second time you've greeted me with that question." His tone cold, Willis came to a sharp halt beside her. "It struck me as impertinent the first time you asked it. Now it strikes me as rude."

"I'm wonderin' who you think you're talkin' to, Willis." In no mood for the haughty side of him she so disliked, Marcy continued flatly, "If I were you, I'd take the edge off my words, or you might find yourself headin' right back to town where you came from."

Willis's smooth jaw hardened. Marcy remembered marveling at the milk-toast quality of his skin the first time she saw him. He had told her once, with particular pride, that he had never done a day's manual labor in his life. She remembered thinking at the time that his faulty pride stuck out of him like quills on a porcupine—sharp and annoying. Right now those quills were quivering.

"You don't like my tone?" Seeming to swell with an anger that flooded his aristocratic features with color, Willis took an aggressive step. "There are a lot of things I don't like, either. I'm your fiancé. I expect to be treated accordingly."

"What's that supposed to mean?"

Towering over her with sudden rage, Willis grated, "It means I do not appreciate being the last person in town to discover that you've been seeing an old flame!"

"Who's been talkin' to you? Hannah?"

Ignoring her question, Willis grasped her shoulders. "Nor does it help to discover that the day you first greeted me in the same insulting manner as tonight was, *coincidentally*, the same day your old lover returned!"

"Take your hands off me, Willis."

"You turned me out that night as if I were a stray cur!"

"I said, take your hands off me."

"We're going to be married in three weeks! I won't have you acting as if we're casual acquaintances."

"Take . . . your . . . hands . . . off . . . me."

Willis pulled her closer. Shuddering, he grated unexpectedly, "Kiss me, Marcy."

Marcy stared up into Willis's flushed face, her throat suddenly tight. Was it only a few days earlier that she had allowed this man to hold her in his arms, that she had let him kiss her, that she had kissed him back? It seemed a lifetime ago.

"Marcy . . ." Willis's voice softened unexpectedly. His fury seeming to drain from him in a rush, he whispered, "Tell me I'm simply being a jealous fool. That's what I'm really here for."

Willis kissed her suddenly, and Marcy controlled the desire to thrust him from her. Steeling herself as Willis's kiss lingered, Marcy waited until he drew back to say with true regret, "I'm sorry, Willis. You're right. I owe you an apology. I haven't been myself for the past few days. Tierney Walsh came back to Harper to claim his pa's things, and it was a shock seein' him again. There's bad blood between Josh and Tierney that goes way back, and Josh and I have been arguin' ever since. I suppose I should've told you about it that first night, but I couldn't think straight. All I could think about was makin' sure no more blood is spilled before Tierney leaves town again."

Marcy's voice unintentionally hardened. "But there're some things that need to be clear. I'm not one of those Eastern ladies you're accustomed to who'll give in to your moods because you're puttin' a ring on her finger. I'm my own woman, and I'm goin' to stay my own woman. I've been workin' side by side with the men on this ranch most of my life, and that's the way I like it. I've got friends I won't give up for any man, and I've got some enemies that'll stay enemies, no matter what. I'm startin' to think that maybe my kind of woman might be hard for you to accept, that maybe I'm not what you were lookin' for in a wife. Maybe we should both think about that for a while."

"What are you trying to say, Marcy?"

"I *said* what I'm tryin' to say."

"We're getting married in three weeks."

"Are we?"

Willis frowned. "You explained away the situation I came here to discuss, and the unpleasantness is over."

"Is it, Willis?"

"My feelings for you haven't changed."

"Willis . . ."

"Yours haven't changed, either. I know that's true, but I won't ask you to confirm that now."

"Willis, I just want—"

"I'm going." Willis took a stiff backward step. "I think it's for the best if we conclude our conversation at this point, before things are said that we might regret."

"Willis . . ."

Marcy was still standing where he left her when the sound of his mount's hoofbeats faded into silence.

Shaking with suppressed emotion, Willis rode stiffly back toward town. His encounter with Marcy had not gone well. He had been too angry, too conflicted, and Marcy had done it again. She had taken the power from him with a cold anger of her own, leaving him only desire. He had been unable to wait another moment to take her into his arms.

Filled with self-disgust, Willis cursed aloud. He would break the power Marcy held over him if it was the last thing he ever did! She had actually toyed with him with her indirect threat to cancel their wedding. She must have thought he was a fool to believe for a minute that she meant it. He was the catch of the county! Every woman within thirty miles dreamed of being in her place. Yet there had been a moment in their exchange when he had almost believed she was going to end it all between them.

No! He'd never let that happen! He would not allow Marcy to humiliate him. The marriage would go on as planned. He would have Marcy for his wife because he wanted her. He always got what he wanted, and this time would be no different.

Willis slapped his mount sharply with the reins. The animal jolted forward, and Willis cut short his angry meandering with that reminder to himself.

Yes, he *always* got what he wanted.

The bastard was gone.

Standing still as a statue as Willis's mount faded from sight, Tierney watched from the shadows as Marcy stared at the barn doorway through which Willis had departed.

Aware that he should at that moment be moving back toward the place where his own mount was secreted, Tierney could not tear his gaze from Marcy's still figure. He didn't want to feel what he was feeling. The torment of seeing Marcy in another man's arms had been almost more than he could bear. He had been one step from charging into the barn and tearing Barnes and Marcy apart when Marcy stepped

back from Willis's embrace. He couldn't hear
what she said to him then, but Barnes had
taken it calmly—too calmly, considering his
immediate departure afterward.

Marcy turned abruptly and reached for the
pail behind her. Yes, she was tending the sick
gelding he had heard about in town. Marcy
was dedicated to the welfare of the ranch
stock. That had not changed since she was a
child.

Marcy turned in his direction, and Tierney's
thoughts stopped still at the sight of silver
streaks glittering on twin paths down her
cheeks.

Marcy was crying.

Recognizing the effort as futile, Marcy brushed
the tears from her cheeks, then swung
Whistler's feeding pail into the bin. Suddenly
overwhelmed, she sank to her knees and covered her face with her hands. She didn't love
Willis. She didn't know how she had ever convinced herself that she *could* love him. She
loved a man who didn't love her—the same
man she had loved as a child, as an adolescent,
and whom she now realized she loved as a
woman. But that man would never be hers for
the deed of blood that stood between them.

Marcy's sobs deepened. She hated to cry. She
hated the weakness of it, the surrender. She
hated the desolation that followed the realization that tears were her final recourse.

"Marcy?"

The familiar voice startled her. She looked

up into the dove-gray eyes she saw so often in her dreams. She felt Tierney's strong arms slide around her as he kneeled beside her, and she leaned into the spontaneous joy of them. Tierney's name was on her lips when his mouth covered hers. His image remained as her eyes closed, and she abandoned herself to the wonder of his kiss.

Long, drugging moments of rapture ended with the abrupt advent of reality, and Marcy jerked herself back from Tierney's embrace.

"What are you doin' here? You shouldn't have come!"

Tierney was breathing roughly. His eyes pinned her. "You know what I'm doin' here."

"Josh could come back any minute now!"

"Do you think I care?"

"I'm not sure I know." Marcy struggled against the hated tears as she rasped, "You had to see me, is that right? But this mornin' in town you hardly bothered to say hello."

"That's right. That's how you wanted it, wasn't it?"

When Marcy could not reply, Tierney rasped, "Or is this the way you want it, Marcy?" He was kissing her again, pressing deeper to separate her lips, to caress her tongue with his in a way that set her heart pounding. Her arms were around his neck, holding him tight, when he abruptly pulled away from her.

"You didn't kiss Barnes like that."

"You were watching!" She attempted to pull back from Tierney, but he crushed her closer. His mouth brushed hers as he rasped, "He's not the man for you, Marcy. Let me prove that to you."

No.

"Let me show you what it feels like to want somebody so much that you ache."

She already knew.

"Then let me show you how to salve the ache, darlin'. Sweet Marcy, let me show you, so you'll remember there's only one man for you."

Marcy closed her eyes as Tierney's mouth again possessed hers. She had always known there was only one man for her, hadn't she?

Marcy's lips parted under his. She had dreamed of his return for more years than she dared remember, hadn't she?

Marcy returned his kiss. She had waited for him in her heart even when her mind denied it, knowing it was unwise.

Soon Tierney's weight was flush upon her, and Marcy accommodated it with joy. His naked flesh was warming hers, and her heart raced with need. He was Tierney, her only love. He was the pleasure of her youth, the joy of her awakening, her dream of the future.

Then Tierney was inside her, and Marcy's gasp echoed loudly in her ears. Needing to mark the moment for all time, she opened her eyes, then clasped Tierney's face with her palms to hold his gaze with hers. Her heart so full she could barely speak, she whispered, "I love you, Tierney Walsh. I always did. I always will."

Tierney swallowed her loving words with his kiss. Tearing his mouth from hers when the passion became too great, he rasped, "You knew. You always knew that I never stopped loving you."

Words of love . . . searing sensation . . . bursting climax.

The sweet-smelling hay beneath them. Tierney's arms around her.

Fulfillment.

Marcy's sweet scent was in his nostrils. Her sweet taste was in his mouth. Her sweet flesh was pressed tightly to his.

Tierney's heart skipped a beat at the beauty of the moment. Marcy's raven-black hair was spread against the straw; her lashes lay in thick crescents against smooth cheeks, where the stains of former tears had faded; her small features were relaxed; her generous mouth was curved with contentment. He had always known that this was the way it was meant to be.

Drinking briefly again from her lips, Tierney whispered, "Open your eyes, Marcy." He waited as she complied. Her whispered words rebounded in his ears.

"*I love you, Tierney Walsh. I always did. I always will.*"

Her eyes were so deep and dark that he could drown in them. He brushed their lids with his lips, then whispered, "We'll wait for Josh to come home. We'll tell him then."

Tierney felt the shock that rippled through Marcy as she gasped, "I can't do that!"

His loving lethargy abruptly dispelled, Tierney shook his head. "You said—"

"I can't!"

"What do you mean, you can't?"

"I promised Josh I would wait."

"Wait? We've waited seven years, Marcy!"

"He said I would be jumping into a decision that I'd regret if I told Willis I couldn't marry him. I had to promise him to give myself more time."

"You said—"

"I know what I said!"

"Give yourself time for what?"

Pain shadowed Marcy's eyes. "Time to be sure how I feel."

The shadows darkened to unwelcome, familiar images in Tierney's mind. Images of doubt. Of denial. He pulled back from Marcy coldly. "You mean, time to be sure you want to give up a rich husband who can save your ranch, for an itinerant cowboy who isn't worth a nickel."

"No, that's not true!"

"A rich husband your brother approves of, so you can all be one happy family."

"Tierney . . ."

A familiar pain cutting deep, Tierney rasped, "I should've remembered: you don't even *know who I am anymore*."

"I was wrong when I said that. I know who you are."

"Do you?" Tierney grasped Marcy's chin with his hand. "Who am I, Marcy?"

"You're Tierney Walsh, and nothin' else matters."

Tierney's heart pounded with sudden, renewed

hope. Refusing to surrender her gaze, he pressed, "Then we'll tell Josh tonight."

"No! Try to understand. Maybe I shouldn't have, but I made Josh a promise. I don't know what he'll do if I break it."

"I don't care what he'll do, and I won't wait, Marcy." His need for Marcy's acknowledgment at that moment imperative, Tierney heard himself say, "It's now . . . or never."

Silent moments stretched long between them before Tierney drew himself to his feet. Marcy was dressed when he turned back toward her. Her face was devoid of color. Yes, she loved him . . . but love never seemed to be enough.

The scene somberly familiar, Tierney left without speaking a word.

Chapter Four

The bank lobby hummed with the muted din of brisk morning transactions and with pleasant exchanges of conversation conducted in hearty Western tones. Behind the closed door of Willis Barnes's office a few yards away, silence reigned.

Seated stiffly behind his wide mahogany desk, Willis scanned the communication in front of him. The letterhead read MONTGOMERY BANKING, LTD., and listed below it was the information he had been waiting for.

Willis's eye ticked with a spasm that had become increasingly frequent of late, and his agitation soared. In two weeks he'd be a married man. The plans were progressing faultlessly, and the celebration stood to be the biggest the town had ever seen for a wedding, but two problems remained.

The first was with his bride. He was not deceived by Marcy's continued avoidance of him. She was annoyed with him because of his behavior that night in the barn. Almost a week had passed since then, yet she still contrived to see him only in the presence of others, or when her watchdog brother was beside her. But he allowed it. The reason was simple. He had made inquiries about Tierney Walsh. The man was a saddle bum and a troublemaker. The fellow was living in a dilapidated shack where his drunkard father had drunk himself to death. He was obviously low on funds. Whatever his reason for returning, he'd leave town when his money ran out. It didn't make much difference in any case. Only a fool would compare a man like that to him, and Marcy was no fool. He would handle the matter when he was no longer distracted by his second problem—which was Larry McNeil.

Willis ground his teeth with a vengeance. In less than a week, McNeil had already come into town and shown himself at the bank twice. It appeared the fool enjoyed Willis's outrage. So obsessed had Willis become with getting free of that degenerate that he had been able to concentrate on little else.

Unconsciously stroking the sheet in his hand, Willis smiled. Yes, he had been waiting for this. It was the stipulated route of a cash shipment that had already left the main branch of Montgomery Banking back East and was traveling by rail to several destinations in Texas. Each point was designated as to the date and expected time of arrival, with his own bank last on the list.

Willis snickered. The shipment would never get that far.

Reaching into the drawer beside him, Willis withdrew a map and scanned it carefully. He had enjoyed planning the previous robberies that McNeil and his cohorts executed. It excited him in a way he had never before experienced to follow the course of the robbery in his mind as it was actually taking place. His meticulous preparations accounted for the success of their joint ventures. Without him in the past two years, he was sure McNeil would've been relegated to minor robberies and bloodshed that would eventually have found him dangling at the end of a rope.

Willis's short laugh was caustic. He enjoyed the thought that McNeil would eventually meet that fate. It was inevitable, after all.

His expression sobering, Willis traced the route of the shipment on the map with deepening concentration. He would need to exert extra care in this last venture. He wanted no complications. He wanted McNeil out of his life forever, and he applauded the stroke of luck that had sent the shipment so he could accomplish his purpose without delay.

An unexpected knock on the door raised Willis's head with a jerk. He stuffed the map into the drawer as the doorknob turned, and he thrust the drawer shut just as the door opened. The rush of heat that colored his face when he saw McNeil in the doorway was almost dizzying.

His exasperation barely controlled, Willis grated, "Come in, Mr. McNeil. Close the door behind you."

The door no sooner snapped shut than Willis hissed, "You're a damned idiot! You'd better hope the sheriff isn't getting suspicious about your hanging around. If he starts looking through his Wanted notices, you're in trouble."

McNeil shook his head with a smile. "No, *you're* in trouble."

"Is that so?" Willis glared. "Well, if your stupidity fixes it so that the sheriff is waiting for you outside the bank door today, you'll end up missing out on the biggest shipment Montgomery Banking, Ltd., has ever sent to this part of the country."

McNeil's smile froze.

"That's right." Holding up the letter, Willis snapped, "Here's the notification I was waiting for, and I don't need you around here to cause any problems. Get out of my office now, and don't show yourself in town again! The money's already on its way. I'll meet you at the cabin as soon as I have the plan worked out."

His color high, McNeil pressed, "When is it comin'?"

"It'll be here in a week."

"A week."

"So you can start getting your saddlebags packed."

"That's fine with me."

Willis stared at McNeil in the ensuing silence, then prompted, "Well?"

"Well, what?"

"What are you waiting for? Good-bye!"

The door closed behind McNeil.

"And good riddance."

"I don't believe a word of it!" Sheriff Dawson leaned back in his desk chair, looked at Tierney a moment longer, and laughed out loud. The sound reverberated in the empty cells across from him as he continued with open amusement, "I tell you, boy, when you was standin' no higher than my elbow, you came up with better tales than the one you just told me. You'll never get me to swallow that story."

"Yeah, only a fool would believe it." Tierney silently smoldered. He glanced at Clarence Cobb. The older man leaned casually back against the closed street door, effectively blocking the entrance, his smile tight. "Isn't that right, Cobb? Only a fool would believe we're Pinkerton agents and that we're here on a case."

Cobb's tone was cool. "That's right . . . only a fool."

"I guess we'll have to show Sheriff Dawson our identification, then. Hand yours over to me, will you?"

Tierney accepted the small leather case that

Cobb withdrew from his pocket, then withdrew a similar case from his own. He placed them side by side on the desk in front of the sheriff and waited.

The sheriff stared at them, then looked up. "Where'd you steal these?"

Tierney's expression tightened. "The same place we stole this letter."

The sheriff's scowl deepened as he opened the envelope Tierney slapped down on his desk and read the sheet inside. He looked up abruptly.

"This here letter is from Montgomery Banking, Ltd. It says it authorizes you and this Cobb fella as representatives of the Pinkerton Detective Agency to investigate the robberies of their shipments from the main office back East." He shrugged. "Hell, this can't be right."

"Why can't it, Sheriff?" Angry, Tierney leaned over the sheriff's desk. "Because you and the rest of this town made up your mind a long time ago what you could expect from my pa and me? Because you all got one look at me when I came back and just took up where you left off?"

"You was nothin' but trouble when you was a kid."

"Right." Tierney drew back, his expression stiff. "But that was then, and this is now. You've got Cobb's identification in front of you, and you've got mine. If that letter doesn't convince you, I suggest you wire Montgomery Banking direct and have them confirm what you've got right in front of your eyes."

"Maybe I'll do that!"

"But you'd better do it right away, and not from the telegraph office in this town, either, because a lot of plannin's gone into the trap Mr. Pinkerton and Montgomery Bankin' have worked out, and if you spoil it, there'll be hell to pay."

"A trap? Who're you intendin' to trap?"

Tierney paused, his eyes gray ice. "A fella named Larry McNeil and his gang."

"McNeil, huh?"

"And Willis Barnes."

"Willis Barnes!" On his feet in a flash, Sheriff Dawson grated, "Now I know you're lyin'!"

Tierney's short laugh was harsh as he turned back to Cobb's impassive expression. "That's right, Cobb. We forgot. Barnes can't be guilty. He has a pedigree."

"I ain't talkin' about no pedigree! I'm talkin' about a man who's so rich he don't need to rob no shipments!"

"His family money's been gone for quite a while—but he's rich again, all right."

"And he's goin' to marry Marcy Tanner in two weeks."

"He'll be in jail in two weeks—with or without you, sheriff."

Walking closer, the sheriff pushed his face up to Tierney's with a frown. "This is some kind of a vendetta thing, ain't it? You're gettin' even with all of us."

Tierney considered the question honestly, then responded. "No."

"Don't tell me you ain't—"

"There's only one thing I'm tellin' you, Sheriff." Tierney's gaze was frigid. "Montgomery Bankin's shipment is goin' to be here in seven days. Nobody out here knows it's on its way except Cobb, you, me, and *Barnes*, so if McNeil shows up somewhere along the line to get it, we'll just have to figure the fella who told him is either Barnes . . . or you."

"You bastard!"

Tierney responded flatly, "We've located McNeil's shack. We know where he and his men are hidin' out. There's no need to watch them until the shipment comes into the area. They're not goin' anywhere right now, but we're goin' to need enough men to set up day and night surveillance at least three days in advance, just in case. Cobb and I are watchin' Barnes for the time bein', but we'll be needin' help to cover him, too. Montgomery Bankin' wants this business settled once and for all. There's no way they'll be satisfied with less, and Mr. Pinkerton's goin' to give them what they want. You can be in on it or not. It's up to you. I'll go to the U.S. Marshal for help if I have to, but this is your town. You have first choice. We're goin' to need time to set things up, so you'd better make up your mind fast. We'll be back tomorrow to get your answer." Turning toward the door, Tierney added in final warning, "I'd be careful who I talked to about this. You've got a lot to lose."

Outside on the street minutes later, Cobb

prompted, "You know that sheriff better than I do. What do you think he'll do?"

A sharp glance his only retort, Tierney walked on down the street.

Willis heard the heavy footsteps approaching his office. He jumped to his feet a moment before the door burst open.

"McNeil!"

"That's right, it's me."

"What are you doin' back here?" Rounding the desk, Willis pushed the door closed behind McNeil. "No more than five minutes ago I told you to get out of town!"

McNeil sneered. "You think you're so smart, tellin' me to stay out of town because that sheriff might recognize me. And all the while you was too dumb to see what's right in front of your eyes!"

"What are you talkin' about?"

"There's Pinkertons in town!"

"Pinkertons?"

"That's right. I recognized one fella the minute I saw his face when he was walkin' out of the sheriff's office. I saw the other one standin' outside your office when I was leavin' that last time, but it wasn't until I saw them two together that I placed him. He's a Pinkerton, too."

"What men are you talkin' about?"

"People around here know the bigger fella by the name of Walsh."

"Walsh." Willis took a shaken breath. "Tierney Walsh?"

"A tall fella with blond hair and eyes cold as steel."

Willis could not seem to breathe.

"But that wasn't the name he used when he put Buddy Jack and his gang behind bars for robbin' the Smithfield Bank a year ago. I was there when he came to El Paso, where Buddy was hangin' out. He was dressed like a preacher and usin' the name Parker. The older one came a couple of days later, and between the two of them, Buddy didn't stand a chance."

Willis rasped, "Everyone in Harper says Walsh is a saddle bum ... without a job ... without money."

"Everybody in El Paso thought he was a preacher, too."

"Pinkertons ..." Willis could not seem to think.

"The Pinkerton Agency don't come cheap, and there's only one reason them two would be spendin' so much time in this town, hangin' around this bank, without lettin' you know what's goin' on. If they was only out to get me and the boys, we'd already be behind bars. They're waitin' for somethin'. To my mind, it ain't no coincidence that they're in talkin' to the sheriff on the same day you got notice about that shipment. My guess is that they're waitin' for proof that you're in on them robberies with us, and they figure they'll get that proof when me and the boys go after that shipment."

"A trap."

"That's right, and all them bigwigs back at

Montgomery Bankin' are in on it with them Pinkertons."

Willis blinked.

"You're so smart," said McNeil.

Yes, so smart . . .

"Me and the boys are gettin' out of here tonight. Them Pinkertons are goin' to be real disappointed with that trap they're settin' when we don't show up. I figure they ain't watchin' the shack, yet. They probably think there ain't no need, bein' as the money don't get here for another week, so I figure me and the boys are goin' to get a week's worth of head start on them."

Willis could not seem to respond.

"If you're half as smart as you think you are, you'll do the same."

His mind was frozen.

The smirking tone of McNeil's voice jarred Willis as he continued, "If I was you, I'd get my money out of that safe outside, and I'd high-tail it someplace where nobody knows and nobody cares who I am. 'Cause, if there's one thing I know, once them Pinkertons sink their teeth into somebody like you, they never let go."

Never let go . . .

"So you ain't so smart after all, are you, *Mr.* Barnes?"

The door closed behind McNeil, and the question went unanswered.

Willis stood numbly in McNeil's wake. He was ruined. Nothing would ever be the same again.

Willis's eyes widened suddenly. Marcy knew! She'd known all along! She had been avoiding him ever since Walsh came to town, holding back from him, trying to separate herself from him without revealing the real reason for her desertion. The witch had betrayed him! She had been preparing to run to her old lover, the man who had come to ruin him, even while he was telling her he loved her!

Tierney Walsh, a Pinkerton.

Tierney Walsh *and Marcy* . . .

"I'm not goin' to let you do it!"

Evening shadows lengthened beyond the living-room window as Josh stared at Marcy. His stance was rigid. His eyes were wild. His breathing was harsh and strained. Marcy had seen it all before, but the sight of her brother's rage still chilled her.

"I'm not goin' to let you do it, I tell you!"

"You don't have any choice, Josh. My mind's made up. I'm goin' in to tell Willis I can't marry him. I'm goin' to tell him tonight . . . now!"

"It's because of Walsh, isn't it?" Josh's hand slipped to the gun on his hip as he continued, "I knew it would come to this. Hell, I knew it had to, sooner or later!"

"I won't listen to this anymore!" Tierney's image flashed again before Marcy's mind, as it had so many times since she had last seen him. It haunted her. She loved him, and she had let him down . . . again. He would never forgive her, and she would never forgive herself.

Her throat tight, Marcy forced herself to continue. "I kept my promise to you. I waited to make my decision, but I won't wait any longer."

"You're makin' a mistake!"

"Josh. . . ." Marcy grasped his hand and clutched it tight. "I don't love Willis Barnes. I never did. I know that now, and I—"

"You know that now—because of Walsh, is that right?"

"What difference does it make *how* I know it? I don't love him!"

"He loves you, Marcy. He'll make you a good husband."

"But I won't make him a good wife!" Josh attempted to pull back his hand, but Marcy gripped it tighter. "I waited to tell him, even when I didn't want to, because you asked me to, but it's cruel to wait any longer, Josh. The weddin' is less than two weeks away!"

"You're makin' a mistake."

"No, I'm not, and I don't want you to make one, either." Locking Josh's gaze with hers, Marcy said, "I love you, Josh. You're my brother, my only kin, but I'm tellin' you now, if you go gunnin' for Tierney, I'll leave the Rockin' T, and I won't ever come back."

"You wouldn't do that." Josh shook his head as if to negate the thought. "You couldn't."

Tierney's image flashed again before her mind, and Marcy said, "I've made a lot of mistakes, Josh. I should've done a lot of things a different way, but I didn't. It's my fault that your breathin' will never be right."

"My breathin's fine!"

Ignoring his protest, Marcy continued, "But I

won't ruin another man's life in order to make
it up to you."

"It's Walsh's fault."

"It isn't."

"I've got a score to settle with him, Marcy."

"Don't do it, Josh." Marcy's heartbeat leaped
to thunder. "Don't make me leave the Rockin' T
forever."

"I warned you what I'd do if—"

"And I'm warnin' you," Marcy interrupted,
aching inside for the truth she knew she was
speaking. "Take a good look at me, Josh,
because if you go out to face down Tierney
tonight, or any other night, you'll never see me
again."

"You wouldn't do that."

Yes, she would.

Josh's jaw was as hard as stone. His face was
bloodless.

In a minute he was gone.

Marcy glanced around her in a moment of pure
panic as Josh disappeared from sight. The
ranch hands had gone to town, and the cook
was off on an errand.

Was Josh going after Tierney, or had he taken
her at her word that he would never see her
again if he did? Strangely, she had always
believed she knew her brother as well as she
knew herself, but at the moment, she was at a
total loss as to what he was going to do.

Her heart pounding and her thoughts racing,
Marcy pulled her saddle from the rack and
threw it on her mare's back. Yes, she had meant

what she said. She had handled so many things poorly, and it was time to set them straight. She had taken the first step in that direction by facing Josh tonight, but she needed to be sure she hadn't accomplished in those few minutes exactly what she had sacrificed seven long years to avoid.

Marcy mounted. She nudged her horse into motion, knowing she could not rest until she was certain Josh was not on his way to a showdown with Tierney. Once she was sure, she would go directly to Willis's house and tell him the truth—that they had been mismatched from the beginning, that she wasn't the woman for him, that they could never be truly happy. If his pride didn't get in the way, she knew he would agree. In any case, she needed to have it over at last.

Marcy's throat tightened. She would then go to Tierney and speak to him from her heart. She would tell him she loved him—that she had always, always loved him, but that it was not until tonight, when she spoke to Josh, that she realized she had been punishing herself *and* Tierney for her guilt for seven long years— when all she and Tierney were truly guilty of was loving each other.

Was it too late? Would Tierney forgive her? Could he put the past behind him? Could he ever truly *trust* her love—the love she wanted to give to him for the rest of her life?

Those questions momentarily too terrifying, Marcy forced them aside as she urged her mount out into the deepening twilight.

* * *

Concealed in the elongated shadows cast by the setting sun, Tierney maintained his watch of Barnes's house. Sitting crouched in the wooded glade, his spyglass to his eye, he followed Barnes's movements back and forth past the windows in his nightly routine. Satisfied that Barnes was preparing to settle down for the night, Tierney lowered his spyglass to the ground beside him. One more week, and it would be over. Barnes and McNeil and his gang would be in custody, and the Pinkerton Agency would add another star to its list of successful investigations.

But it wouldn't be over for him.

"I love you, Tierney Walsh. I always did. I always will."

Yet love did not seem to be enough. There were so many obstacles between them. Would Marcy's love for him be forever damaged when she discovered that even while their love was hot and sweet between them, he'd allowed others to perpetuate the lie about his true reason for returning to Harper? Would she hate him for the many deceits and evasions that had followed?

Questions . . . with only one answer he had ever wanted to hear.

Seven more days.

Willis walked to the window. Cautiously hiding himself from view, he peered outside into the twilight. He saw it then: a flash in the wooded glade across from the house—the last rays of the setting sun glinting against metal.

Willis raised his spyglass to his eye. He cursed aloud as the shadows within the glade moved, briefly forming a male figure with light hair that was immediately recognizable. Tierney Walsh! Damn if the man wasn't looking back in his direction with a spyglass exactly like the one he himself was using!

Willis took an unsteady step backward. So it was true, all of it, everything McNeil had said. How many days had Tierney been secreted in that spot, watching him?

Willis took a shuddering breath, then turned toward the dresser behind him. Pulling out the drawers in a near frenzy, he dumped the contents into his carpetbag, then tossed the drawers aside. He halted when the bag was full, then snapped it closed.

Standing motionless, Willis reviewed his plan. He had concealed his saddled mount behind the house, where it was not visible from the street. He would light the lamp beside his bed as soon as it was fully dark. He had already dumped enough oil from the wells of the house lamps to ensure they would burn no more than an hour before they went out, making it appear he had retired for the night. He would then slip out the back door, make his way to the bank, and hide his horse behind the bank while he went inside. No one would give his after-hours presence in the bank a second thought if they saw a lit lamp. He so often worked late. The only difference this time would be that his "work" would be more profitable than ever before, when he emptied the vault, rode to the next town, and boarded a train for California.

Money opened all doors in California. Yes, he'd be fine.

Twilight had faded into night when Willis stood poised at the rear door. He waited impatiently until the moon slid behind a cloud bank before slipping out into the yard. Grasping his mount's reins, he drew the animal behind him as he moved stealthily into the darkness.

Bawdy music spilled out through the swinging doors of the Last Stand Saloon as Marcy observed the brightly lit interior from the street. Maintaining a discreet distance, she had followed Josh to town a half hour earlier. He had headed directly for the bar against which he was now leaning. She had watched him drain one glass after another brimming with red-eye, far too many for her to believe he had any intention of confronting Tierney Walsh that night.

Relieved, Marcy silently mounted her horse. She did not enjoy the prospect of facing Willis. He loved her in his own way, she was certain, but she somehow believed his pride would play a greater part than love in any exchange between them. She wanted it to go well. Willis had always been generous to her, and she was repaying him poorly for his kindnesses.

Marcy rode down the street, her uncertain thoughts turning anxious at the unexpected sight of a lit lamp in the bank. Willis. It could be no one else. He often worked late. She had wanted to speak to him in his home, where the surroundings were less formal, but she could not—she would not—allow another night to pass before setting things right between them.

Dismounting in front of the bank, Marcy paused for a stabilizing breath, then dropped her horse's reins over the hitching post and approached the door. She peered inside, took another breath, and knocked.

Something was wrong.

His brow furrowed, Tierney stared through his spyglass at Barnes's bedroom window. The light was lit, but there had been no visible activity for some time.

A prickly feeling moved up Tierney's spine—a familiar warning he had learned not to discount during his years as a Pinkerton. His agitation increasing, he peered carefully through his spyglass, scanning the other rooms that were still lit. The pragmatic side of him mentally listed the possible reasons for a lack of movement in the house. Barnes might be doing paper work somewhere out of sight. He might be reading. He might have dozed off somewhere.

Tierney's frown became a scowl. He couldn't afford to jump to conclusions that could endanger the success of their plan. He needed to be patient. Barnes would undoubtedly show himself again within the hour.

Patience.

* * *

A knock on the bank door!

Willis leaned back against the vault door, his hands trembling as he stuffed the last of the bank funds into his bag. He slid one hand into his pocket, where the smooth handle of the derringer he had put there caressed his palm.

Another knock.

Pulling himself erect, Willis snapped the bag shut, then peered around the corner toward the street entrance. Marcy! He silently cursed. He could have turned anyone else away with a wave of a hand without causing any suspicion at all. But not Marcy. He couldn't afford to respond to her in any way that might send her back to her lover with suspicions. A head start was crucial to his escape plan.

Another knock.

Cursing aloud, Willis slipped his bag under a desk, adjusted his jacket, then paused only long enough to wipe the perspiration from his forehead before stepping into sight.

His fury mounting with every step he took, Willis barely restrained himself as he reached the door and pulled it open.

"Willis . . ."

Marcy's smile was strained, but she was beautiful despite the shabby Western garb she wore so proudly. He had been a fool not to press himself on her when he had the chance—before her lover came back. He remembered the scent of her skin, the taste of her mouth. It galled him that he'd never know more.

"Are you all right?" Marcy searched his face, her smile fading. "You look pale."

"I'm fine. It's a little warm in here." He paused. "I'm quite busy, Marcy. Perhaps we can visit another time."

"No, I . . . I need to talk to you now."

Marcy's uncharacteristic hesitation raised hackles of suspicion on Willis's spine, and he responded sharply. "I suppose I'll have to make myself clearer, then. I don't have time to talk to you tonight, Marcy. So if you'll excuse me—"

"I need to talk to you now, Willis." Color touched the smooth skin of Marcy's cheeks. Stepping past him, she pushed the door closed behind her and walked into the bank's interior.

Forced to follow, Willis halted when Marcy turned abruptly toward him. Her expression suddenly penitent, she said, "I'm sorry, Willis, but I've put this off too long already. It won't wait another day. Willis . . . I'm so sorry, but I can't marry you."

"You can't marry me." Willis's control was rapidly waning. "May I ask why you cannot? Have you found a more favorable prospect? Your old lover, perhaps?"

Marcy took a backward step, her color mounting. "Willis, please . . . I hoped we could end this in a friendly way."

"Friendly?" Willis's caustic laughter resounded in the silent room. "I never felt *friendly* toward you—didn't you know that, Marcy?" He sneered. "I disliked you when we first came into contact. Then I came to desire you. But *friendly* never once entered my mind. Did you feel *friendly* to me, Marcy? Did you feel *companionable* when you decided to betray me?"

"Betray you?"

His control all but dissipated, Willis grated, "Walsh didn't send you here tonight, did he? He's too busy watching my empty house, where he thinks I've retired for the night. You came here to do a little detective work on your own, didn't you?"

"I don't know what you're talkin' about! I—"

"You knew all along, didn't you!"

Marcy stared at Willis. His color was suddenly high. There was a feral quality to his gaze. Confused by his unexpected rage, by his irrational questions, she responded bluntly, "I knew *what* all along? What are you talkin' about?"

"Don't pretend! I saw the difference in the way you treated me after Walsh came to town. You were in league with him against me, weren't you?"

"In league with Tierney—"

"You knew he was a Pinkerton! You knew the board of directors back East was suspicious that I had a part in the robberies of bank shipments. You knew the Pinkerton Agency sent him out here to trap me!"

Tierney, a Pinkerton? Willis, a thief?

Stunned, Marcy gasped, "I don't understand."

Willis advanced menacingly. "I told you I loved you, and you lost respect for me, didn't you? That was my mistake, wasn't it? I should have turned my back on you like Walsh did. I should have walked away from you when you tried to avoid me, just like Walsh. Then you would have come running back to my arms—like you went running back into his the first chance you got!"

Willis's eyes were glassy. His breathing was ragged.

Tierney, a Pinkerton? Willis, a thief? Was Willis insane?

Marcy glanced around her. The bank was dark except for the lamp that was lit farther back, near the vault . . . near the vault door that stood partially open.

"That's right. You're not seeing things. The vault is open." Willis leered. "And it's *empty*."

Incredulous, Marcy stared. "What are you sayin', that you're stealin' the bank money?"

"I'm sick of your pretense!" Grasping her arm, Willis shook her roughly. "You were in on this with Walsh from the day he got here, but you won't profit from my ruin! I'll see to that! I'll be out of this town and on my way to safety before anyone realizes I'm gone. No one will find me, because my money will protect me, just as it always has!"

He *was* crazy.

"No, I'm not crazy." Willis cackled wildly. "I could see in your eyes what you were thinking. Or perhaps I am—crazy like a fox! A fox who is going to take you with him part of the way when he leaves this town—as insurance."

"I'm not goin' anywhere with you, Willis."

"Oh, yes, you are!"

"You're goin' to have to make me come with

you, and to my mind, there's no way you can do that."

"Will *this* change your mind, Marcy?"

Marcy stared at the gun Willis withdrew from his pocket. The gun was small, but it was real, and its bullets were no less deadly for its diminutive size.

"I see you have the proper respect for firearms."

"I do." Marcy struggled to control the shuddering that gradually beset her. "But I'm not goin' with you."

"You are!" Willis's gaze was suddenly frenzied. "You will come with me even if I have to drag your dead corpse all the way!"

"Drop your gun, Barnes!"

Tierney's booming command echoed in the silent room, turning Willis toward the rear door as Tierney stepped into view, gun drawn. He repeated, "Drop it, now!"

Her heart pounding, Marcy stared at Tierney. His powerful size was menacing, his strong features were tightly drawn, his gaze was deadly, but he had never been a more welcome sight.

His voice quavering, Willis grated, "Don't come any closer. I'll shoot her . . . you know I will."

"You'll never get out of here alive if you do." Tierney's eyes were gray ice. His words were all the more threatening for their emotionless tone as he continued, "There's only one way you'll get out of here now . . . and that's if I *let* you."

"If you let me." Willis sneered. "As if you would!"

"I'll let you leave, and I'll let you get that head start you wanted, too. All you have to do is put that gun down now, and you can walk right out that back door. I won't stop you. I give you my word on that."

"Walk out that back door—without Marcy and the money, of course!" Willis laughed aloud. "You don't fool me! I know what you'd do then. You'd take the money and say *I* stole it. No one would believe I left it behind! Bastard!" Willis was shuddering visibly. "You want it all, and you want it all on your terms!"

"Think what you like. It's my terms or nothing at all."

"You think so?" Willis's gun hand was trembling. Marcy saw Tierney's eyes shift in silent warning. He was going to—

The sudden crash of sound as the street door burst open left Marcy gasping. Swaying unsteadily, Josh stood in the opening, the muzzle of his gun aimed directly at Tierney as he shouted triumphantly, "I've got you now, Walsh! You can't get away! Barney Ross said he saw you slinkin' around by the bank. I figured you were goin' to try somethin', and I was right. You're goin' to jail this time!"

"No, Josh! You've got it all wrong!" Aware that Josh was too drunk to see the situation as it truly stood, Marcy rasped, "Willis is robbin' the bank, not Tierney!"

"Willis! Are you crazy, Marcy? He—"

Distracted, Marcy did not see Willis's subtle movement toward her until it was too late. Jerking her back against him in an imprisoning grip, Willis jammed his gun barrel against her breast, halting all sound and movement in the silent room as he said, "Thank your brother, Marcy. Without his ill-timed interference, you wouldn't be in my arms right now." Pressing the gun painfully tight, he glared with venom at the two men opposite him and spat, "Drop your guns, both of you, or I'll shoot her now!"

Shaking his head in obvious confusion, Josh slurred, "W . . . what's goin' on here?"

"You drunken fool! What do you think is going on?" Willis's tone was scathing. "It was a stand-off between Walsh and me, until you came in and tipped the scale in my favor. I'd thank you for your stupidity, but I don't have the time. Drop your gun, now!"

Willis darted a tight glance at Tierney. "You, too, Walsh! I'll shoot her if I have to!"

Her attention diverted when Tierney's gun hit the floor, Marcy was unprepared as Josh lurched forward, yelling, "Bastard! You ain't takin' Marcy nowhere!"

A gunshot rocked the room. Knocked from Willis's grip, Marcy felt Tierney's strong arms close around her as they struck the floor together. Stunned, motionless under Tierney's protective weight, Marcy saw Josh standing nearby, staring at Willis's bloodstained shoulder as Willis slumped weakly to the floor.

Cobb stood in the doorway, smoking gun in hand. He advanced toward Willis as Tierney rasped, "Are you all right, Marcy?" His voice ragged, his eyes anxious and searching, Tierney turned her toward him with shaking hands. "Tell me you're all right."

"I'm all right, but—"

Crushing her close, his lips against her hair, Tierney whispered, "That's all I want to know. Nothing else matters. I love you, Marcy. I made the mistake of lettin' you go once before, and I almost lost you again. But you're in my arms to stay this time. No matter what you say, that's the way it's goin' to be."

Sweet words . . . loving words . . . interrupted by Josh's unsteady step toward them as Tierney raised her to her feet.

Josh questioned uncertainly, "Wha . . . what happened here, Marcy?"

What happened? Still dazed, Marcy was silent as Josh's question rang in her mind. How could she answer him? Willis wasn't the man everyone thought he was. Tierney wasn't, either. The masquerade had been twofold, and the deception had been complete.

Tierney's dove-gray eyes held hers as he waited for her reply.

"You're in my arms to stay this time."

Marcy's throat was suddenly tight. How could she explain to Josh that she didn't really know how everything that had happened a few minutes earlier came about, but that the explanation didn't matter? How could she make him comprehend that those terrible moments just past had clarified the only important truth— that Tierney was the part of her that had been lost for so many years, and that she could never be truly whole without him? How could she find the words to relate that, when all was said and done, loving Tierney was all she had ever wanted—and at that moment, her greatest joy was that Tierney's gaze was speaking those same words straight to her heart?

"You're in my arms to stay this time."

Yes, she was.

How could she make Josh understand?

Dispensing with words, Marcy responded in the only way she could. Her heart filled to bursting, Marcy stepped into Tierney's waiting embrace.

Epilogue

It wasn't the biggest wedding Harper ever saw, but it was the talk of the town.

Tierney Walsh, a Pinkerton!

Willis Barnes, a thief!

Incredible!

Unbelievable!

It can't be true!

The astounded whispers still resounded as Marcy scanned the familiar faces in the crowded church. Focusing her gaze on Tierney, who awaited her at the altar, Marcy started down the aisle.

I love you, Tierney.

Marcy glanced at Josh, who stood beside Tierney, a sober and silent best man. She had never been more proud of her brother than she was when he brought the animosity between

Tierney and him to an end by speaking simply and humbly.

"I was wrong about Willis Barnes. I was wrong about you, too, Tierney. I'd like to be your friend."

Peace, at last.

She had felt no pity for Willis when he was removed from Harper's local jail, heavily bandaged, and remanded to the custody of the U.S. Marshal. She knew that if Cobb's second sense as a Pinkerton agent hadn't brought him to the bank at that time, and if his bullet hadn't stopped Willis before he could fire his gun, her life might have been changed forever. She also knew that although McNeil and his gang had gotten away, the law—or a Pinkerton—would get them eventually.

The aisle seemed endless. Tierney's eyes were solemn gray velvet when she stood beside him at last.

"I love you, Marcy."

Whispered words. Cherished words.

"I love you, Tierney."

Words engraved in her heart.

With this ring, I thee wed . . .

Something old. Something new.

At last, Marcy and Tierney, just as she had always known it should be.

SOMETHING NEW

Constance O'Banyon

This one is for you, Kathy Baker, for helping me come up with the plot for "Something New." Congratulations for winning Bookseller of the Year!

Chapter One

Charleston, South Carolina—1850

Gabriel T. Merrick stalked across the marble floor, his eyes blazing with anger. When he called for his secretary, his voice echoed against the vaulted ceiling, manifesting the intensity of his anger. "Dammit, Niles, where are you?"

Niles Edger hurried from the library, stepping gingerly around the green Persian rug as was his habit; the rug, a thing of beauty, cost more than ten years of his salary, and he cringed at the thought of walking on it. "I was just sorting through the mail, sir," he said, taking the hat Gabriel thrust at him and passing it to the butler, who had just hurried into the foyer behind him.

Niles's employer, the heir of Merrick Shipping

and Ship Building, stood a good head taller than he. Although the ladies called Gabriel Merrick handsome, with his dark hair, chiseled features, and unusual golden eyes, at the moment, Niles imagined Gabriel would frighten any shy young miss. Gabriel's golden eyes swirled with anger that made them appear to darken to deep brown, and his jaw was clamped tightly, while a muscle pulsed in his throat.

"Have you gotten any responses to my advertisement for a baby nurse?" Gabriel asked impatiently.

"No, sir, not yet. But this came in the post." The secretary thumbed through the papers he was carrying and extended an envelope to his employer. "It's from Cyrus Larson. Since it's probably of a private nature, I didn't open it."

Gabriel took the letter and frowned. "I don't care how much the man rants and raves, or how demanding he becomes, I will never surrender the baby to him! My nephew stays here. He's my only heir, and he will inherit from me one day."

Niles knew that his employer was sought after by many ladies, and he expected Miss Sarah Maxwell was the leading contender for the prize. Certainly Mr. Merrick was wealthy as well as handsome. He would someday be married and have children of his own. However, the secretary did not feel it was his place to point out the obvious. "Perhaps Mr. Larson merely wants visitation rights with the child," Niles suggested.

Gabriel's jaw set in a firm line. "I might consider that." He glanced down at the letter and began to read:

Sir,
As to the matter of the baby my daughter bore your brother, my wife and I have no interest in the child now nor anytime in the future. Do not contact me again, because I disowned my daughter, Mary Ann, when she married your worthless brother. Pursuant to the death of my daughter, I enclose a bank draft to cover the expense of her burial. I assume you have had her laid to rest beside your brother. This will preclude any further correspondence between us.

Cyrus Larson

Gabriel wadded the letter in his clenched fist. "I needn't have worried—that cold hearted bastard wants nothing to do with my nephew! His own daughter dies, and he doesn't want to see her baby."

"There will be no reply to his letter, sir?"

"No. I think not." Gabriel glanced toward the stairs. He had been at the docks since before sunup, arranging for cotton shipments to France and England. He wanted nothing more than to go to his room and sleep the night through. But there were many demands on his time, and correspondence he must answer before he'd see his bed this night. "How is the baby's wet-nurse working out?"

"Mrs. Whitlow isn't too pleased with her, but she has not told me why. I checked on the woman twice today, and she seemed capable to me."

Gabriel had always trusted his housekeeper's instincts, and if she didn't like the wet-nurse, there must be a reason. "I'll talk to Mrs. Whitlow about it later. Perhaps I should just dismiss the woman right now."

"Sir," Niles said, lowering his voice, "Mrs. Jenkins can't leave until you have someone to replace her. Who would nurse the child?"

Gabriel shook his head wearily. "Accompany me to the library. I have letters to write."

Niles followed his employer into the book-lined room and closed the door behind them.

"Did you ask Mrs. Whitlow if she would continue to look after the child until I can find a suitable nurse?"

"I did, Mr. Merrick. She told me to remind you that running your house is a tedious task without the added burden of the child. But, seeing how she coos over the baby, I think she does not mind too much."

"Did you tell her that I'd pay her for the extra work?"

Niles cleared his throat and studied his fingernails. "To quote her exactly, sir, she said to remind you that she has been in service to your family for thirty years, and she has been paid quite well, thank you very much. She did ask that you be purposeful in your search for a nurse."

"I get the feeling from the look in your eyes

that you have more bad news for me. What is it, Niles?"

"The head gardener quit this morning. It seems he ran off with the upstairs maid."

Gabriel ran a hand through his thick black hair in agitation. "I hope you have come to the end of your worrisome news. I'm gone for three days, and the whole damned place falls into chaos."

"I have nothing further to report at this time."

"What am I to do, Niles? There is no one to take care of my nephew. I don't know anything about taking care of a baby."

The secretary shook his gray head. "There is always hope that some suitable woman will respond to the advertisement you placed in the newspaper."

Gabriel stalked out the door and walked toward the stairs. "If anyone applies for the position of nurse, let me know at once. But if they do not have the proper credentials and recommendations, send them away. I don't want another Mrs. Jenkins on my hands."

"Yes, Mr. Merrick." Niles adjusted his bifocals on the bridge of his nose and walked softly back into the library, while Gabriel went up the stairs and disappeared into the baby's room.

Mrs. Whitlow had just laid the baby in the cradle and turned to her employer with a finger to her lips.

Gabriel moved silently to the cradle and stared down at his brother's child. His heart wrenched with pity for the tiny infant, who was only three months old. There was no mother to tenderly hold him, to sing lullabies and kiss his hurts away.

"How is he doing?" he whispered, glancing up at the housekeeper, who wore a neat black uniform with a white apron, her hair covered with a stiff white cap.

"He's a little angel, Master Gabriel. Never a peep out of him unless he's hungry." Her gaze went back to the baby. "I want to speak to you about the wet-nurse, sir. I have reason to believe that she's tipping the bottle."

"You mean drinking?"

"Her breath would knock a sailor down."

"What am I to do, Whitlow? There is no one else to feed him."

"I know. You had a hard time finding this woman. Where will you get someone to replace her?"

"How should I know?" he said with irritation. "I'll have to let her stay until I can find someone more suitable. If only I could get a nurse to watch over him, that would help with the problem."

Gabriel touched a golden curl that fell across the child's forehead. His dead brother's son was the only family he had left, and he'd be damned if Cyrus Larson or any of Mary Ann's family would have any part of the child's life! He'd felt obligated to let them know about the baby, since he was their grandson, but he had fulfilled that obligation, and they were never to be allowed to set foot in this house.

The woman stepped down from the carriage and stared for a long moment at the imposing red brick mansion. She swallowed hard. With its three stories and three flanker additions, it would take a fleet of servants to make sure it ran smoothly.

She started to reenter the carriage when she stopped herself. She couldn't let anything intimidate her—her mission was too important!

She turned to the driver. "I won't be needing you. You can leave."

The craggy-faced driver looked at her with doubt in his gray eyes. "What about your trunk, miss?"

"Leave it at the inn. I will send for it." She added under her breath, *"If I am allowed to remain."*

The driver respectfully tipped his hat to her and urged the horses forward. She wanted to call out to him to come back, but she straightened her back and set her foot on the path that led to the front door.

Should she have thought to wear a wedding ring to make her appear older and more responsible? It was too late now. If only she'd worn gloves, then Gabriel Merrick would not be able to tell if she wore a ring.

She stopped halfway up the walk. Perhaps she should come back tomorrow. She didn't even know if Mr. Merrick was in residence.

She shook her head as she approached the wide front door. Before she lost her nerve, she reached for the brass doorknocker. She'd come too far to back out now. If he was home, she intended to see Gabriel Merrick!

Gabriel had just finished his dinner when Niles appeared at the dining-room door. "There's a Mrs. Amanda Lord to see you, sir."

Gabriel wiped his mouth on a napkin and stood. "I don't know anyone by that name. What does she want?"

"She's come about the position of baby nurse, sir."

Gabriel's golden eyes flashed as he straightened his gray waistcoat. "Show her into the library, and tell her I'll attend her straightaway."

The woman walked the length of the library, scanning the titles of books in the vast bookcases. The many tomes had not been purchased just for show; it was easy to see from the frayed covers that they had been read, and often, and many of the pages had been dog-eared.

The maroon-colored leather couches and chairs were placed so that a reader could catch the light from the wide bow windows. Papers were neatly stacked on the smooth surface of the heavy oak desk, while an inkwell and several pens lay in an orderly row. The room bespoke wealth and good taste. But there was nothing here that would tell her anything more personal about the man she was about to meet.

She walked to the window and gazed out on the vast lawn that, like the library, was neat and trim. Her heart was thundering within her breast as she anticipated her meeting with

Gabriel Merrick. She had to convince him to let her look after the baby—she just had to!

She tried to remember everything she'd been told about Gabriel Merrick. His family had lived in Charleston for five generations. They had made their money in trade, starting out with one ship and then acquiring a fleet of ships in Gabriel's great-grandfather's time. Since then, their riches had increased considerably. Like most families of wealth, they had their enemies, but they were highly respected if somewhat standoffish. Gabriel, the only remaining son and the last of the Merrick clan, was reported to be arrogant, ruthless, and a formidable enemy. Beyond that, she knew little else.

Amanda straightened her blue silk bonnet and nervously unfolded the newspaper and reread the advertisement. She just had to convince Mr. Merrick to employ her to look after the infant!

The door opened, and there was no mistaking the man who entered as anything but the head of Merrick Shipping. He was so tall, he filled the doorway. He was powerfully built and the most imposing man she had ever encountered. Muscles strained against the gray cutaway, and his tight-fitting trousers outlined a long, lean body. He moved with muscular grace and with the assurance of a man who was accustomed to walking the deck of a ship. Dark hair framed a handsome face, and his chin was square and stubborn. His eyes were the most remarkable golden color, and the long, dark lashes would be the envy of any woman.

Amanda drew in her breath under his intense scrutiny, feeling as if he'd just stripped her last secret away. She didn't know if the fluttering in the pit of her stomach was from fear of the impending interview or because of his strong male presence.

"You are Mrs. Lord? Mrs. Amanda Lord?"

She dipped into a quick curtsey, hoping she demonstrated just the right amount of deference. "I am, sir."

"And your business with me is . . . ?"

"You advertised that you need a nurse to care for an infant, and I would like to be considered for the position."

He stood between her and the window, cutting off the sunlight. "And you think you have the qualifications I am looking for in a nurse?"

She raised her chin. "Yes, I do. I believe I can tend this child better than anyone else you might find."

His lip curled sardonically, and he indicated that she should be seated on the sofa in the sunlight so he could better observe her. He watched her cross the room with a stately, graceful stride. She moved to the end of the sofa that was cast in late-afternoon shadows, rather than the place he had indicated. He was annoyed, because he couldn't see much of her face as she kept it tilted downward, a trait that irritated him. He certainly didn't want a timid or perhaps even devious woman looking after his nephew. He was good at stripping away pretenses, and he would know the truth about her before she left this room.

Gabriel's lids drifted down over golden eyes. Since he'd entered his study, a restlessness stirred within him, and he didn't know the cause. Because of the depth of his reaction to her, his voice came out harsher than he'd intended. "What makes you think you are the right person for this position?"

She almost balked under his searching stare. "I . . . you will find no one more dedicated than I am."

He was silent for a long moment, and she tried to look directly into his eyes, but it was like staring into the eye of a storm.

"Tell me about yourself," he said, becoming fascinated by her graceful and delicate movements. "Tell me all, so I can decide for myself if you are qualified to look after my nephew."

Her heart was drumming with fear, because the aura he projected was one of overwhelming power. He seemed to have the ability to see right into her mind. He must not know her true identity, lest her chances of being the baby's nurse diminish.

Her voice trembled when she replied, "What would you like to know?"

Chapter Two

Gabriel watched the woman fold her hands demurely in her lap. "I suppose you have brought references, Mrs. Lord?"

She avoided his eyes. "I...have never worked outside my home, Mr. Merrick; therefore, I have no one to recommend me."

Gabriel seated himself across from her, propped his chin on his laced fingers, and studied her intently. His voice had an edge to it and verged on sarcasm. "No references? Then perhaps you know someone of good standing in Charleston who can vouch for your character?"

Now she did meet his gaze and felt the pull of those golden eyes. "I have just arrived in Charleston and know no one here."

"And you are from...?"

"Savannah."

"What about your husband? Did he come with you?"

"I . . . he . . . John is dead."

Gabriel assessed her clothing. Her blue silk gown and matching bonnet were nicely styled but worn and out of date. Her clothing was certainly not in keeping with what a grieving widow would wear. His gaze dropped to her hand, and he saw no ring on her finger. "How long has your husband been dead, Mrs. Lord?"

Untruthfulness did not come easily to Amanda's lips. "He . . . David has been gone these last two months."

"David? I distinctly heard you call your husband John."

Her face reddened, and she feared that she'd ruined her chances to convince Merrick to hire her as the baby's nurse. "His name was John David," she blurted out. "I often called him by both names."

"I see. Then accept my condolences, Mrs. Lord." Gabriel fell silent, watching her as she shifted uncomfortably, allowing his silence to stretch ominously before he asked, "Did you have a happy marriage with John . . . David?"

Amanda was shocked by his question. She had always spoken her mind, even though it had often gotten her into trouble, and she did so now. "That would not be any of your concern, Mr. Merrick. Just because I apply to you for employment does not give you the right to pry into my personal life."

"You are mistaken, Mrs. Lord. If you want to look after my nephew, everything about you is my concern." His golden gaze became hard, penetrating. "Now, did you have a happy marriage, Mrs. Lord?"

"I still don't see that my marriage is any of your concern."

He liked to see a person's eyes when he questioned them, it allowed him to ferret out lies and get straight at the truth. But this woman's bonnet shaded most of her face as well as her eyes. She was hiding something, and he intended to find out what it was. "Was your marriage a happy one?" he repeated.

She couldn't imagine that anyone would be capable of withstanding those probing golden eyes for very long. "Of course. I cared for John."

"Yet you do not mourn his death," he observed blandly.

Her head snapped around, and she replied with indignation, "Why should you draw such a conclusion? You don't know how I feel."

"You say you loved your husband, who has been dead only two months, but you do not wear the trappings of a widow. Why do you not wear black, madam?"

She lowered her gaze, her hands clenching and unclenching in a reflexive action. "I thought you might not hire me if I was in mourning."

His voice was soft now, but with a sharp edge; he knew she was not being truthful with him. "Remove your bonnet, Mrs. Lord. I will see your face before I consider whether to entrust the well-being of my nephew to you."

Not wanting to provoke him, she reluctantly untied the silk ribbon from beneath her chin and slowly, hesitantly, removed the bonnet.

Gabriel stared at her for a long moment. She was much younger than he'd thought. If he was any judge of age, she couldn't be any older than twenty. Her hair was red with golden streaks, and she had pulled it away from her face in a tight bun—he imagined it was an attempt to make her seem older than her years. He stared into her eyes, which were the greenest he'd ever seen. To say that she was beautiful was not enough—she was breathtaking. If she had a flaw, it was hidden in a place he could not see.

Amanda wondered why Mr. Merrick was staring at her so strangely, and she felt her panic returning. The room was so silent that Amanda began to squirm until, finally gaining control of her nervousness, she met his gaze squarely. "I love children, and they seem to respond to me."

Her voice was deep and throaty, and for some reason, every nerve in his body tightened at the sound of it. Gabriel wondered how it would feel to loosen her silken hair and allow the strands to drift through his fingers. He could imagine the softness of those luscious full lips. He pushed his lustful thoughts aside and tried to discern who she was and why she was there.

"Since you don't seem inclined to talk about your husband, perhaps you won't think it's too presumptuous of me if I inquire about where you live," he said, breaking eye contact and glancing at her hands, which were clasped so tightly in her lap that the knuckles were white. "Perhaps you can convince me to place my nephew in your care."

There was desperation in her eyes when she looked at him. Was he toying with her? It seemed so. "I will love this child as much as any mother would. I will give him the best of care. You will never have reason to regret it if you place him in my care."

Gabriel settled back against the chair and watched her twist the ribbon of her bonnet around her finger. "Why should I trust you? You come to me with nothing to recommend you, and you are unwilling to talk about yourself. Would you place your own child with a woman who is as secretive as you are?"

She shook her head and admitted with honesty, "No, I probably wouldn't. But if you let me watch over the child, you won't be sorry."

He felt the sincerity of her words, and he saw tears gathering in the corners of her eyes. Eyes that dilated with . . . what? fear? Hope? She either loved children, or she was destitute for money. Or was she simply a madwoman?

Amanda reached out a hand and then hopelessly withdrew it. "If I could just see the child and know that he is . . ." She shook her head and, as if reading his thoughts, said, "You must think me mad."

With a sudden jolt, he stared at her, taking in every feature. What a fool he'd been. He'd seen green eyes like hers before, although not as deep a green. He'd seen hair the same color as hers—red, shot with gold. He'd seen her likeness in Robert's wife, Mary Ann. Mary Ann had been lovely, but older, and without the same delicate beauty this woman who called herself Amanda Lord had. He stared up at the ceiling to gather his thoughts.

Dear God, this woman was Mary Ann's sister!

Gabriel stood, making a quick decision. "I have decided to trust you, Mrs. Lord. Come; I will take you to the child."

Amanda pressed a hand over her pounding heart. "Do you mean I can care for the child?"

Gabriel wasn't about to turn the entire care of his nephew over to her until he found out her reason for being there. For all he knew, this woman might have come to take the child away. But something about her compelled him to trust her. After all, the child was her nephew as well as his. He already knew that her father and mother didn't want anything to do with the child. Amanda Lord must be watched at all times, and the best way to do that was to have her in his home.

"I will allow you to stay if you understand that you will be supervised at first. Then, if I find you to be suitable, I may allow you to care for my nephew on a more permanent basis."

She gripped her bonnet and hurried after him. "You will never regret this, Mr. Merrick."

"That, Mrs. Lord," he said, turning back to her and allowing her to precede him, "remains to be seen."

Amanda hesitated at the door of the nursery

with Gabriel just behind her. She took a deep breath and moved into the room and toward the cradle. She could hear the soft sounds of the child and willed herself not to cry.

Standing over the cradle and staring down at the child, she was blinded by tears. She reached out and ever so gently touched the golden, downy hair on the baby's head. "Oh," she said as her hand slid down the smooth arm to touch the tiny hand that curled around her finger. "Oh, how very beautiful he is."

She'd almost forgotten that Gabriel Merrick was beside her until he spoke. "You have walked into a terrible tragedy here, Mrs. Lord. The child's mother and father were killed in a carriage accident. Mary Ann, the baby's mother, lived only long enough to give him life. It was as if she refused to die until he was safely delivered."

Amanda ducked her head and drew in a deep breath. Grief welled up inside her, and she managed to push it aside, fearing that if she started crying, she wouldn't be able to stop. Dazed by her inner pain, she slid her fingers along the baby's cheek. "That is a tragedy. But out of death came this precious life."

"Would you like to hold him?"

"Yes. Yes, I would." She lifted the baby in her arms and held him to her cheek, loving him to the very depth of her soul. "He is so new and smells so sweet. I never knew a baby could be so precious." Her eyes met Gabriel's. "What is his name?"

"Rob."

"Short for Robert?"

"Yes. We seem to have fallen into calling him Rob." Gabriel looked slightly bemused. "The whole idea of raising a child is a bit daunting to me. I have had him for only three weeks." He touched the child's cheek. "When he was brought to me by the doctor who delivered him, he had no name, and it seemed only right that I name him after my brother."

Amanda's lips brushed across the baby's head. "I'm sure your brother and sister-in-law would have approved."

Gabriel stepped back and watched her with the child. There was no mistaking the love in her eyes when she looked at the infant, nor the tenderness of her touch. "Yes, I believe you are right, Mrs. Lord."

"He seems healthy."

"So the doctor assures me." Gabriel leaned against the doorjamb and crossed his arms. "I have decided to trust you, Mrs. Lord. Although, I might point out, you have given me no reason to."

There was joy in her eyes as she laid the baby down and turned to Gabriel. "Thank you, Mr. Merrick. I promise you the baby will be in loving hands with me."

His voice hardened, and there was the hint of a threat when he said, "I will expect you to always put the baby's welfare ahead of everything else. And never take him away from this house. Do I make myself clear?"

She nodded. "Of that you have my assurance, Mr. Merrick."

"I'll send the housekeeper, Mrs. Whitlow, to you so she can get you settled." He was relieved to relinquish the details concerning the baby's daily care. "Mrs. Jenkins is the wet-nurse, and I don't want her to be left alone with the child. Is that understood?"

"Yes, of course. But why?"

"Let's just say that she's on trial, as you are."

She lifted her chin. "And who will be watching me?"

His eyes met hers. "I will. And when I am away, my secretary, Niles, will be watching you. I should tell you that he's a very capable man, so take care of this child, Mrs. Lord."

"You will find no reason to mistrust me."

Gabriel nodded, feeling somehow relieved. "It is not easy to have parenthood thrust on one. I'm satisfied for the moment to place the baby under your care." He turned to leave but paused. "I find it strange that you did not inquire about your wages, Mrs. Lord."

"Whatever you deem appropriate will be fine with me."

He looked at her strangely. "I will be gone for a week. Should you need anything, just ask Mrs Whitlow or Niles to help you."

"Mr. Merrick?"

"Yes?"

"I am grateful to you."

He frowned. "Don't be. If I find your care of my nephew inadequate in any way, I will not hesitate to show you the door."

"You will not have to do that, sir."

He turned away abruptly, and she watched

him disappear down the corridor and heard his boots on the stairs.

Amanda closed her eyes and leaned against the wall. She had accomplished her goal. She had the care of the baby.

Chapter Three

Amanda walked to the cradle where the baby slept and smiled gently down at the tiny infant. "I will love you with the tenderness your mother would have, had she lived," she whispered, bending to touch her lips to the downy head. "This I swear."

The child stirred, stretched, and yawned. Amanda gathered him in her arms and settled into a rocker. She loved the way the baby curled against her, and she felt an overpowering love and protectiveness toward him.

She hummed a lullaby her nurse had sung to her as a child. Then softly she sang the words that came to her memory. "Little one, so new and warm, little one, so far from harm. Little one, for you I pray and sing this song at end of day."

The baby stared into her eyes, and she cuddled him close to her heart as tears rolled down her cheeks. She was thankful to Gabriel Merrick for giving the baby a home and glad that she would now have a place in the child's life.

He was a powerful man with deep insights, and, no doubt, he would be a formidable enemy. What would he do if he discovered her deception?

The housekeeper, Prudence Whitlow, appeared at the door of the nursery. She turned out to be a practical, no-nonsense kind of person, and Amanda liked her at once. She had an ample figure, cheeks the color of cherries, and twinkling blue eyes.

"The wee babe needs loving hands to tend him," Mrs. Whitlow stated as she entered the nursery and stood at Amanda's shoulder. "Such a sadness has touched the little one's life. But he's fortunate in his uncle. Master Gabriel intends to see that nothing harms the wee one."

"Did you ever meet the baby's mother?"

"No, but Master Gabriel did." Her eyes were reflective. "He said that his brother had married above him, and that his wife would be a good influence on him."

"In what way?"

"Master Robert was kind of wild at times. Oh, there was no harm in him, you understand. He just needed a good woman to gentle him. Such a pity that he didn't live to see his son." She blew her nose in a handkerchief, which she then stuffed into her apron pocket. "He'd have been so proud of little Rob."

"I understand there are some concerns about the wet-nurse."

"Indeed. I refuse to leave that woman alone with the wee one. She comes every three hours to feed him and always smells like strong spirits."

Amanda's mouth opened in horror. "Well, we can't have that!" Her eyes went to the sleeping child and softened. "I don't want such a woman to touch him, much less feed him."

"You love children—I can tell. I'm glad you will be looking after this child." Mrs. Whitlow nodded toward the connecting doors. "Come; let me show you to your room."

Amanda laid the baby in the cradle and followed the housekeeper into the next room. It was quite pleasant, decorated in creams and bright yellows. But she quickly decided that it must be rearranged. "Mrs. Whitlow, I need to have my bed positioned so I can see the baby at all times."

Prudence Whitlow looked puzzled. "Surely you don't intend to keep your door open at night."

"Just until the baby is older, or we have a wet-nurse I can trust."

"Yes, I see what you mean. I'll attend to it immediately."

With quick efficiency, the housekeeper arranged for two workmen to move the furniture and arrange it the way Amanda wanted it. In no time at all, her trunk had been retrieved from the inn and unpacked, her garments hung in the huge wardrobe.

Amanda looked about the room that would be hers as long as she remained in the household, and she vowed to stay as long as Gabriel Merrick would allow it.

It was only a short time later that Mrs. Jenkins arrived to feed the baby. Amanda was horrified at the woman's condition. Somewhere in her late thirties, the woman wore a soiled apron, and dark, greasy hair hung from beneath her cap and lay against her ruddy cheeks. Amanda remained beside the woman the whole time she fed the baby and was relieved when Mrs. Jenkins finally left.

When the housekeeper entered later, carrying Amanda's dinner tray, Amanda spoke of her concerns about the wet-nurse. "We have to find someone trustworthy to feed little Rob. I don't want that woman around him. What can we do? Obviously, advertising in the newspaper hasn't helped."

Mrs. Whitlow looked thoughtful for a moment. "Simmons, the cook, just told me about a niece of hers. It seems the young woman's baby was stillborn. Simmons swears that her niece is kindhearted and trustworthy. Says she cries because her breasts are swollen with milk, and she has no baby to feed. I could speak to Cook about sending her around."

Amanda's eyes brightened. "Yes, do that! Get her here as soon as possible."

Mrs. Whitlow looked worried. "Master Merrick left and won't be home for a few days. Do we dare get rid of Mrs. Jenkins without his approval?"

"I'll take full responsibility for my actions."

"Cook's niece lives just down the road. I'll have Simmons send for her straightaway." She looked at Amanda with concern. "Are you sure you shouldn't wait until Master Gabriel returns?"

"No. I will not have that woman near the baby if I can help it."

Mrs. Whitlow's face broke into an amused smile. "I have a notion you'll be able to handle Master Gabriel just fine." She walked to the door. "Yes, I believe he's met his match in you."

An hour later, Amanda was interviewing the cook's niece. Sally Brown was in her mid twenties, a tall, raw-boned, country girl. Her apron and cap were spotlessly clean. It was clear to Amanda when she looked into her sad gray eyes that the young woman was still grieving for the child she'd lost.

When Sally saw Rob, her gaze softened, and she touched his hand. "My breasts are full of milk, and I can give him the nourishment he needs."

"Can you move into the room across the hall so you will always be at hand to feed Rob?"

Sally looked concerned. "I am married and can't leave my husband, madam."

"What does your husband do?"

"He is the second gardener here on the Merrick estate. Of course, he may lose his position now that the head gardener left. Mr. Merrick has a fearful temper and may blame my husband because the work has not been done. Poor Jonathan helped the head gardener move out of his cottage and got behind on setting out the bedding plants and trimming the hedges."

"I don't think you need worry, Sally. You say the gardener's cottage is empty?"

"Yes, madam."

"Then I want you and your husband to gather your belongings and move them into the head gardener's cottage. If Mr. Merrick objects, we will find other quarters for you. I need you nearby so you can feed the baby."

"Oh, miss, bless you!" Sally said with tears sparkling in her eyes, and she looked trustingly at Amanda. "Thank you! Thank you so much!"

"Don't thank me, Sally. Whether you remain or go will depend entirely on Mr. Merrick." She smiled reassuringly when she saw the fear in the young woman's eyes. "At the moment, you are more important to Mr. Merrick than his garden. I will take full responsibility for your moving into the cottage."

Amanda was less sure of her actions when Sally Brown dashed from the room to tell her husband the good news. Oh, she'd have to answer to Gabriel Merrick—she had no doubt about that. But she would face that problem when he returned. For now, little Rob had a proper wet-nurse, and that was all that mattered.

The ballroom at the Valley Green Plantation was crowded with dancers, but Gabriel was seated in the study, holding his wineglass up to the candle, watching the amber liquid catch and hold the light. His mind was far away from the festivities. He was thinking about the green-eyed enchantress who occupied the bedroom next to the nursery. How long would he allow her to get away with presenting herself as a widow when he knew perfectly well that she was Mary Ann's unmarried sister? She might have succeeded in fooling him had she not so closely resembled her dead sister.

Mary Ann had never spoken to him of her father and mother, but Gabriel had made inquiries into the Larson family's background when Robert had married Mary Ann. The Larson family was respectable enough and lived in Savannah, where Cyrus Larson owned a small shipyard. He had a reputation of building ships of inferior quality. Gabriel remembered his father once telling him that he'd blocked a sale Larson had negotiated with France. It seemed Mary Ann's father still carried a grudge against the Merrick family.

Gabriel had heartily approved of the marriage between his brother and Mary Ann. It was a pity that they'd had so little time together, because it had been a true love match.

Taking a sip of his drink, he tried to recall just what Mary Ann had said about her sibling. He remembered now that she'd often spoken about a younger sister whom she'd adored and called Mandy. That same sister was now situated in his home. He wondered why he hadn't exposed her from the beginning.

"Gabriel, there you are," Sarah Maxwell said, sitting down beside him. "Why are you hiding here in the study?"

Gabriel glanced at the pretty blonde, wondering why her beauty had never stirred him. She was petite and slender and had a pert little nose, soft gray eyes, and skin as smooth and creamy as satin. She was the personification of a Southern belle in both looks and behavior. Everyone, including Sarah and her family, expected them to marry, but Gabriel had, as yet, made no offer for her. Suddenly he knew he would never marry Sarah. She would make some man a perfect wife, but not him.

She feigned a pout, her eyes lustrous in the candlelight. "If I thought you were trying to avoid me, it would break my little old heart."

"No, Sarah, I was not trying to avoid you. I was thinking about my nephew and his new nurse."

She opened her ivory fan and peered over the top at him. "Oh, is that all? What you need is a good woman to set your house to rights and see to the care of Robert's baby."

He quirked a dark eyebrow at her. "My house runs smoothly under the direction of a very capable housekeeper."

"But that's not the same as having a wife to see to all the tiresome details for you." Her eyes met his, and she inched closer to him.

Gabriel studied Sarah for a long moment, trying to visualize her as mistress of his home. Though she would be a pretty adornment to any man's household, the vision did not suit him. "I would not make you a good husband, Sarah. I am too much away from home, and any woman who married me would grow weary of the loneliness."

She leaned closer, and he could smell her perfume, which was too sweet for his taste. "If you had the right wife, she could keep you closer to home and change your habits."

He took her hand and said kindly, "That's what I'm trying to tell you, Sarah. We are not suited to one another."

Her hand clamped on his arm. "You have met someone, haven't you, Gabriel? This is your way of telling me that you are in love with someone else."

He came to his feet, hoping to change the subject, which was becoming uncomfortable. He didn't want to hurt Sarah. And if he'd never met Amanda Larson, he probably would have married Sarah. Hell, he thought, looking out the door at the dancing couples, he didn't even know Mary Ann's sister. Why was she occupying so much of his thoughts?

"Would you care to dance, Sarah?" he asked, bowing gallantly.

Sarah's eyes narrowed, and her lips thinned into a frown. She understood very well that he didn't want to speak of marriage with her. "Yes, I would," she answered, placing her gloved hand on his outstretched arm.

As he whirled her around the floor, it was not her soft gray gaze that lingered on his mind, but a pair of green eyes—Amanda's eyes.

Sarah raised her head to Gabriel. "I am so

looking forward to our hunt ball in three weeks. You will be attending, won't you?"

He smiled down at her, wondering why he had a sudden urge to return home immediately. "You will be the prettiest woman there, Sarah."

She gazed longingly into his eyes. "Do you really think I am pretty?"

"Of course I do. I'm not blind."

Her hand tightened on his, and she licked her lips. "I want to be pretty for you."

Gabriel wanted to tear his hand from her clawlike grasp, but he didn't. "Every gentleman in this room wishes he was dancing with you at this moment."

His statement was true. Many gentleman had offered Sarah marriage, but until now, she had turned them all down because she was waiting for him.

The music had stopped, and with a bold move, Sarah laced her fingers through his and led him toward the door. Good manners prevented him from pulling away from her.

When they stood on the veranda, she slid her hand up his arm. "You must know I love you, Gabriel—everyone else does. You may think I'm forward, but if I don't tell you how I feel, how will you know?"

"Sarah, you must not say these things to me," he answered, regret welling up inside him because he knew he would never return her love. "You don't need my heart to add to the collection of beaux vying for your affection."

She stepped away from him as if he'd

slapped her. Her eyes became sad. She said the first thing that came to her mind. "Does this mean you won't be coming to my family's hunt ball?"

He touched his lips to her cheek and shook his head. "No, I will not be attending the ball, Sarah."

"I somehow knew," she said in a resigned voice. She raised her head proudly, her good breeding coming to her rescue. "Who is the woman who has your heart, Gabriel?"

He wondered if it would be kinder to keep his feelings to himself, and then he knew that he owed Sarah the truth. "You don't know her."

She sighed with relief. "Well, that's a blessing. I would have been mortified if you had fallen in love with one of my friends." She managed a smile. "Or, worse still, one of my enemies."

Gabriel had never liked Sarah better than he did at that moment. "Some man is going to be very lucky to get you."

Her coquettish smile was back in place. "Won't he, though? I'm the catch of the county!"

Gabriel took her hand and raised it to his lips. "That you are, Sarah Maxwell."

Without another word, he turned on his heels and walked down the steps toward his horse. He wanted to go home. He wanted to see the little green-eyed temptress who had unsettled his life and dominated his thoughts. He doubted if Amanda even knew how he felt

146

about her. She certainly had not flirted with him. Her mind had been on the baby and nothing else.

Gabriel rode away from Green Valley Plantation, knowing that if Amanda Larson were his wife, he would rush home to her every night just to touch that sweet body and kiss those tempting lips.

He shook his head. If Robert were alive, he'd say that his elder brother had lost his mind. So this was what love felt like!

Well, it hurt like hell!

Chapter Four

"Dammit," Gabriel roared, taking long strides toward his study. "Niles, who in the hell put the Browns in the gardener's cottage?"

The secretary stood in the door, shaking his head. "She did it, sir. But I think you will agree that—"

"She? She who?"

"Mrs. Lord, sir."

Gabriel felt the heat of anger coursing up the back of his neck with fierce intensity. "Just who gave her the power to take over the running of the grounds while I was away?"

Niles shifted his gaze nervously toward the stairs as if he half expected to see the baby's nurse appear and explain her own actions. "Well, when she dismissed Mrs. Jenkins and replaced her with Mrs. Brown, she had the

Browns move into the cottage. She wanted Mrs. Brown to be near the baby."

Gabriel was stunned into silence. When he found his voice, it cracked with anger. "She dismissed the wet-nurse?"

"Yes, sir, but with good reason."

Gabriel's long strides took him toward the stairs, which he covered two at a time. When he entered the nursery, he found Amanda rocking the baby.

"Shh," she whispered.

Her warning trapped the angry questions Gabriel was ready to fire at her. She stood, carrying the child to the cradle and gently laying him down. Then she motioned for Gabriel to follow her into the hallway.

"If you have come to inquire about your nephew, he is doing wonderfully. He sleeps the whole night through since Sally Brown has become his wet-nurse."

He glared at her. "That's what I wanted to speak to you about. Who empowered you to take over the running of my gardens and the hiring and dismissing of servants?"

She tucked a stray curl behind her ear and gave him a sweet smile. "I knew that if you understood my reasoning you'd approve of what I did. Actually, it solved two of your problems with one stroke."

He was surprised to find his anger melting away and astonishment taking its place. "Do you mind explaining to me just what you mean?"

"Well," she said, running a hand down her

pink-flowered gown as if pressing out imaginary wrinkles, "I knew you wouldn't want Mrs. Jenkins around the baby when you fully understood her problem. She was most unsuitable, and"—she leaned closer as if afraid someone would overhear—"she drank."

His lips twitched, but he tried not to smile. "I see. And what about the gardener's cottage?"

"The Browns had no place to go, and since Mr. Brown was your under-gardener, and the cottage was empty, it just seemed the sensible solution to have them move into it."

He shrugged his broad shoulders and said, attempting sarcasm, "Of course. A perfect solution."

Again she blessed him with a smile that curled through him with the warmth of a warm August wind. "I knew you would see it that way."

Amanda gazed into Gabriel's eyes and found them most disturbing. There were depths to him that she'd never felt in any other man. She trembled to think what he would do when he discovered she was deceiving him.

Before he could protest, the baby began to cry, and she hurried back into the nursery. Gabriel shook his head, wondering at what point he'd lost the argument. Grumbling to himself, he went downstairs to find Niles waiting for him.

"That woman has a mind of her own," Gabriel said in exasperation.

Niles nodded in agreement. "So I have

noticed, sir. The servants like her very much. She is a most extraordinary woman."

"Gather the ledgers and let me go over the accounts before she decides to replace you with a secretary of her own choosing."

Niles smiled. "Yes, sir."

"I'll just see for myself this Mr. Brown who calls himself a gardener."

"Shall I come with you, sir?"

"No. Stay here and see if you can keep our little nurse from changing my whole household."

Again Niles suppressed a smile. "As you say, sir."

Gabriel was ready to find fault with the under-gardener, but after spending several hours with the man and seeing the results of his work, he had to admit he was pleased. Jonathan Brown and his wife, Sally, had, two years earlier, come over from England where he'd worked on a huge estate as head gardener. And his experience showed. Merrick's grounds had never looked better, and the hedges had never been so neatly trimmed. After meeting Sally Brown and observing her kindness with the child, he had to admit that Rob was better off than he'd been with Mrs. Jenkins. But it hadn't helped Gabriel's temper any to find out that Amanda had made a wise choice in both the Browns.

The hour was late, and everyone was in bed by the time Gabriel entered the house just ahead of a storm that lingered over the sea.

Thunder shook the windowpanes, and lightning streaked across the sky ominously.

His boots fell silently on the stairs as he made his way to his bedroom. Gabriel's thoughts were on the new ship he'd be launching on the first of the month. He wearily unfastened his tie and unbuttoned the first button on his shirt. All he wanted was his bed and a few hours of sleep. But when he reached the landing, he saw light spilling into the hallway from the nursery. Apparently the baby was awake.

Gabriel stopped at the nursery door but pulled back into the shadows when he heard Amanda's voice. The soft rain seemed to whisper against the rooftop, and the flickering candle spilled a halo of light around her as she rocked the baby in her arms. He was mesmerized by the sight of her red-gold hair cascading down her back to her waist. She had the expression of an angel when she smiled at the child, and her voice was lovely, piercing his heart as she began to sing a lullaby.

When she fell silent, Gabriel watched her gather the baby to her and plant a kiss on his rosy cheek.

"I will love you forever, little Rob. If I can prevent it, you will never lack the love your mother would have given you." She closed her eyes as tears crept through her long lashes and down her cheek. "Oh, Mary Ann, I will take care of your son for as long as I live."

Gabriel felt his heart contract, and his throat tightened. She didn't see him when he stepped into the room. He knew what he must do.

"Amanda," he said, coming up beside her. "Put the baby down. I want to speak to you."

She looked up at him with a startled expression and nodded. She placed the baby in the cradle and then fumbled with her hair, trying to secure it atop her head.

"Don't worry about your hair," he told her. "I like it as it is."

Amanda raised her gaze to his, wondering if he'd heard her speaking to the baby. There was something dangerous about him, and it made her blood stir hotly in her body. "You want to talk to me?"

He turned abruptly, moving out of the room into the hallway. "Come with me to the study."

Amanda rushed after him, having to run to keep up with his long strides. He was angry about something, and she had to make sure he didn't send her away from the baby.

When Amanda entered the study, Gabriel indicated that she should be seated, while he leaned back against his massive desk in an intimidating pose.

She silently watched him as if she knew what was coming.

"Your real name is Amanda Larson, and you have never been married; therefore, you couldn't be a widow. I believe your sister, Mary Ann, called you Mandy."

She lowered her head as fear gnawed at her. "You won't take the baby away from me, will you? Please don't make me leave!"

"Why did you tell me you were widowed?

Why didn't you just tell me your real name? I would have understood your need to see the baby."

She raised her head and met his golden gaze. "I'm sorry about the subterfuge. I was afraid you wouldn't let me stay if you knew who I was." Her eyes were wide with worry. "Are you going to send me away?"

"That depends on why you are here. If you have come to take my nephew away, then you can leave now."

She shook her head. "I would never do that. You are kind to my sister's baby. Knowing he is the only family you have, I would never take Rob away from you. I understand what it feels like to have no family."

He was puzzled. "But you have a mother and father."

"Rob is the only family I have." She stood up and walked over to him. "My father told me that if I came here he never wanted to see me again. I am the same as dead to him, and I know him well enough to be certain he'll never change his mind."

"And your mother?"

"She always agrees with my father."

"Yet you still came."

"I had to." There was raw passion in her tone. "I owed it to my sister!"

He could feel the hurt in her, and he wanted to take her in his arms and hold her until the hurt subsided. Instead he asked, "Why did you risk so much by coming here?"

"You must understand that Mary Ann and I were closer than most sisters. I have been devastated by her death. I only want to give the baby the love she would have given if she had lived."

He was quiet for a long moment while he looked into misty green eyes. "You know I cannot allow you to stay on as the baby's nurse now that I know who you are. Your reputation would suffer if it became common knowledge that you, an unmarried female from a good family, resided under my roof."

There was desperation in her eyes when she placed a small hand on his arm. "No one need ever know. Everyone but you thinks I am a widow. Please don't send me away. I will do anything you say if only you will let me stay with the baby!"

"Anything?"

"Almost anything," she qualified, pride tilting her chin at a stubborn angle.

"I suppose there is a man somewhere in your life who wants to marry you." He watched her face carefully. "Is there?"

"No. There is no one I care about."

Relief washed over him like a flood tide. "Then, Amanda Larson, would you be willing to become my wife?"

Her lips trembled, but she met his gaze steadily, and she felt almost faint at the thought of being his wife. "Surely you jest."

"I can assure you I am in earnest."

She considered his words and didn't hesitate

as she said, "If marrying you is the only way I can remain with my nephew, then I have no choice."

His lips curved into a whimsical smile. "Don't try to spare my feelings—say what's on your mind."

He was the most handsome man she had ever met, and just being in the same room with him made her feel giddy. But there was also something dangerous about him, something powerful and intimidating. His name alone struck terror into the hearts of most people. What would it be like to be his wife and be exposed to his driving personality daily? But did she have a choice?

"You will not change your mind and allow everyone to think I am the widowed Mrs. Lord?"

"I can assure you, I will not. I am prepared to do the honorable thing toward you."

"This isn't necessary. We have done nothing wrong."

He shook his head. "Do you think anyone will believe that when they learn who you are?"

He reached out and touched a red-gold strand of hair that curled near her breast, and she felt as if a bolt of electricity went through her body. Amanda felt so alive when he was near, felt things she'd never experienced before. She wanted to run from the room and out the front door into the driving rain. At that moment, she could think of nothing more frightening than being this man's wife.

Why would he want her when he could have any woman? she wondered, and she said as much. "Surely a gentleman such as yourself could have any woman he wanted."

"Perhaps I want only you."

She glared at him, not finding his statement in the least humorous. "Do not expect me to believe that. We hardly know each other. Why would you want a reluctant wife when you could have any number of willing ones? I am not even sure I like you."

His eyes were swirls of golden light when he gazed at her. "Perhaps I can change your mind about me."

"I don't want to marry you."

"Then you will have to leave. I want no scandal to touch my nephew's life, even if it's only from the voices of the local gossips."

The thought of leaving Mary Ann's baby was like a physical ache in Amanda's heart. "If I did agree to marry you, would you expect . . . will I have to—"

"To answer your question, yes. I do not want a wife in name only. I intend to have but one wife throughout my lifetime, and my bed would become extremely lonely over the years if I had to grow old alone in it."

Her eyes widened with fear, but she also felt pleasure wash through her, cutting off her breath. She dropped her gaze so he wouldn't see her expression. "What if you were to discover, after we're married, that you don't like me?"

He laughed, and she watched him change

from the man she half feared to a man exuding charm. She'd never seen this side of him and imagined that no woman would be immune to that potent charm.

"I already like you, Amanda. I don't know of any other young lady who would sacrifice her whole future to raise her sister's child. Had it occurred to you that we are of the same mind—that we both want what's best for the baby? Who else would love him as much as we will?"

She bit her lip and nodded. "That much is true."

His voice deepened. "I intend to change the way you feel about me. Do you think that's possible, Amanda?"

Her face reddened, and she dropped her gaze to study the hem of her gown. "I didn't mean it when I said I didn't like you. You are a good and honorable man, Mr. Merrick." She raised her head and looked at him. "But I am not ready to be a wife."

Seeing her uncertainty, Gabriel was quick to assure her. "I will, of course, give you time to get to know me, Amanda, before I ask anything of you. And don't you think you could call me Gabriel?"

"Well, Gabriel, I can't believe this is happening. All I wanted to do when I came here was to care for my sister's baby."

"And all I want is a wife, so marriage-minded mothers hereabouts and their daughters will choose some other poor fool for their victim."

"Marriage to a woman you hardly know does

not seem the right solution to your problem, Mr. Merrick—er, Gabriel. Let me see if I have this right: you want to marry me so other women will not expect you to marry them?"

He grinned. "It does sound a bit strange, but, yes, that's partly the reason."

"There are other reasons?"

His gaze fused with hers. "Oh, yes, Amanda Larson. I'll tell you the other reasons someday when you trust me more and like me better." He held a hand out to her, disarming her and tilting her world with his irresistible charm. "Do you accept my somewhat unconventional marriage proposal?"

She gave him her hand and felt his warm clasp engulf her trembling fingers. She surprised herself when she heard her own voice. "I . . . yes, I will."

Amanda thought she saw relief in his eyes, but it was so fleeting, she wasn't sure.

"I suppose you will want a proper wedding. Most women seem to desire all the trappings."

When they were young girls, Amanda and Mary Ann had endlessly planned the elaborate weddings they would one day have. But poor Mary Ann had been forced to elope with Robert, and now Amanda had just agreed to embark on a marriage with a man she hardly knew. "My father will be furious when he hears."

"Does that matter to you?"

She tilted her head up to a proud pose. "Not in the least."

"Then is it to be a small wedding?"

She, like her sister before her, was about to tie herself to a family her father despised. "Yes," she said at last. "I will not invite guests. Still, every woman wants a proper wedding."

He arched a dark eyebrow. "Shall we set the date for two weeks hence?"

It was obvious that he was a man who liked to control every situation. He had overcome all her objections in the space of a few minutes and had gotten her to agree to marry him. What was she getting herself into? She could hear her own strained breathing and feared he could hear it, too. "Two weeks is so . . . soon."

His golden gaze settled on her mouth as he raised her hand to his lips and placed a warm kiss on the palm. "It doesn't seem all that soon to me."

A sudden gust of wind blew open the French doors, snuffing out the candles, and lightning splashed a patch of brilliance across the floor.

Amanda stiffened with fright until she felt a firm hand on her arm and she was drawn against a hard chest. "No need to be frightened. It's just the wind."

In the faint light Gabriel's eyes glittered. He tilted his head, and Amanda knew he was going to kiss her, but she could not pull away.

His mouth was soft against hers, and she felt a sweet yearning awaken inside of her. He applied the merest pressure to her lips, and she swayed toward him.

Gabriel suddenly broke off the kiss and rested his lips against her hair. When he spoke,

160

his voice was deep, and it sounded to her as if it trembled a bit. "That wasn't so bad, was it?"

She tore herself out of his arms and ran for the stairs. When she reached her bedroom, she closed the door and leaned against it. She was shaking all over, not from fear of him but from her overpowering reaction to his kiss!

Chapter Five

Mrs. Whitlow helped Amanda into the most beautiful white silk wedding gown she'd ever seen. The housekeeper chattered like a magpie while she laced the gown up the back.

"The dressmaker can be proud of this creation—it's beautiful! You make a lovely bride. It's no wonder Master Gabriel chose you for his wife. Imagine our surprise when we discovered who you really were. Imagine, two brothers marrying two sisters." She was quiet for a long moment. "I had just about despaired of Master Gabriel's ever taking a wife."

"Has he never been engaged or betrothed?" Amanda asked the question that had been nagging at her mind.

"No, not him. Although he's had plenty of chances. The ladies love him sure enough, but he's never given his heart to any of them." She frowned sadly. "Many people may not know this about him, but he's been lonely without a family. Because I know him so well, I have seen this loneliness in him. It lessened some when he was with the baby. But as grand as the little one is, he alone cannot take the edge off Master Gabriel's loneliness or cheer his sorrow."

Amanda wanted to ask the housekeeper why Gabriel had chosen to marry her if he could have any woman he wanted, but she clamped her lips tightly together.

Mrs. Whitlow stood back and observed Amanda with satisfaction. "You are just beautiful." Then she looked pensive, dug into her apron pocket, and withdrew something, which she extended to Amanda. "Will you wear my brooch for something borrowed?" The little woman held out a plain blue cameo for her inspection.

Amanda was touched by the housekeeper's kindness. "I would be honored. Will you pin it at my neck?"

Mrs. Whitlow beamed. "This can serve as something old, too, because it was my grandmother's, as well as something borrowed and something blue." Mrs. Whitlow frowned. "But what have you got for something new?"

The baby had started fretting, and Amanda moved out of her bedroom and into the nursery, where she lifted the tiny infant into her arms. The baby fell silent at once and laid his head against her breast. When she tried to lay him back down, he bellowed, kicking his little legs and thrashing his arms. Amanda picked him up, and he became silent immediately. With a half smile, she looked over the child's head at Mrs. Whitlow. "My nephew, Rob, will be my something new. He will be as my first-born son." She blushed at the thought of having other children and kissed the baby soundly.

The housekeeper looked startled. "Surely, miss, you don't intend to hold the baby through the wedding."

"That's just what I intend to do." Her chin jotted out stubbornly. After all, it was because of Rob that she'd agreed to marry Gabriel. "Why shouldn't he come to the wedding?"

Mrs. Whitlow nodded reluctantly while she arranged the gossamer veil on Amanda's head and secured it with a pearl and silver pin from the chest of Merrick family jewels that had been delivered to Amanda just that morning.

"It's no wonder Master Gabriel loved you at first sight—you are breathtaking," the housekeeper said softly. "And so sweet with the baby."

Amanda felt her heart flutter within her breast at Mrs. Whitlow's words. Of course, Gabriel didn't love her, but she wondered why the housekeeper should think so. "What makes you say Gabriel loved me at first sight?"

Mrs. Whitlow shook a crease from Amanda's silk gown and smiled brightly. "Why, my dear, hadn't you heard? Merrick men are known for falling in love at first sight. It's a family habit. It was so with the grandfather, the father, Master Robert, and now Master Gabriel."

Amanda felt her heart thud. She could not bear to tell the sweet little woman that Gabriel Merrick had broken with tradition. He had not fallen in love with her at first sight. He didn't love her at all.

Gabriel ran a hand across his brow in thoughtfulness. Soon Amanda would be his. But what did he really know about her, outside of the fact that she'd cut herself off from her family to take care of her sister's baby? That act bespoke character, but what was she really like? What was her favorite color? Did she like to sleep with the window open or closed? He stared at his hands. They were trembling. He was acting like a timid schoolboy who had just discovered love.

He took a deep breath and remembered exactly when he'd fallen in love with Amanda. It had been the moment she'd removed her bonnet the first day they'd met. In that instant she had become the one woman in the world for him. She was different from any other woman he'd met. For one thing, she had easily resisted his charms. He wasn't arrogant, but he'd always known he could have any woman he wanted. All of them except the one who had stolen his heart.

He clasped his hands behind him and drew an understanding glance from Niles. Gabriel moved to the door, grasping the brass doorknob in his hand. The woman he loved would soon be his, but would she ever love him?

* * *

Flickering candlelight spread warmth over the marble floor in the formal sitting room where the wedding was to take place. Only the servants would be in attendance.

Amanda stood at the top of the stairs, feeling as if she were living a dream. Here she was, swathed in the most beautiful wedding gown she'd ever seen, about to marry an incredibly handsome man she knew little about, and holding a beloved infant in her arms. As her foot touched the top step on her descent, she had the strongest urge to flee the house and never return. But she couldn't. She had to go through with this for the baby's sake. Little Rob had curled contentedly against her, unaware that he was about to attend a momentous ceremony.

She took a step and faltered. Raising her head, she let her gaze meet Gabriel's, as if she expected him to object about her bringing the baby. He looked quizzical for a moment, and then a soft smile curved his lips. She tried to read what he was thinking, but he was not a man who displayed his feelings on his face.

When she reached the bottom step, he advanced toward her. With a wink at Mrs. Whitlow, he offered Amanda his arm, then led her across the room to stand before Reverend Potter.

If the minister thought it strange that the bride held a baby in her arms, he did not show it. He smiled with humor and opened his prayer book, spreading it across his huge hands. He spoke in a clear voice:

"Dearly beloved, we are gathered together to unite this man and this woman in holy matrimony."

Suddenly Gabriel took Rob from Amanda and handed him to Mrs. Whitlow. He then clasped Amanda's hand tightly. She looked into golden eyes, which glistened as if they had caught a sliver of the sun in their tawny depths. Amanda found that her thin veil was no protection from his probing glance, and she felt her knees go weak as his mouth eased into a smile—not a smile of mirth, but the smile of a man who had conquered and won what he wanted.

When the time came for her to repeat a vow, she did so in a small voice. But Gabriel repeated the vow with conviction, his gaze drawing and holding hers. She could feel his sensuality, and her mind shied away from the thought of the wedding night that loomed ahead of her. She knew so little about intimacy between a man and a woman. She'd always thought she would one day marry a man who would love her, not this tall, handsome creature who could reduce her flesh to quaking jelly with just the touch of his hand.

The reverend's voice floated to Amanda, penetrating her woeful musing. "I now pronounce you husband and wife. You may kiss the bride!"

When Gabriel lifted Amanda's veil, he paused a moment, his gaze locked with hers. To this point they had shared no more than a fleeting kiss and the touching of hands. She could sense the leashed power within him. He leaned forward, touching his lips to hers so softly that her heart thudded against her rib cage. Her mouth trembled, and she could not suppress the small sigh that slipped through her lips.

Hot passion coiled through Gabriel's body as he kissed his virginal bride. Her innocence dictated that he should court her slowly and keep that coiled passion under control until she matched his desire. Slowly he raised his head, his eyes gleaming with hidden depths. He could feel the untapped fire within her, and he could hardly wait to bring it to full flame. "For better or worse, you have me for your husband, Amanda."

"Yes," she said, turning to take the baby from Mrs. Whitlow and holding him in front of her like a shield. "So it would seem."

The household surged around them, offering them their well wishes, until finally Gabriel took the baby from Amanda and handed him to Sally.

"Are Amanda's trunks packed, Whitlow?"

"Just as you ordered."

He took Amanda's hand and led her out of the room. "The servants will celebrate for most of the night." He raised her hand to his lips and felt her gasp when his mouth traveled up to her wrist and the pressure point there. "Amanda, when I saw you coming down the stairs with the baby in your arms, you took my breath away."

She gave him a timid smile. "I'm sure there has never before been a bride who carried a baby to her wedding."

His eyes were like melted moonlight. "You still take my breath away."

She lowered her head, unable to look into his brilliant eyes.

Seeing her discomfort, he abruptly changed the subject. "I have made plans that I hope will please you."

"I know we are going on a journey, since Mrs. Whitlow packed my clothing."

"I asked her to keep our destination a secret. Have you ever sailed on a ship, Amanda?"

Her eyes widened with pleasure at the thought. "No. But I have always wanted to."

"I have a new ship in my fleet that is beginning her maiden voyage. How would you like to be one of her first passengers?"

She could not contain her joy. "Oh, could we?"

"Why don't you run upstairs and put on something more appropriate for travel, and I'll have the carriage brought around front."

"I'll just get the baby and—"

He placed a finger to her lips. "The baby will not be coming with us, Amanda."

She took a step away from him, suddenly afraid to be alone with him. "I thought—"

"Rob will have the best of care while we are away. I want to have you all to myself. After all, this is our honeymoon."

She reminded him of a frightened bird about to take flight. He took two steps that brought him against her and drew her into his arms. "You have nothing to fear from me, Mandy. I want only to make you happy."

She felt his warmth surround her and resisted the urge to lay her head against his broad shoulder. Taking a steadying breath, she glanced up at him. "You will not . . ."

He laughed softly. "Not until you are ready." He tilted her chin up and forced her to look into his eyes. "But I think you will soon welcome me as your husband."

Cook had made a feast for the newly married couple, and it was served in the formal dining room. But Amanda barely tasted the capon baked in orange sauce or the wedding cake that went mostly uneaten on her plate.

Gabriel, however, didn't seem to suffer from a lack of appetite. He even offered Amanda a bite of cake from his fork. She took it in her mouth and tried to smile, but it stuck in her throat, and she had to wash it down with a sip of wine, which made her cough and lose her breath.

At last the ordeal was over, and Amanda stood, moving in a swirl of silk and quickly climbing the stairs. Gabriel made her feel things she'd never known she was capable of feeling. When he touched her, her heart raced. When he looked into her eyes, she felt faint. What would she do when they were alone together?

Gabriel frowned as he watched her ascend the stairs. He wanted to fill her with his seed.

He wanted to feel her come alive with passion beneath him. Since she'd arrived at his house, she'd won all the servants with her sweetness, and she'd chased all the sadness from his heart.

Amanda reached her bedroom and stared down at her golden wedding band. She had no memory of Gabriel sliding it onto her finger. She closed her eyes to steady her heartbeat.

Her husband was a man of passion. What if she could not give him what he wanted? What if he was disappointed in her as a wife? He had known more mature and sophisticated women. How could she, with her inexperience, hope to satisfy this marvelous man who had given her a home and his name?

She heard the baby stirring in the next room and went to him, lifting him in her arms. "I won't be away long, little love. Mrs. Whitlow and Sally will take good care of you while I am away."

She kissed his soft cheek and laid the baby back in the cradle, knowing she was going to miss him terribly. Sally entered the room, and Amanda said to her, "Take care of him."

"I will, madam. It won't be the same as your being with him, but I will take the tenderest care of him."

With a last kiss on the satiny cheek of her nephew, Amanda reluctantly returned to her room and picked up the green hat that matched her gown, setting it at an angle on her head. Today had been like a dream, but the crumpled wedding gown across the bed attested that it had been real enough. There was nothing of hers left in this room. Her meager belongings had been moved to the master's suite, which she would occupy when she returned from the voyage.

Pulling on her leather gloves, Amanda left the room. She was more frightened and unsettled than she'd ever been in her life. She was a bride, and she would soon have to meet the demands of a husband.

She paused in the doorway, a feeling of belonging hitting her full force. Everything had happened so quickly that she'd forgotten to take the measure of the man she'd married. He was a man who loved children, so much that he'd taken his brother's baby and made him his own. Then, when she'd arrived at his home, he'd taken her in and made her a part of his family.

He'd even married her.

He was a man of integrity, kindness, and deep commitment. Her hand suddenly flew to her heart, a tight knot lodged in her throat, and her mouth went dry.

She was, she abruptly realized, in love with her husband!

Chapter Six

When Gabriel escorted Amanda up the gang-plank and onto the deck of the ship, the crew glanced at her with mild curiosity, but a stern glare from Captain Merrick made them scamper about, returning to their duties.

His hand remained on Amanda's shoulder in a possessive gesture. "Later, when their duties allow it, I'll introduce you to my first mate and my second-in-command."

The ship was so new that Amanda could smell the heady aroma of new lumber. Everything was clean and sparkly, and she loved it!

"Where do we sail?" she asked, glancing up at her new husband.

"We will be sailing to Boston. This is her test to see if she is seaworthy."

"You do this with every ship your workers

build?" she asked, knowing her father had never done such a thing.

"I do. Not all shipbuilders test their ships personally. But I want only the best to bear the Merrick name," Gabriel informed her as she paused at the railing to watch the sun-washed shores of Charleston. "We will be under way with the evening tide. I want you to see the sunset. On land, sundown happens rather lazily, but here at sea the sun appears to drop into the water, painting the sky with brilliant colors and making the sea blood red. It has to be seen to be appreciated."

Gabriel spoke with such passion that Amanda caught his excitement. She was suddenly afraid, not of him, but that she would not be able to match his passionate nature. She didn't want to bore him or to become a wife to be shoved in a corner and forgotten.

Moments later, he pointed to the western horizon, and she saw the brilliant sunset, just as he had described it. "It's magnificent!"

"Yes, isn't it?"

Amanda glanced about, expecting other passengers to be enjoying the spectacle, but there was no one on deck other than the crew, and they seemed to be unaware of the wonderful sight. Probably they had seen it all too often. "Where are the other passengers, Gabriel?"

The raffish smile he gave her melted her bones.

"We are the only passengers. I believe it is significant that this is the ship's maiden voyage. And"—he touched her cheek gently— "your maiden voyage as well."

She blushed at his innuendo and lowered her head.

He laughed heartily and turned aside. "It's time to get under way. Would you like to watch me take her out of the harbor, or would you prefer to go to our cabin?"

"You are the captain?"

He smiled. "Of course. I always take my ships on their maiden voyages." There was humor in his voice. "But don't fret, my dear. I have able-bodied men to stand at the helm if I'm otherwise occupied."

She turned away as heat crept into her face. "I will go to the cabin and get my shawl. It's a bit cool."

He placed a hand in the small of her back and guided her to the captain's cabin. With a chaste kiss on the forehead, he bowed to her, his eyes seeking and brilliant. "Hurry if you want to watch us catch the wind, Amanda."

She stood at the door, feeling trapped. Why had she agreed to marry Gabriel? When she'd discovered that the baby was being well cared for, why hadn't she left? She stepped to the middle of the room and took in her surroundings. It was not a large cabin. Maps were spread across the top of the desk. A huge bed took up most of the room, and two wooden chairs looked more serviceable than relaxing. A table stood in the corner, and her trunk rested at the foot of the bed alongside Gabriel's.

Opening her trunk, she was surprised to find the clothing was all new. Puzzled, she lifted a crimson hooded cape and ran her hands loving over the soft velvet. When had Gabriel had all these garments made for her? She had no doubt that they would all fit to perfection, because he was a man who left nothing to chance.

She slid the cape across her shoulders, and it fell about her like a whispering caress. She then opened the door and stepped onto the deck.

As Amanda climbed up beside Gabriel, she excitedly watched the lights of Charleston disappear in the distance, and night enfolded her. She welcomed the salty spray on her face as the ship caught the tide and moved away from land.

"Do you feel the least bit sick?" Gabriel asked, dropping his gaze to her.

She listened to the snapping of the canvas as the wind caught the sails, and she shook her head. "No," she answered with pride. "I find it exhilarating! I could sail on forever and never touch land again."

He laughed lightly. "Highly impractical, Mrs. Merrick."

That was the first time she'd heard herself referred to by her new name, and warmth spread throughout her body. "Yes, I suppose it is." She turned to him. "But perhaps we could sail often."

One of his hands rested on the wheel, and he

placed the other on her shoulder. "That I can promise you. Since I am often at sea myself, I would like it if you could accompany me."

She knew that he was wealthy, but she'd never given it much thought. "Do you have many ships?"

"I do. Counting this one, I have nineteen ships that sail to every corner of the globe. Of course, that number varies from time to time. I also build ships to sell to the government."

"Any country's government?"

"No. Just ours. I have an aversion to selling my ships to other nations; I don't want to see my ships coming against us if we're ever at war with the other countries."

"Yes, I see the sense of that." She thought of her own father, who had been willing to sell to anyone who would buy from him. "But it isn't true of all American shipbuilders."

"Unfortunately not."

He removed his hand from her shoulder, and he pointed to the right. "You see the last of the lights of Charleston. We are ready to come about and veer to our larboard side. When we pass that point, you will no longer be able to see the lights." His hand came back to her shoulder.

All Amanda could think of was the intimacy of his touch, and how it turned her knees weak and made it difficult for her to breathe. "How amazing," she managed to say. "It all seems so small from here."

He was quiet for a long moment as the ship

gently turned to the left, and as he'd predicted, the lights were lost from sight.

Amanda relished the wind in her hair and the taste of salt on the wind. "Had I been born a man, I believe I would have wanted to sail the world."

He chuckled, drawing her closer to him and wrapping her in his warmth. "If you had been born a man, it would have been a great loss."

Again she had an overwhelming urge to lay her head against his broad chest, so she stepped away from him. "I am weary. I believe I'll retire now."

"Yes," he said, glancing into the snapping sails that had caught a sliver of moonlight. "You have had a tiring day. I will join you later."

Amanda lay on the big bed, listening to the wind in the sails. Silvery beams from the full moon spilled through the porthole, bathing the room in soft light. The gentle swaying of the ship made her drowsy, and she had forgotten to be apprehensive about her wedding night. She was sure it was near midnight. Perhaps Gabriel was going to stay at the helm all night. So much had happened today. She had gotten married, and she was now on her first sea voyage.

She yawned, wondering if she should have left the lantern burning for Gabriel. She turned to her side, her eyes sliding shut, and was soon asleep.

Moments later, Amanda heard the door

open. She heard Gabriel mutter an oath as he bumped into the desk. Sliding down beneath the covers, she inched as close as she could get to the wall. Squeezing her eyes tightly closed, she heard him undress, and soon she felt the bed dip as he joined her.

"Are you asleep, Amanda?"

She thought about not answering, but that would be dishonest. "I was," she said in a small voice.

He reached out and touched her face, and she froze. "What are you going to do?" she asked.

He shifted his weight so he was facing her. "Nothing you don't want me to do, Amanda. The reason I wanted to bring you on this voyage was so we could become better acquainted."

"Oh."

"I am not insensitive to the fact that I'm a stranger to you."

"And you don't know me, either," she was quick to add.

"Ah, there you are mistaken. I know quite a lot about you."

She raised herself up on an elbow. "You do?"

"Indeed I do. When you were sixteen you went away to finishing school to learn to become a young lady. By the time you were seventeen, you had been sent home for climbing a tree to rescue a stray cat, and the headmistress wrote your parents that you were a hoyden and would never be a lady." He smiled slightly. "The headmistress was wrong."

179

"How did you know that?"

"Mary Ann told me." He clamped his hands behind his head and stared at the ceiling. "She also told me that your father angrily carted you back to the school and insisted the headmistress reinstate you, and she refused."

She closed her eyes for a moment. "My father is often an angry man, and my mother indulges him. He was so angry when Mary Ann married Robert that he swore he never wanted to see her again. He didn't even attend her funeral, and he wouldn't allow my mother and me to go, either."

"And now your father will have to adjust to the fact that his second daughter has also married into the enemy camp."

"I don't care what he thinks." Her voice became forceful. "I would do anything to be with Mary Ann's baby."

He was quiet for a long moment. "Even marry me, Mandy?"

"I didn't mean that. I . . ."

His hand settled on her shoulder. "We have much in common, Amanda. You lost a sister, and I lost a brother. We share a nephew, and . . . we are man and wife."

"Yes, that is so," she said worriedly.

His hand lifted from her shoulder to rest against her cheek. "I want you to know that you have nothing to fear from me, Amanda. I told you I would do nothing until you are ready."

Just the touch of his hand was sufficient to

turn her insides to jelly, and as if that weren't enough, the thought of him lying next to her made her want to jump into his arms, to be held against that strong body. He smelled of fresh sea air, and she wanted to touch his dark hair, to feel his hand clasped in hers, to press her body against his.

His voice brought her back to reality.

"I would like for us to honor a tradition that my mother and father practiced every day of their married life. Would you mind, Amanda?"

"I . . . what is it?"

"My mother and father had the ideal marriage, and they had one habit that probably contributed to their happiness more than anything else."

"They did?"

"Uh-huh. They vowed on their wedding night that they would never go to sleep angry with each other and that they would always end the day with a kiss. They kept that vow to the end of their life together." His voice deepened, and his hand swept into her hair. "Can we make that same vow to each other tonight, Amanda?"

Her heart felt as if a warm hand had just closed around it. Gabriel was a powerful man who seemed to need no one, and yet there was this bit of sentimentality instilled him by his parents that was touching and sweet.

"I would like that, Gabriel."

He drew her into his arms slowly so he

wouldn't frighten her. His arms tightened about her, and he rested his lips against her cheek. "I'm going to like this vow, Amanda."

She felt the heat of his body like a drug, and she trembled from the strange sensations that started at her toes and worked their way up to her heart. She tingled, burned, and felt weak all over.

Slowly he drew her closer, his lips so close to hers that she could feel his breath against her skin. She wanted to strain toward him, but she didn't need to, because he brought her even closer, and she fit against his hard body as if she belonged there.

The gasp that started in her throat was never uttered because his mouth closed over hers, making her go weak. The touch of his lips on hers and the feel of his body as he pressed her against him rocked her whole world. She could feel him swell against her, and his hands slid down to her thighs, and he fit her more tightly against him.

Her lips trembled, and her arms slid around his shoulders, and she felt the muscles beneath her fingers. She had never known a man could be so muscled and yet so gentle. Amanda opened her mouth and groaned as his kiss deepened. He had awakened something that had lain dormant within her, just waiting for him to bring it to life. The tightening ache inside her demanded something he could give her, but she wasn't sure what it was.

Just when she thought she would faint, he

released her and moved away. His voice was deep with feeling. "Good night, Mandy. Sleep well."

How could he say such a thing? How could she sleep when he had stirred up feelings in her that made her yearn and tremble all over?

She moved away from him until she felt the wall against her back. She touched her lips, still soft from his kiss, and resisted the urge to reach out to him. He seemed to have felt nothing from the kiss and appeared to be drifting off to sleep, while she lay there a long time staring into the darkness, wishing her heart would stop drumming in her ears and wishing she could find forgetfulness in sleep.

Gabriel closed his eyes, trying not to tear off Amanda's nightgown and bury himself in her. He had wanted many women—he'd had many women—but none of them had stirred him as deeply as his innocent, green-eyed wife. He was in torment; just lying next to her ripped him apart inside. He felt himself swell anew, just thinking about how sweetly her soft body had fit into his.

He gripped the side of the bed, wondering how in the hell he was going to get through the next few hours without ravishing her. He had stirred her to life tonight, but that wasn't enough. He wanted her to ache for him as he did for her. He wanted her to beg for his kisses, and she would, he knew that, because he knew just how to make her want him. But he wanted more from her than just her body. He wanted her heart. And that must be won with patience, which wasn't his strong point.

He had begun a campaign tonight that would intensify tomorrow. And he hoped she would willingly offer herself to him by tomorrow night.

Chapter Seven

The sun was streaming through the porthole when Amanda awoke to the aroma of coffee. Raising herself up in bed, she saw that Gabriel was dressed in a blue cutaway and trousers. He looked so handsome that it left her breathless.

"It's about time you woke up, sleepyhead. You missed a brilliant sunrise."

She pushed her tumbled curls out of her face and pulled the covers to her neck. "Is that food I smell? I'm hungry."

"The sea gives one an appetite. I believe Cook has outdone himself today, wanting to please my lady."

He noticed how her red-gold hair spilled down her back to her waist, and he resisted the urge to touch the curl that hung over her shoulder. "When I was a boy," he said, pouring her a cup of coffee, "I loved the mornings best of all. I'd get up when it was still dark so I wouldn't miss anything."

"I have the impression you sprang to life as a full-grown man—I can't imagine you ever being a child."

His laughter was deep with amusement. "I had no idea that my wife had a sense of humor. This added to all your other attributes—what more can a man ask for?"

A smile played on her lips, and she swung her feet to the floor, draping the bedcover about her. "You are something of a surprise to me, as well. My father is an angry man who never smiles. I like the way you laugh at life."

He held a chair for her, and his hand came down on her shoulder. "What else do you like about me, Mandy?"

"No one but my sister ever called me Mandy. I like it when you do."

He sat down opposite her and handed her the cup of coffee. The smoldering gaze he gave her told her that he was remembering the night before, and she responded with wild emotions ricocheting through her body. She ached and tingled all over as she glanced down at his strong hands, remembering how tenderly he'd touched her. She felt her nipples harden, and she wanted him to kiss her so she could feel those wonderful lips fitting against hers.

Amanda's thoughts shocked and frightened her, and she lowered her eyes to the cup of coffee.

His hand covered hers, lifting it and bringing it to his mouth. She jerked her head up and stared at him, unable to speak for the tightening in her throat.

He placed a kiss on her palm and smiled at her. "I have already eaten. I'll leave you to dine in peace." He stood, towering over her. "When you have finished eating, get dressed and come on deck. The lookout spotted several whales off the starboard bow. You might enjoy watching them swimming alongside the ship.

She nodded, watching him leave and waiting for her heartbeat to return to normal. Would she ever be able to act normal around him?

She tore off a piece of hot bread and popped it into her mouth. Was this empty ache inside her . . . love? Oh, she had wanted him to touch her, to take her to bed and pull her body against his again. She wanted him to make her his wife in every way.

Taking a sip of coffee, she stood. She would get dressed and join Gabriel, because she had a burning need to be near him.

Gabriel stood on deck, allowing the cool breeze to hit him in the face. When he was with Amanda it was difficult to keep from throwing her onto the bed and driving inside her. He didn't know how much more he could take of being near her and playing the gentleman. He'd never desired a woman as he did her. The old Merrick curse had hit him full force in the gut: he had fallen in love with her in one sweeping, breathtaking moment, just as his grandfather had loved his grandmother, as his father had loved his mother, as Robert had loved Mary Ann. He needed to make love to Amanda and show her the depths of his ardor. But what if she didn't love him? She might become mindless with desire for him, but that was because he knew just how to play her innocent body to make the passion spring to life. But love was something else. And he vowed he would have nothing less than her heart.

Amanda stood at the railing, amazement etching her expression. "I never knew whales were so huge!" A giggle escaped her lips as she watched the three mammals leap and dive in the water. One was a baby, but it was almost as big as the ship. "It's almost as if they were performing for us."

Gabriel stood at her side, more enchanted by her reaction to the spectacle than by the whales themselves. "Whales often behave this way. I believe they like humans and like being near them." He shook his head. "Sadly their closeness to us will probably eventually lead to their extermination. The whalers slaughter them mercilessly." He shrugged. "There is nothing that can be done."

"Can't someone stop them?"

"No, Amanda. The whalers have that right. That's just the way it is."

Her eyes were sad as she watched the largest whale guide and nudge the baby. They dove underwater and were lost from sight.

"I am glad I got to see that," she said, looking into Gabriel's eyes. "They looked like a family."

"They are a family, Amanda. Just like you, Rob, and me."

A feeling of warmth and belonging spread through her. She loved the thought that she was his family. "You have no one left in your family, do you, Gabriel?"

He touched her cheek with one finger. "I have you, Mandy." His voice deepened. "Or I soon will have."

Her face reddened, and she glanced back to sea, watching the whitecaps foam and disappear against the side of the ship. "What is the name of this ship?" she asked, needing to say something.

He grinned down at her. "I was wondering when you'd get around to that question. This ship is the *Amanda*." He took her hand and led her to the helm, where he quickly introduced her to his first mate. "John Taylor, it's time you met my wife, Amanda."

John was tall and stout. His face was like old leather from a life spent aboard ships. His gray eyes danced with joy as he quickly removed his cap and presented Amanda with a very graceful bow. "It's surely my pleasure to make your acquaintance, ma'am. We—the crew and me—want you to know how happy we are to have you aboard, Mrs. Merrick."

She smiled at the crusty old sailor. "It's my pleasure, John."

Gabriel nodded at his first mate. "I'll take the helm. You get some rest."

"Aye, Captain." The big man lumbered away, and Amanda watched him disappear down the companionway.

"I like him," Amanda said with feeling. She raised her head and felt the salty spray on her lips. "I love the sea!"

He drew her into his arms, one hand on the wheel, the other on her shoulder. "It's a good thing you do, since your husband is a sailor."

She smiled up at him. "How did you come to name the ship *Amanda*?" She could feel his chest expand, and she eased back against him.

"I named her after you." He lowered his head so his mouth was near her ear. "See how she responds to my slightest touch?"

His voice was seductive, and she watched his hand move over the wheel caressingly.

"My slightest wish is her command." He rested his cheek against Amanda's, and his lips touched her brow. "This is the way I want you to respond to me, Mandy. I want you to feel my hands on you, to move as I instruct you. I want to make love to you."

Her body went weak, and she pressed even tighter against him. His hand moved to her waist, and she could feel the heat through the thin material of her gown. "I . . . must go," she whispered in a shaky voice.

To her surprise, he released her immediately. "There is nowhere to run, Mandy. And if there were, you wouldn't need to run from me."

She moved away from him, her heart beating so loudly that she could feel it drumming in her ears. If she didn't make it to the cabin, she would crumble into a hundred pieces. She half hoped he'd come after her, but he didn't.

She closed the cabin door and threw herself on the bed, aching and trying to push sensuous thoughts about Gabriel to the back of her mind. She was still yearning for his touch when sleep carried her away on velvet arms.

Gabriel's warm breath stirred her hair. "Are you going to sleep all day and all night, too?"

She blinked and stared into laughing golden eyes. "I didn't mean to fall asleep."

Before she knew what he was doing, he joined her on the bed, pulling her unresisting body close to his. She curved into him, and she heard his breathing becoming labored.

He remembered feeling this same aching emptiness the first day he'd met her. At that time it was as if he'd discovered something very precious that really didn't belong to him. But now she was his wife. She was his!

His hands moved to her hips, and he brought her against him, fitting her to his hardness, pressing her tighter and tighter. He felt her arms slide around his shoulders, and she raised her head to him. With a mutter, he dropped his head, his mouth covering hers, his body grinding against her softness. He felt her gasp and go limp, and he knew he could have her at that moment if he wanted to. He chose to wait, although he wasn't through with her yet. He only hoped she would come willingly to him before he lost his mind from wanting her.

Amanda felt as if she were drowning in a sea

of wild sensations. She felt his hardness, his muscled shoulders, the maleness of him pulling at her, tugging at her to give herself to him.

Her lips opened beneath his probing, and he slid his tongue into her mouth, and a gasp escaped her. If she was so willing, why did he hesitate?

Groaning inwardly, he stood and pulled her up with him. "I thought we could have lunch together. Would you like that?"

Her eyes were big and round in her face, and he knew what she was feeling. Tonight she would willingly be his.

He ate a hearty fill of fried fish and fresh vegetables, while she merely picked at her food. He thought to put her at ease by talking about her sister.

"Mary Ann was so soft-spoken and amiable, I doubt she ever raised her voice. Did she?"

"No, my sister never raised her voice. She was kind, considerate, and a lady."

"I sensed that about her. She was exactly the kind of woman who would have won my brother's heart."

Suddenly Amanda's eyes gleamed like green fire. "Well, Gabriel, you should know this about me. I'm nothing like my sister was. I have a temper, I always speak my mind, and I am not in the least amiable. If you wanted that kind of woman, you should not have married me."

He laughed loudly and laid a hand on hers. "I chose you because you had fire inside you. You have emotions that have never been tapped." He massaged her palm with his thumb and gloried in the way her eyes flamed with passion. "I don't want someone who will agree with everything I say, as you say your mother does with your father. I want a woman who will stand toe-to-toe with me and tell me when she thinks I'm wrong, which you have done on numerous occasions." He raised her hand to his lips and placed a kiss on her wrist. "I want you to come alive in my arms, Mandy."

Her breath caught in her throat, and her chest tightened. He knew he could keep her bound to him through pleasures of the flesh, but that wasn't enough for him. Before she could answer, Gabriel said, "I am needed on deck. I will see you sometime after sundown."

After he'd gone, Amanda paced the cabin floor. He said he wanted her, and yet he never did more than kiss and caress her. She was feverish with wanting him, aching for his touch and his possession of her body.

Didn't he know that she was ready for him to make love to her?

Chapter Eight

Amanda paced the floor, gazed out the port-hole, and paced some more. Dinner came and went, and still Gabriel did not return. The dinner that was delivered to her cabin went uneaten, and at last she became so weary that she undressed and got into her nightgown. At first she touched the pillow where his head had lain; then she took it and embraced it, inhaling Gabriel's musky male scent, which still clung to it.

Tears gathered on her eyelashes. If just holding his pillow made her ache for him, what would she do if he ever made love to her? She would lose control, that's what she'd do. She would behave shamelessly, and then he'd be disgusted by her.

She turned her face to the wall, praying she

would fall asleep before Gabriel came to the cabin.

And she did.

Moonlight stabbed through the porthole, casting part of the cabin in its light. Gabriel stood over his wife, watching the way the shadows played across her face. She looked so beautiful, so innocent in sleep. He was hit with the strangest feeling—that he'd been waiting for her all his life, but that she had come into his world so suddenly that it had confused him at first, yet somehow he'd known from the beginning that she would belong to him eventually. He knew she was half fire and the other half vinegar, and he liked that about her. He could never love a woman who parroted his words and agreed with everything he said.

He removed his jacket and draped it across the back of a chair. His shirt and trousers followed. He eased into bed beside Amanda and bent over her, his lips lightly touching her brow.

Her eyes opened, and she stared back at him. He was afraid he had frightened her, but there was no fear in the green depth of her eyes, only hunger and naked passion.

Amanda stared into golden, predator's eyes, and her bones melted. He drew her to him and turned her so his mouth fit against hers.

With wild abandonment her hands slid around his shoulders, feeling the corded muscles that rippled with each movement he made.

"Sweet, sweet Amanda," he whispered. "Did I

tell you that Merrick men always make up our minds right away when we find the woman we want to marry? I knew you were the one for me that first day when you removed your bonnet and stared at me with those misty green eyes."

She trembled as his hand slid down to her waist, and he gathered her gown, raising it upward. "Is that true?" she asked, her mind more on his wonderful hands than his words.

"Every word of it." He lifted her up and removed the gown, tossing it to the floor. "All that remained was to convince you."

She ached with pleasure as he gently touched her breasts, stroking, kissing, suckling, and kissing again.

Amanda felt her toes curl, and any resistance she might have had melted away. "Oh," she said. "I . . . want, I need—"

His hand slid across her stomach, and his mouth covered hers, smothering whatever she might have uttered. He kissed and stroked her until he was mindless and she was arching beneath him. His woman was all fire, and he would stoke it into a flame. "You are my sweet, sweet madness."

He gently parted her legs and slid between them, touching her ever so lightly. She groaned and tossed back her head, and he pressed his hardness against her. Instantly she opened her legs to allow him access.

He gave her a slow smile that melted her heart, and desire coiled in her like a ring of flames about to flare out of control.

"Easy, sweetheart," he murmured against her

ear. "I don't want to hurt you, since this is your first time."

His finger glided into her to discover that she was tight and moist, ready for him. He hovered above her, easing into her by slow degrees. She closed around him like a sheath to a sword, accepting him and arching her back, wanting more.

"Sweet, sweet Mandy," he said in a husky voice. "How much I have wanted this."

Amanda's eyes were luminous as she lay in his arms. "Gabriel, may I ask you something?"

He smiled at her, lacing his fingers through hers and lifting them to his lips. "Ask anything you want. I am in a generous mood. Can I get you the moon, or is the sun more to your liking?"

She frowned. "You don't understand—this is serious."

He released her hand. "All right, what is it you want? You have my full attention."

"It's about the baby." She stood and moved to the porthole and looked out as if afraid to meet his eyes.

He came up behind her. "What is it you want, my love? Truly, I can deny you nothing."

"I want us to adopt Rob. I know we will have other children, but I want him to know he's special and that he is as well loved as any other children we might have." She spoke so softly that he had to lean closer to catch her words. "Of course, when he's older, we would tell him about his real parents and how they loved him as much as we do."

He turned her to him, his eyes gentle. He loved her so much, it hurt. "If that's what you want, I'll see to it as soon as we get home."

She smiled brightly, and the dimples danced in her cheeks. She threw her arms around him and pressed her cheek to his shoulder. "You are the most wonderful man I have ever known! You can't know what this means to me."

"Say you love me," he demanded, raising her chin and staring into her eyes.

"Love you? Oh, my dear heart, I love you so much, I never want to be away from you for a moment of the day!"

He laughed and lifted her in his arms. "I think I can promise you that you will see my face all of this day." He carried her to the bed, laid her down, and joined her, one hand moving across her breast. "In fact, I think I'll keep you in bed all day and all night."

She slid her arms around his neck, feeling his arousal and gravitating toward his warmth. "Yes, I would like that," she said.

He laughed and buried his face in her hair. She came to him eagerly, accepting his need for her. "You are all I want."

"Love me, Gabriel."

He couldn't answer for the knot that was forming in his throat. He wanted to bind her to him with ropes of passion, and keep her with him with ropes of love.

Amanda groaned, accepting his hardness into her body and riding with him on the wings of passion.

Something New

Gabriel crushed Amanda's lips beneath his, and they made love while the ship sailed across the golden sea and long into the night, when the sea turned to silver.

Epilogue

Rob had just passed his third birthday, and he had sensed an excitement in the house, but he didn't understand what was happening. He watched his father pacing back and forth worriedly, and then Mrs. Whitlow came to get him, and he hurried upstairs.

The young boy tugged at Mrs. Whitlow's apron with a concerned frown on his face. "Is my mother going to die?"

The kindly housekeeper bent to the boy. "Goodness, no, young master. In fact, your mother is very well indeed."

At that moment, Gabriel came downstairs beaming and lifted Rob in his arms. "Come," he said gently. "Your mother wants to see you right away. She has a happy surprise for you."

Mrs. Whitlow wiped her tears on a handkerchief and tucked it back into her pocket. Young Master Rob had been adopted by the master and madam, and they loved him as much as if he'd been born to them. Everything had changed about the house since Amanda had entered it. There was laughter and happiness here. The biggest change of all was in Master Gabriel. It was plain to everyone who had eyes that he deeply loved his beautiful Amanda. She had softened him and brought joy to his life.

She watched father and son disappear into the master suite; then she went about her appointed duties. She would not allow the servants to be lax in their tasks just because they were excited about the young mistress giving birth.

Rob climbed up on the bed and moved into his mother's outstretched arms, throwing his chubby little arms around her neck. "Mommy sick?" he asked, knowing it was unlike her to be in bed at this time of day.

She shook her head. "No, dearest, I am quite well. Look what I have for you." Amanda pulled back the covers and revealed a tiny bit of humanity that was kicking and squirming.

Rob looked puzzled. "What is it?"

"This is your new baby sister," his father told him, sitting down beside him. "Isn't she beautiful?"

Rob looked at the red-faced baby who didn't have much hair or any teeth. He didn't want to hurt her feelings by saying she was not beautiful, so he bent to kiss the small cheek. "I will love her anyway," he said magnanimously.

The tiny infant clasped Rob's finger, and his expression softened. He stroked the tiny hand and gently touched her head. "Yes," he said, changing his mind, "she is beautiful."

Gabriel and Amanda laughed and looked into each other's eyes, the love they felt for each other there for anyone to see.

"She'll grow up to be a beauty like her mother," Gabriel said, leaning forward and kissing his wife. He whispered in her ear so no one but she could hear. "Hurry and heal. I want you back in my bed."

Amanda laughed delightedly as she looked at the family she loved so much. "I have missed you, too, my love."

Rob was still holding his sister's tiny hand. "When can she play with me?"

"Not for a while," his father told him. "She will need you to help look after her until she is stronger."

"Yes, she will need me," he said, yawning and curling up beside his mother.

Amanda looked down lovingly at her son, then up into the golden eyes of her husband. Gabriel was a powerful, yet gentle and infinitely lovable man, and she blessed the child who had brought her into his life—and created a happy family.

SOMETHING BORROWED

Evelyn Rogers

*To Tina Woods—an incredible bookseller
and a treasured friend.*

Chapter One

Word was that emigrants on a wagon train could buy anything they wanted or needed in the jumping-off place of Independence, Missouri.

On Celinda Cheney Ward's first full day in town, she found out that word was wrong. To take her place in the long, snaking line moving west, she needed a man.

It was the wagonmaster himself who told her, not two hours past when she approached him at the livery stable.

"I'll hire a teamster to handle the oxen," she had said. "I won't be a problem. I won't be asking for anything special."

"Nope. Single woman, single man traveling together? Definitely not. Only a husband will do. Ask around all you want. You won't find anyone to tell you different."

"But I heard that if I got the proper supplies and could come up with your fee, I'd have no trouble joining the train."

"You heard wrong."

"I'll pay extra." Desperation had laced her voice, and she hadn't cared who among the passersby heard what she said.

The wagonmaster's steely eyes looked her over. Nervous, she tugged at her black bombazine gown and fought the urge to straighten her best black bonnet.

"You're talking money," he said.

"Of course," she said, not sure she wanted to know what else he thought she could give him. Persevering, she provided her name and the hotel where she was staying. "You can send word if you change your mind."

"Not likely," he said. "You'd be more trouble than you could pay for."

With a shake of his head, he had turned and quickly walked away, leaving her to desultory wandering down the center of Independence.

The news was bad. Even if a dozen likely suspects had suddenly put themselves on the marriage market, she wouldn't be interested. Having just lost a spouse, she wasn't interested in taking on another.

Wandering in and out of the stables, blacksmith shops, and mercantile stores that had sprung up in Independence, she pondered her predicament. Everywhere she looked she saw people preparing for the journey, or trying to make a few dollars off the travelers. Hurrying around her on the busy walkway were enough sharp-eyed hustlers to fill the saloons along the river near her St. Louis home.

Her former home, she amended. She had sold out after Charles Ward's sudden death left her a widow, rendering her able to fulfill her dream of going west.

But dreams, evidently, were not so easily realized.

"You'd be more trouble than you could pay for."

No matter where she went, the wagonmaster's insinuation kept haunting her. She knew what he was getting at. She was too tall, too scrawny, her face too gaunt to turn a man's head, but she was a widow woman and might be considered easy pickings on the long nights that lay ahead.

There might be trouble, too, with the teamster. What if the man she hired got a little lonesome in the night? She had always performed her wifely duties, no matter what they had included. But she wasn't a wife anymore.

Enough maundering. It was doing her little good. Making her way down the wooden walk, she put her long legs to work in the brisk, swinging strides that used to irritate Charles.

Her progress halted at the edge of a crowd blocking the way. Using her height to advantage, she stood on tiptoe to see what was going on. Someone was nailing a crudely drawn sign on a post in front of a blacksmith shop. WANTED was written large across the top, and, directly underneath, KILLER SHARK, and underneath that, REWARD—DEAD OR ALIVE.

The drawing under the words was not of a denizen of the deep but rather of the meanest-looking villain she had ever seen—hair past his shoulders, a scraggly beard covering half of his emaciated face, beady eyes, everything about him dark and menacing. She shivered at the sight.

"Shark didn't shoot that marshal," a thin, whiny voice declared from somewhere at the edge of the crowd.

The words brought hoots and catcalls.

The whiny voice wasn't done. "I've known him a powerful long time. I never seen him cheat, never heard him lie."

"He ain't accused of cheating or lying," someone yelled back. "It's killing he's done. The shcriff's got proof."

The second speaker received a loud chorus of support. A gray-haired, gray-eyed man standing close to Celinda added his opinion. "Well said, sir. This Shark must indeed be a villain. He should be shot on sight, to protect our women and children."

Another round of support answered the harsh words. The man glanced sideways at her, as if waiting for her personal agreement. Short and spare, he was dressed as a gentleman, but a sharpness in his gaze caused her unease, and she hastily looked away.

The crowd scattered, most onlookers speculating as to the reward, and Celinda was left staring at the Killer Shark's lone defender, a wizened derelict who hitched up his baggy pants, wiped his nose on his sleeve, and stared back at her.

"Shark ain't no killer." In the absence of the bigger audience, his voice sounded stronger, more sure.

His pinpointy eyes made Celinda feel guilty.

"I don't know anything about it," she said with a shrug, thinking that, given her own problems, she ought to be hurrying on.

"They say he gunned down a United States marshal last night, behind one of the saloons. Warn't no witnesses, but that don't matter. If they find him, they'll hang him fer sure."

"But someone mentioned proof."

"A puny little two-headed coin Shark called his good-luck piece. It was under the body." He spat on the ground beside his scuffed brogans. "It ain't bringing the poor bastard much luck today."

"Have you talked to the sheriff about him?"

"Naw. I'm what's known as a ne'er-do-well. If'n I was to speak up, I'd do Shark more harm than good. Wherever he's found a hidey-hole, he best stay put for the next year or so."

Celinda's gaze drifted back to the Wanted poster.

Despite the limited talent of the sketch artist, the menace of the accused killer came through. Again she shivered. If she had one thing to be grateful for on this gray spring afternoon, it was that the man known as Shark was not her concern.

Shaking off her disquiet, she hurried on

down the busy street and into the crowded hotel lobby. When she arrived by train yesterday, she had been fortunate to find the small room here. In this spring of 1852, with seemingly half the country wanting to head west, Independence was swollen with travelers, most of them begging for accommodations.

She stopped by the desk to make sure the wagonmaster hadn't sent word that he'd changed his mind.

"No messages, Mrs. Ward," the clerk reported. "You gonna be moving out soon? We got folks wanting that room."

She smiled sweetly, though it made her cheeks ache. "I'll let you know."

Slowly she went up the stairs to her third-floor quarters, each step driving her deeper into despair. Early this morning, before the fateful scene at the stable, she had put her money into the best team of oxen she could find, then the best wagon, supplied by the best outfitter in Independence. She still had money for the wagon train, with an adequate sum left over for additional expenses. She had the heart and courage for the journey. She had the will. What she did not have was the way.

Right now that was all-important.

She had to jiggle her key a few times to get it to open the lock and admit her to the darkened room. Strange, she remembered opening the curtains before she left, but they were drawn closed now. Securing the door behind her—a single woman couldn't be too cautious—she tossed her bonnet onto the bed, shook out her hair, and took a step toward the window.

Lightning quick, a hand clamped over her mouth, an iron arm wrapped around her waist, and she found herself imprisoned against a solid body directly behind her. Terrified, she flailed out with her fists, but she made contact with only air. Her scream caught in her throat. She tasted salt, dirt, the acrid hint of leather, and her heart pounded until she thought it would burst.

Still, she struggled, twisted, went limp, then struggled again in a vain attempt to catch her assailant by surprise.

In everything she tried, she failed, her discouragement matched only by her continuing terror. Finally she ceased struggling, the fight gone out of her. Tears came; they streamed down her cheeks and onto the punishing hand. She couldn't stop them. She didn't try. If crying was the only response left to her, she would do a first-class job of it.

"I'm letting go of your mouth." The voice in her ear was thick, deep, menacing. "But don't scream, or I'll shoot."

She nodded to show she understood.

The hand moved, and she licked her bruised lips, wanting to spit out the taste of him.

"I won't scream," she managed in a shaky voice. "Just don't smother me like that again."

Under the circumstances, giving orders was not the smartest thing she could have done, but it was the most honest. All her life she had been under the control of men. To end her days on earth the way she had lived them seemed particularly cruel.

She waited for the hand to clamp back into place or to start roaming over her body. Shooting wasn't the only way he could hurt her. She held herself very still, thinking too late that he had probably enjoyed the struggle she put up, rubbing her body against his in her pitiful attempt to get away.

"When I let go of you, turn slowly to face me. I don't want to hurt you. I want to talk."

Talk? Is that what he called it? Celinda would have laughed if she hadn't been so caught up in fright. When she went to her Maker—very shortly, if she was lucky—it would be at the hands of a madman.

Maybe she could wrestle the gun from him and shoot herself, hastening the whole thing. She abandoned the idea in an instant. He was the mad one, not she. Despite all her woes, she very much wanted to live.

The iron band around her waist eased, allowing her to pull away. Wiping the tears from her cheeks, she turned, gasped, and with a few stumbling steps backward sat heavily on the edge of the bed. The outside light seeping around the closed curtains was dim but adequate for her to get a fair look at her captor—and to realize the desperation of her situation.

The eyes that watched her were the same eyes that had peered out from the Wanted poster, the scraggly hair and beard likewise the same. There was no mistaking who the intruder was.

"Killer Shark," she whispered.

"Shark will do."

The deeply resonant, almost sardonic voice seemed incongruous, coming out of the man who stood before her. Tall, lean, hairy as a mountain man, his black suit covered in dust, dark streaks staining his once-white shirt, he was not a sight to give a woman courage.

She cleared her throat and clasped her trembling hands in her lap. Calm. She must remain calm.

"Mr. Shark—"

Was that a twitch of a smile in the midst of all that dark beard?

"As I said, Shark will do."

Her temper flared. "Nothing will do as long as you're in this room. I am Mrs. Celinda Cheney Ward, in case you're interested in the identity of the woman you're frightening half to death. I must warn you, my husband is a strong man and an excellent shot. He will be here at any moment."

"Not unless he's come from the grave."

She started. "How did you know Charles was dead?"

"I overheard you at the livery stable. I was hiding in one of the back stalls."

"When I was arguing with that mule-headed wagonmaster."

"He could have said the same thing about you."

Celinda rubbed her temples. "I don't believe this conversation."

"I don't believe you're not fluttering about in hysterics. Most women would be. I figured I'd have to bind and gag you before you'd listen to reason."

She covered her eyes, peering at him from between her fingers. "Reason?"

"Reason."

Her hands returned to her lap, and she stared at him in relative calm, caught by the absurdity of the situation.

"You're a killer. Why would I listen to anything you had to say?"

"I'm not a killer, Mrs. Ward. I'm a gambler, and lately I've come close to being a drunk, but I am not a man given to violence of any kind. And I'm not stupid, which I would have to be to shoot a lawman in the back and leave evidence I had done it."

He did indeed sound reasonable. But Celinda knew that reasonable men could be just as mean as unreasonable ones. She had been married to such a man.

"I'll bet you were drunk last night. How do you know what you did?"

"I know what I didn't do."

"So you don't remember the details."

He scratched his beard, then dropped his hands to his sides, as if he would show her he intended her no harm.

"There are some blank spots, I admit. I know I was gambling—"

"And drinking."

"And drinking. But I wasn't so far gone I would forget killing a man. I slept it off in the livery stall and woke up to the talk about the shooting. The stablehand's a friend. He came back and gave me the details, told me to lie low. Before too long, you and the wagonmaster came along. Not having much else to do, I listened in."

"You heard me say where I was staying."

He nodded, then took a step forward. She jumped.

"Relax. I don't plan to touch you again," he said. "Unless you give me no choice."

"You can shoot me without touching me."

Again his lips gave every appearance of twitching.

"True. It's something you ought to keep in mind."

She eyed the door behind him.

"Don't even think it," he said, leaving her to do nothing more daring than stare at him in disgust.

He moved sideways to the window, eased the curtain open a couple of inches, and peered outside. When the light fell across his face, she got her first good look at his eyes. They were watchful, sharp even, but they were also the clearest blue she had ever seen. The bloodshot whites distracted a bit from their clarity, but all in all they didn't look nearly so mean as they had on the wanted poster.

When they shifted to her, she looked away nervously, as if he had caught her doing something she shouldn't.

"What are you doing here?" she asked. "If you plan to have your way with me, get it over with and be gone. I've got problems, as you very well know, and I need to start working on them."

He dropped the curtain and turned to face her. "I want my way, all right, and you're very much involved, but what I have in mind is not what you're thinking."

For some reason she remembered the ne'er-do-well on the street. *"Shark ain't no killer."* He was also, according to his defender, not given to cheating or lying. She stiffened her spine, her fright reduced by half. But that still left her trembling inside.

"All my life I have prided myself on my patience, sir, but you are a trying man. Spit out what you're thinking," she said.

"Let me introduce myself properly, Mrs. Ward. Around the gambling tables I'm known as Shark, but my name is Reed Bayard Porter. I want you to consider being Mrs. Porter. I want you to be my wife." Reed watched the shock in Celinda Ward's expressive brown eyes, watched it turn to disbelief and at last scorn.

"You're madder than I suspected."

"No offense, Mrs. Ward, but I'm more desperate than insane."

"Meaning you would have to be desperate to extend a marriage proposal to such as me? If *proposal* is even the right word. I'll try not to be insulted. But neither can I take it as a compliment."

"Call it what you like. It's meant in all earnestness. I have learned something about myself over the past few hours. I'm not afraid of dying, but I do not want to do it in dishonor."

"And marrying me will save you from such a fate?"

He looked at the way she sat straight-backed at the edge of the bed, her fine brown hair falling softly around her shoulders, her eyes deep and wide and wondering. She was tall, a little spare for his tastes, but she was strong. She had given him more difficulty in her struggles than she realized.

And she was levelheaded. The question was whether she was levelheaded enough to consider the sensibleness of his suggestion.

"You need a husband. I need a way to get out of town for a while, to let the dust settle so I can figure out how to clear my name. I'm a traveling man who earns his money at the poker table. An honest reputation is about all I've got. And the freedom to move about as I want."

Her eyes showed her calculations. "I have been married once. I harbor no intention of getting married again."

"I'm not speaking of a true marriage. Look at it this way. I borrow you for a while," he said. "You borrow me. We each get what we want."

"What do you mean for a while?"

"Until we're too far along on the trail for you to be sent back. A few weeks, a month at the most. By then the furor here will have died down, and I can work at finding the truth."

She looked him over. He pulled back the curtain to give her a better view, taking care to step well away from the window.

"You're far too hairy and dirty," she said. "The wagonmaster would never believe I had married such a man."

"I clean up well."

The calculations in her eyes turned to skepticism. And then another thought struck.

"What else would you want, Mr. Porter, besides a way out of town?" She cleared her throat. "I refer, of course, to the . . . conjugal bed."

"Again, no offense, but I have no intention of touching you other than when we are in public and a helping hand on your arm seems appropriate. As a lad, I was taught my manners. I've not become a complete reprobate."

"How encouraging."

"We would, of course, dissolve the marriage when it is no longer of benefit to one or the other of us. I am by no means seeking anything permanent."

He could see her weakening, then stiffening again.

"This is truly mad. You could very well be a killer."

"You'll just have to take my word that I'm not."

A weariness settled on him, and a disgust that he had come to this—he, who wanted most in life to be left alone. He picked up his hat from where he'd tossed it to the floor and shoved it onto his head, twisting his hair up underneath so the length didn't show.

"Forget what I suggested. Forget I was here. You go back to dreaming about a wagon train that's denied you, and I'll go back to dodging the law."

He opened the door and peered into the hallway.

"Wait," she said.

He closed the door.

"I must be losing my mind," she said. "But you're beginning to make sense."

He kept quiet, having said all he'd come to say.

"A man on the street said you were innocent. He said he never saw you cheat or heard you lie, and he knew you weren't a killer."

"Did he look like a tramp? Short, wrinkled, with a whiny voice? That's Pitiful Pete. He was the one laid the moniker Shark on me. I gave him his."

She stared at the worn carpet for a moment, then directed her expressive brown eyes at him.

"Have you ever had a dream, Mr. Porter?"

It was a question that once would have hurt. "Not in a long while."

"Mine is new, but it's powerful. I'm all alone in Missouri now that my husband is gone. My brother has written, asking me to join him in California. It is what I want more than I want to breathe."

Her honesty moved him. And it irritated

him, too. He didn't want to be moved by anything about her.

"Have you any idea how dangerous these wagon trains can be? How hard you'll have to work? The miles you will have to walk to preserve your team?"

"You sound as if you're trying to discourage me from going."

"I don't like stupidity or ignorance. A woman alone is a needful creature. I'm all on that wagonmaster's side."

"I've lived a safe and proper life," she said, as if that answered him. "Charles was a physician, and I helped him when I could. Not once did I ever do or say anything that wasn't expected of me, anything that wouldn't be approved by the strictest Methodist in town."

She continued to interest him, continued to irritate him.

"If you're working up to accepting my proposal," he said, "you're taking a long time getting to it."

"If I'm to put my fate in your hands, I have the right. At least for now. Chances are we will never talk so honestly with one another again."

"You can bet your oxen on it."

"How would we go about the marriage? It would have to be genuine. The wagonmaster will be skeptical enough about the situation."

"There's a justice of the peace down the block. You be there by mid morning tomorrow. I'll take care of the paperwork."

She looked at him for a long while, then looked down at her hands. "I need to think this over. 'Borrowing each other,' as you put it, is all so sudden. So . . . bizarre."

"Tell you what. You be there and we'll go through with the ceremony. If you're not, I'll be on my way."

She stood, and he put out his hand.

"You say you clean up well," she said. "I'll wait until you've done so before we shake hands." She gave him a wide berth as she went to open the door. "I don't know how you managed to get in here without being seen, and I don't know how you'll leave. If you manage to do so safely, there is a very good chance I will stand with you before the justice of the peace. Shall we say ten o'clock?"

Celinda Cheney Ward wasted no time in getting him out into the hallway and closing and locking the door behind him, Reed noted. This possible Mrs. Porter was not a woman to dilly-dally, though she talked a bit more than he would have liked. When he had come up with the idea of marriage he had thought it crazier than she had. But no other plan had occurred to him, and he had figured it was worth a try.

Would she show up? He wouldn't want to bet either way.

Pulling a pair of wire-framed glasses from an inside coat pocket, he settled them into place. Strange how such a simple thing could disguise a man, make him look like one of those preachers who never shaved instead of the killer he was supposed to be.

Rounding his back and stiffening one leg, he

limped down the stairs and through the crowded lobby. All the while he kept thinking that by this time tomorrow he could very well be a married man. It was enough to give a determined bachelor the shivers.

The easiest part of the whole thing would be keeping his promise to leave his bride alone. A woman who had dreams, especially one willing to sacrifice for them, was a complicated creature, and he had troubles enough without adding her to the list.

Chapter Two

Celinda combed her hair six different ways before ending up with the usual bun at the back of her neck. On her wedding day, a woman wanted to look her best, even if it wasn't a true wedding and she would be a borrowed bride joining herself to a borrowed groom.

She threw the comb down onto the scarred top of the hotel dresser and stared into the mirror. A sleep-needy, sunken-cheeked, troubled woman stared back. It wasn't just any groom she was borrowing. Reed Bayard Porter was a man wanted by the law far more than he was wanted by his would-be wife.

She twisted back and forth, checking over her reflection. She had packed away her best dress, the bombazine, deciding widow's weeds were hardly appropriate, even for a bride as unorthodox as she. The blue silk was second best. It used to fit snugly. It hung on her now.

Her grief for Charles had been genuine, if not deep, deriving mostly from the fact that he had never become the man he should have been. But it had caused her to lose her appetite. She had to start eating more, if for no other reason than to keep up her strength. She already knew what Mr. Porter had warned her about: A wagon train moving west offered dangerous challenges, long hours, demands on stamina most people would never have to face.

With a sigh she turned away from the mirror. The time was a quarter to ten. She needed to pry herself away from the hotel.

Donning a blue bonnet that matched her dress and slipping on a pair of lace-trimmed gloves, she grabbed up her reticule and hurried out the door. In the lobby the clerk motioned to her from behind the desk, but she answered him with a wave and hurried on. She had to keep hurrying. Once she stopped, she would turn coward and dash back to her room.

Outside, she forced herself to slow down. If she arrived in front of the justice of the peace breathless and disheveled, Mr. Porter would think she was eager to be his wife.

Even dawdling, she got to the small, one-room office early, and the judge, a round-bellied, full-bearded potentate, promptly introduced himself.

"The clerk here will be your witness. Unless you came up with one of your own."

She shook her head.

A Special Offer For Leisure Historical Romance Readers Only!

Get Four FREE* Romance Novels

A $21.96 Value!

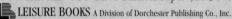

GET YOUR 4 FREE* BOOKS NOW—
A $21.96 VALUE!

Mail the Free* Book
Certificate
Today!

4 FREE* BOOKS 🌺 A $21.96 VALUE

Free Books Certificate*

YES! I want to subscribe to the Leisure Historical Romance Book Club. Please send me my 4 FREE* BOOKS. Then each month I'll receive the four newest Leisure Historical Romance selections to Preview for 10 days. If I decide to keep them, I will pay the Special Member's Only discounted price of just $4.24 each, a total of $16.96 ($17.75 US in Canada). This is a SAVINGS OF AT LEAST $5.00 off the bookstore price. There are no shipping, handling, or other charges*. There is no minimum number of books I must buy and I may cancel the program at any time. In any case, the 4 FREE* BOOKS are mine to keep—A BIG $21.96 Value!

*In Canada, add $5.00 shipping and handling per order for first shipment. For all subsequent shipments to Canada, the cost of membership is $17.75 US, which includes $7.75 shipping and handling per month.[All payments must be made in US dollars]

Name _____

Address _____

City _____

State _____ *Country* _____ *Zip* _____

Telephone _____

Signature _____

If under 18, Parent or Guardian must sign. Terms, prices and conditions subject to change. Subscription subject to acceptance. Leisure Books reserves the right to reject any order or cancel any subscription.

(Tear Here and Mail Your FREE* Book Card Today!)

Get Four Books Totally
F R E E* —
A $21.96 Value!

PLEASE RUSH
MY FOUR FREE*
BOOKS TO ME
RIGHT AWAY!

Leisure Historical Romance Book Club
P.O. Box 6613
Edison, NJ 08818-6613

AFFIX
STAMP
HERE

"Your intended is not with you," he added, somewhat needlessly she thought.

"He will be shortly," she said with a smile.

But would he? For all she knew, Reed Porter had been captured by the sheriff and was now ensconced in the bowels of the Independence jail, contemplating the awaiting gallows.

An embarrassing few minutes of silence passed. Unbidden, her thoughts went back to her first wedding, the simple ceremony in the country church where the Cheney family had worshiped for years. Friends and family had surrounded her. She had harbored no doubts about what she was about to do.

She hadn't loved Charles Ward when he rode up to her Tennessee farm and asked her father for his youngest daughter's hand. But she had known him—or thought she did. The disillusionment had come later, after they moved to St. Louis and he set up his physician's practice.

With Reed Porter, whom she neither knew nor loved, there would be no illusions that could be crushed, not even if he had taken another man's life.

She stopped herself. He was no killer. She had believed in his innocence last night. She must believe in it on their wedding day.

Their wedding day. The enormity of what she was about to do struck her like a splash of cold water in the face. This was absurd. It would never work. She turned to leave.

The door opened, and a stranger walked in. He was tall and lean but obviously well muscled beneath his chambray work shirt. His trousers were black, as were his polished boots and the loosely tied bandanna at his throat. His clean-shaven face was marked by a strong jaw, firm mouth, and prominent cheekbones that hinted of an Indian ancestry.

He doffed his hat to reveal neatly trimmed black hair. *Why couldn't this be Reed Porter,* she asked herself morosely. Then when she looked into his blue eyes, she saw that he was.

"Oh." It was the most she could say.

He stepped forward to take her hand. "Dearest, my apologies for being late, but there were so many last-minute details to see to. I'm sure you understand."

She didn't, not for sure. He probably meant the cleaning up had taken a longer time than he had allotted. It was time well spent, though. He did indeed clean up well.

Her heart pounded at the sight of him. She didn't want to react to Reed Porter in any way, but at the moment she could not control it. Worse, he must know what was happening to her. It showed in his very evil smile.

"You're forgiven," she said. "I know how much our marriage means to you."

His eyes narrowed. "And to you." He turned to the justice of the peace. "Shall we get on with it? We expect to leave town by the end of the week, and there's much to be done to get ready."

If the judge was in the least suspicious about the proceedings, he gave not a sign. The ceremony was brief, to the point, nothing flowery about love and commitment and the sanctity of marriage. She wondered if Reed Porter had told the man him to leave all that out.

She was grateful for one thing: Porter had managed to get a simple gold band to slip onto her finger. He was, she was learning, a man who saw to details.

It was a trait they shared. She tucked her gloves into her reticule, leaving the ring uncovered for all the world—and the wagonmaster— to see.

The proceedings ended with five ominous words. "You may kiss the bride."

Celinda turned to leave, caught her new husband's eye, and felt dread ripple from her head to her feet.

He wouldn't dare.

He would.

Wrapping his arms around her, he brought his lips down on hers. Wanting to struggle, to kick him in the shins, she could do little else but submit to whatever he wanted to do. Right away she figured out what he wanted: to kiss her more thoroughly than she had ever been kissed before.

His lips were warm, insistent, and so was the tongue that teased her tightly closed mouth. In an instant buds of hot emotion blossomed within her. Instinctively she opened herself to him, leaning against his strength, aware of nothing but the smell, the feel, the taste of him. Her heart pounded in her ears, and she felt the blood course through her veins, all with an immediacy and power that rendered her weak and bold at the same time.

He broke the kiss and pressed his lips against her temple.

"Dearest," he said.

The buds closed, the warmth fled, and she was left standing in his arms humiliated and ashamed. When her thoughts cleared, she also became furious. She understood now how men killed in a rage. It was a good thing she wasn't carrying a gun.

Pushing away from him, she managed to meet his gaze. "Darling," she said. "We've kept the gentlemen far too long."

Outside on the busy walkway she opened her mouth to tell him what she thought of him, his lack of character, his dubious ancestry—to throw in his direction every insult she could come up with.

He took her by the arm and guided her into an alley next to the judge's office.

"It's not a good idea to have our first argument so soon after the ceremony," he said. "And in front of witnesses. My dear Mrs. Porter, you must be more circumspect."

"I have more than arguing in mind, you bastard."

She drew back her arm. He caught her wrist and pulled her hard against him.

"My little honeybear," he said. "You are insatiable."

He proceeded to kiss her again. This time she tried to squirm away from him, but the squirming only intensified his embrace. It also increased her awareness of his body, of hard, masculine contours she wanted to know nothing about.

The emotional buds started opening again. Why did he have to feel so good? She didn't like sex. She certainly didn't like him.

Her only defense was to hold herself very still and keep her lips tightly closed. His tongue had gotten its last taste of her.

At last, he lifted his head from hers, shot her a warning look that quelled invective, and glanced toward the street.

"Good morning," he said, full of good cheer. "We meet again, Mr. Dalton." He stepped back a pace from Celinda. "Look, dearest, it's the wagonmaster. I established our place in line with him early this morning, hoping to make it a wedding surprise. But I've been found out."

"*She's* your bride?" the wagonmaster asked, more than a little incredulous.

Celinda stiffened. As much as she did not want to be Mrs. Reed Porter, she took offense that anyone would find it so difficult to believe.

"Allow me to introduce you two," the new bridegroom said smoothly. "Celinda, this is Buck Dalton. Mr. Dalton, Mrs. Porter."

Celinda stepped well away from her groom and managed a smile. "Mr. Dalton, you and I have met, have we not? I'm so glad the situation between us has altered. When we spoke before, I wasn't sure the wedding would take place so quickly. But now that it has, right here

229

before the justice of the peace, as a matter of fact, I'm the happiest woman on earth."

Dalton did not completely lose his skeptical frown.

"Reed," she said in her most wifely voice, "could you show the wagonmaster our marriage certificate?"

Her husband reached inside his coat pocket.

"That won't be necessary," Dalton said. "I'll talk to the judge. We'll be pulling out ahead of time, in two days. We start assembling at dawn. Make sure you're in place."

He moved on, leaving the newlyweds to return their attention to each other.

"Honeybear?" she said.

He shrugged. "It was all I could think of. I thought it was pretty nice. I've never called a woman honeybear before."

"It's not nice at all. And please leave off with the endearments. They remind me too much of what a fake marriage this is."

"Don't say fake. Dalton might overhear."

"Temporary, then." She smiled sweetly. "I've got just one more thing to take care of."

"What?"

She slapped him, fast and hard, before he had a chance to stop her.

"Don't you ever kiss me again."

With that, she turned her back to him and in long strides returned to the walkway, leaving him to either follow her to the hotel or pick his own destination, she did not care which.

* * *

Reed was not a man who sought revenge against anyone, no matter the offense. Still, the new Mrs. Porter was a worthy candidate for a comeuppance. Maybe he had deserved a reprimand for the kiss before the watching judge, at least for the manner of it. He certainly hadn't for the second one—that had become a necessity the instant he saw Buck Dalton staring down the alley at them.

His too-slight bride packed a wallop. She had to learn when and where to deliver it. Never at her husband. That was rule number one. He hadn't quite decided on rule number two, but he knew he would think of something, knew that over the next few weeks a long list of rules was sure to develop.

She made the short trip to the hotel fast. He had to hurry to keep up. Beneath the folds of her skirt she had long legs, which she put to good use. She would soon have need of that healthy stride. He wondered how long she would keep it up as she crossed the plains.

He also thought about those long legs, and about the feminine swishing of silk when a woman walked. Feminine, too, was the way his bride had returned his kiss, at least the first one. He tried not to think for long of the softness of her lips, or of the warmth of her response. She had not been the only one heating up from the brief encounter. But they had made a bargain that did not allow for heat.

She kept him waiting outside her room while she changed into a plainer gown and bonnet.

When she joined him in the hallway, he took her arm. She tried to pull away.

"Careful. I'm a wanted man, remember? You have to make the world think *you're* the only one who wants me."

He released her long enough to put on the wire-framed glasses. This time she took his proffered arm, though a little too stiffly for a genuine show of affection, and walked beside him down the stairs.

The opportunity for her comeuppance came when they went to inspect their wagon and team. She had bought six fine, strong oxen, four to pull the wagon, two to plod along behind in reserve. With the help of the outfitter who had sold her the team, Reed soon had them yoked to the canvas-covered wagon.

"Why don't you try your hand at the reins?" he suggested. "I won't always be around, you know."

She glanced worriedly at the outfitter.

"There will be days when I'll be out hunting for food," Reed added quickly. "Unless you're handy with a gun."

"Not yet, but I intend to be." She spoke sweetly. He was not deceived.

"And I've already taken the reins," she added. "When I bought the team."

She spoke confidently enough, but he could see the fear in her eyes.

He looked to the outfitter.

"That she did," the man confirmed. "Needs practice, though. Best get used to the feel of 'em here 'stead of out on the trail."

"Needs practice" turned out to be an under-

statement. At first the oxen refused to move, and when Celinda at last got them under way, after a feeble attempt at cracking the whip over their massive rumps, they chose a direction that was clearly not to her liking.

They proceeded to plod in a wide arc, pulling the wagon and a very reluctant driver behind them. Moving as slowly as they were, Reed had no difficulty pulling himself onto the wagon seat at Celinda's side. He expected a fight when he reached for the reins. Instead, she handed them over right away.

"Teach me what I need to know," she said, staring straight at him. "I can't let pride keep me from doing this right."

It wasn't the comeuppance he had envisioned. Somehow she managed to make him feel in the wrong for even wanting it.

When he took the reins, he noticed her reddened hands.

"You need gloves," he said.

"I guess the lace ones won't do."

He started to make a sharp remark, then noticed she was smiling at him, or as close to smiling as she could get under the circumstances. Within the circle of the bonnet, her face looked delicately formed, her ivory skin far too vulnerable, her deep brown eyes far too expressive and needy. The urge to kiss her struck him again, and it had nothing to do with putting on a show for anyone watching.

Returning his glasses to a shirt pocket, he turned his attention back to the oxen. Who was getting the comeuppance here, him or her?

He soon had the beasts headed in a straight line down the road, grateful that the dust they stirred up masked the sweet scent of the woman by his side. Nothing could mask her attentiveness, her questions, her observations, or the way she agreed to place her hands over his to get the feel of how he worked the team.

By the time he got the team, the wagon, and his wife back to the outfitter, Reed's sense of being in charge was pretty much shattered. Dropping to the ground, he helped Celinda down beside him, holding her waist, enjoying touching her, thinking about what it would be like to touch her more intimately.

Their eyes met. Neither of them looked away.

"Thank you for the lesson," she said.

"You're welcome."

He bent his head toward her; she raised her lips as if in invitation. One little kiss . . .

"Well, hello there," a feminine voice trilled. "Looks like we're going to be traveling together."

Celinda jumped away as if she'd been burned, and Reed turned toward the voice.

Two young women stood behind him, one fair, the other dark-haired, both shapely, both too flamboyantly dressed in bright silk for emigrants on a wagon train.

"I hope we didn't interrupt anything," the fair one said with a giggle. "I'm Mary Ellen Hudson, and this is my sister, Lodisa. We're traveling with our aunt and uncle—"

"He's just an uncle by marriage, understand," Lodisa said.

Mary Ellen shot her sister a dark look for interrupting. "He took sick a couple of days ago, so he's been holed up in the hotel. Any chance you've seen Aunt Dorothea around? She's a big woman, not at all like us, kind of bosomy, you understand, and tall, really tall." She batted her eyelashes at Reed. "Not quite as tall as you, of course. I do like a man with height."

"You like 'em short, too," Lodisa said.

"Well, so do you."

"Girls!"

This feminine voice did not trill, it boomed, and Reed watched as the big-bosomed, sturdy Aunt Dorothea approached across the field where the outfitter kept his stock, taking care to watch where she stepped.

"Pardon my nieces," she said. "They are silly girls, but they mean no harm. I'm Dorothea Clapp. And you are . . ."

"Reed Porter," he said with a slight bow. "This is my wife, Celinda."

It was the second time since the ceremony that he had introduced her. With the wagonmaster, he had felt as if he were lying. This time the word *wife* fell more naturally from his lips.

"I'm pleased to meet all of you," she said, avoiding his eyes. "But please excuse me. I've developed a terrible headache, and there's nothing to do but lie down and rest until it goes away."

"I understand," Mrs. Clapp said, while her nieces were too busy looking at Reed to listen to his wife.

Celinda glanced at him but still did not meet his gaze. "Please forgive me for not helping with the team and wagon, but I really do feel in need of rest. I'm sure you understand. Don't bother escorting me back to the hotel. I'll be fine."

He watched her walk away, her bonnet bobbing, her skirt moving in the rhythm set by her long stride. He thought about the lesson, about her eagerness to learn, about the genial way she accepted instruction and correction.

He thought, too, about the more than genial way she had lifted her lips to him after he helped her to the ground. That was indeed a complication. Judging from the look in her eyes when she turned to leave, she was as bothered by that fact as he.

As quickly as he could, he separated himself from the Hudson sisters and their formidable aunt, unhitched the team, and hurried back to the stables, where Pitiful Pete was supposed to meet him. Pete had agreed to circulate through the town, asking a few questions that Reed had suggested, serving as his investigator.

Finding the marshal's real killer was the only issue that mattered to Reed, but he could hardly move around freely, despite the alteration in his appearance. The sheriff had a reputation of being not only honest but also smart. He would figure out in short order how easy it would be for his only suspect to shave and give himself a haircut.

Reed scratched at his bare cheek. He missed his beard. He missed drinking, too. But getting drunk would be dumb. Almost as dumb as becoming infatuated with his wife.

The last time he had cared for a female he was seventeen, son of a lowly shopkeeper. She was the mayor's daughter, the prettiest girl in town. She had broken his heart. He'd thought he would never recover. Funny, right now he could not remember her name.

But he knew Celinda Cheney Ward Porter. He knew the sting of her hand and the warmth of her lips. He knew far more than he wanted to know.

Chapter Three

Celinda did not see her husband for the rest of the day and all of the next. She did not care in the least. In fact, she was relieved. He unsettled her far more than Charles ever had. She couldn't say exactly why, except that there seemed so much more of him, though that didn't make sense. Charles had been heftier and probably outweighed him by twenty pounds.

A small voice inside reminded her that a man was not measured by the pound. The voice also told her that she did miss this new husband of hers, that she worried about his well-being, even about his going through with the bargain they had made.

She did not listen to the small voice. She had enough worries packing her supplies in the wagon, making sure she had purchased wisely for the long trek, arranging for additional purchases when she saw what others had bought.

Taking the advice of one of the women, a mother of three who had done a great deal of research on the matter, she was sitting in the wagon bed, a half dozen pins in her mouth as she sewed pockets inside the canvas cover, when she felt someone watching her from the back opening.

She knew who the watcher was without looking. She almost swallowed a pin.

He climbed into the wagon and sat beside her. She looked at his folded legs and black boots, at the plaid shirt, the black bandanna, and at last into his eyes. Unable to breathe, she removed the pins and stuck them into the cushion beside her with more force than was strictly necessary.

"I was beginning to doubt you would show up," she said.

"You missed me?"

"I need you, that's all."

She smoothed her hair from her face, wishing her bun weren't so untidy.

"You need me," he said softly, "but do you want me?"

He was teasing her, goading her, taking pleasure in observing her discomfort.

She dared to look at him. "No more than you want me."

She saw no point in letting him know that she had been unable to get a good night's sleep worrying about him. There was no telling what

239

he might say or do. He wasn't a killer—she felt it in her bones—but he probably was a lover and leaver, the kind who could break a woman's heart.

Even hairy, he hadn't looked bad.

He looked around the wagon. "What's in the barrels?"

"Cornmeal and flour. I've got eggs tucked down in one and smoked bacon in the other. We've got coffee, sugar, some dried beef, a little bit of this and that to get us started—enough, I hope, to get us to Fort Laramie. We can restock there."

She fell silent. He probably wouldn't stay around that long. He had far more important matters to deal with than a temporary wife.

The silence lengthened awkwardly, and she knew his thoughts were the same as hers.

He dropped a small package into her lap. "I brought you something."

She stared at it, for some reason embarrassed.

"It's not a wedding gift, if that's what you're thinking," he said.

"I wasn't thinking anything of the sort." She lied. "Mostly I was wondering if it might bite."

She tore off the paper and looked at a pair of sturdy leather gloves. "Oh." For some stupid reason she felt like crying. "I had meant to buy a pair, but I forgot." She stared at her reddened palms. "I always took pride in my hands. That seems silly now. I've never been particularly vain."

He was probably thinking it was a good thing, since she had little to be vain about.

"Try them on. See if they fit."

She did. "They're perfect. Thank you. I got something for you, too." She opened the small trunk she had placed directly behind the seat and pulled out a hat.

"The brim's wider than on the one you've been wearing. It'll give you more protection from the sun and rain. It's not a wedding gift or anything like that. I saw it and thought you needed it."

She didn't go on to say that the black felt reminded her of the black bandanna at his throat and the way his long, black-clad legs tapered into a pair of polished black boots.

He settled the hat low on his forehead. "Perfect," he said.

"Not quite."

Taking off her gloves, she reached out for the brim. He jerked back, as if her touching him would be a terrible experience. She did not let his reaction stop her from adjusting the hat to a slight tilt. All the while, she was far too aware of the way he was looking at her. She made sure she touched only the hat and kept well away from any part of him.

He would not appreciate her desire to experience the warmth of his skin or the texture of his lips. She didn't appreciate it much herself.

"There," she said, trying to keep her voice light. "Now it's perfect." He had no idea just how much. "It covers your eyes," she went on in her most practical voice. "I don't know if you realize it, but they're quite recognizable. Even the glasses you sometimes wear don't hide them enough."

He thumbed the hat to the back of his head, and her heart did a thumpety-thump.

"You ought to hide your eyes, too," he said. "They reveal too much of what you're thinking."

"I'm not thinking anything."

"Not true. You're always thinking. Right now you're edgy. Something about me has made you fidgety. Are you afraid of me?"

He spoke harshly, still goading her. If that was his goal, he was succeeding very well.

"Afraid? Maybe. A little."

The truth was, she was afraid of herself and of the itchiness he started inside her when he got close. But she could hardly reveal something so intimate, being a woman long used to keeping her own confidences.

Besides, under the circumstances, itchiness was a weakness she could ill afford. Reed Porter was not a man to tolerate any kind of weakness if it got in his way.

"Having second thoughts about my innocence?"

His voice was growing sharper. She had angered him. Good. The more distressed he became, the calmer she could feel.

"Your innocence is not an issue. We are married, and we are about to set out on an adventure. That's all the worry I can handle right now. I don't care what my eyes tell you. Listen to what I say."

With that, she turned her attention to the sturdy needle that was dangling by a strand of thread from the last pocket she had to sew.

"I'll be here well before dawn, Mr.—"

"You'd better start calling me Reed."

"I will. When it matters."

"I'm going to plunge right in and call you Celinda. Unless you prefer honeybear."

There he was, teasing her again, jerking her back and forth the way a child might a kite on a string. She simply did not understand the man.

"You'd best not. I bought a gun."

"Do you know how to use it?"

"About as well as I can take the reins."

"I'd better warn the others."

"I won't be shooting at them."

"Not intentionally."

He reached out to touch her, then dropped his hand.

"I'll see you in the morning," he said abruptly. Turning his back to her, he dropped out of the wagon and was gone.

Reed showed up early, ready to hitch the oxen to their yokes. He brought with him a surprise: a milk cow, which he tied to the back of the wagon. Celinda showed up shortly afterward, carrying a small valise. Lanterns hanging on the surrounding wagons allowed him to see the simple gown and sturdy shoes she wore. A bonnet hid most of her face.

She stared at the cow, a question in her expressive eyes.

"You bought everything else," he said, and then, before she could express her gratitude—he didn't like it, didn't want it—he glanced at the valise. "That's all you're bringing?"

"I've got a couple of dresses and some extra

shoes and bonnets. It's all I need. I'm not a woman who's used to fancy things."

"Your husband didn't buy them for you?"

"He devoted his life to caring for the sick. I was his helpmeet."

Reed grunted. She must have been a damned good one. He cursed himself. What the devil was he doing thinking such a thing? She was nothing to him, a borrowed ruse to save his neck. Why he kept teasing her, taunting her, he did not know. The way her ivory skin turned pink when he did so, the attractive blush creeping up her slender neck and staining her cheeks, was a pathetic reason.

He hadn't been around a woman who blushed in too many years to number. She was a curiosity, that was all.

Still curiosity could kill a man. It was a fact he'd best keep in mind.

"You're wearing the hat," she said.

He shifted uneasily. "Wide brim."

No need to tell her that, except for an occasional beer, it was the first thing anyone had bought him since he was a youth. No need to thank her, either. She had bought the thing to hide his eyes, to keep his identity a secret and protect their place in the wagon train. He had no delusions about how she regarded him.

It was the same way he regarded her, as a means to a very important end. But he wished she wouldn't blush.

She looked past him to the eastern horizon, where the sun was sending its first tentacles of light into the cool spring air. The rays mingled with the surrounding lantern light to cast a gentle glow over the scene. Around them they could hear people stirring, talking, the words carrying through the stillness the way they did when most of the world slept. Occasionally a whip cracked over a team of mules or oxen as they balked at their traces. A baby cried. A woman laughed.

A tense excitement was like a sharp scent in the air. He could see it in the fine brown eyes peering out from the depths of Celinda's bonnet. His heart beat a little faster. Cursing to himself, he went to claim their oxen, which were staked in a nearby field.

He made quick work of yoking the oxen in place. Heading to the back of the wagon, he heard voices. His wife had visitors. He recognized one—the wagonmaster, Buck Dalton. The other he couldn't identify until he rounded the wagon and saw the shiny badge on the man's vest. The sheriff was busy engaging his wife in earnest conversation, saying something about her being a new bride. It was enough to send a wanted man running.

Instead, he smiled, eased to a halt beside Celinda, and draped an arm around her shoulders.

"I am a lucky man, am I not?" he said, keeping his eyes cast down toward her.

"Indeed you are," the sheriff replied.

The milk cow, bound to the far side of the wagon, mooed and swished her tail.

Buck Dalton spoke up. "I was telling the sheriff here how you two got hitched yesterday, just in time to join us this morning."

"You know how women are," Reed said. He felt his wife stiffen, and he held her even tighter.

"No," the sheriff said. "Being a bachelor myself, I don't reckon I do." He spoke slowly, as if he weren't quite bright, but Reed knew his reputation to be the opposite.

"They like to keep a man dangling, making him worry, before she finally says yes. I can tell you my honeybear was worth the wait."

He gazed down at his wife, willing her to return the gaze and at the same time looking out of the corner of his eye at the lawman.

"Mrs. Porter?"

She did not respond, and the sheriff repeated her name.

Reed gave her a small pinch. She jumped.

"Oh," she said. "My goodness, I must seem addled. I was thinking about being a new bride and setting out on this grand adventure and hoping I had made all the right preparations."

She started listing all she had done, from her first purchases to the pockets she'd sewn inside the wagon's canvas. He had never heard her prattle on quite so much. He could have kissed her for it.

"Pardon, ma'am," the wagonmaster said, "but we got to make the rounds. Sheriff here is looking for this man." He pulled a Wanted poster from his pocket. "You seen him anywheres?"

Reed stared down at the unflattering likeness of himself and shook his head. Celinda shuddered. She had the right.

"Goodness," she said, "he looks evil. Killer Shark. I haven't seen anyone who looks anything like him. If I did, I'd probably start screaming."

Don't overdo it.

As if she could read his mind, she shut up.

The wagonmaster took the poster and turned to leave, but the sheriff seemed reluctant to move on.

"Honeybear," Reed said, "did you get that shirt I asked you to?"

"Of course. Now don't fuss, but I bought a few other things, too. Let me show you. I just know you're going to love what I got."

He smiled down at her in the best simulation of husbandly indulgence he could manage. "I'll look at anything you want to show me."

Turning his back on the men, he helped her into the back of the wagon and climbed in beside her. When he looked outside, the sheriff was gone.

Her hands trembled as she took off the bonnet and smoothed back her hair. He fought an urge to help her.

"I was so scared," she said.

He motioned her to be quiet, but she didn't pay attention. "When he came up—"

Reed silenced her in the only way he knew how. Tossing his hat aside, he kissed her. She jerked once, but he made the kiss persistent, and it didn't take her long to settle down. The next thing he knew, she was leaning into him, and he was kissing her for real, and it didn't matter who was around or where they were or whether they even liked each other. He liked kissing her, and it was clear she liked kissing him, and for the moment that was all that mattered.

It was a lingering kiss, soft and sweet and as provocative as any kiss he could remember. It wasn't only the touch of her lips that he liked. She was delicate and feminine, needful in a way that brought out similar needs in him. When she trembled in his arms, he felt an answering tremble that threatened to take control.

He didn't know which of them pushed away first. It seemed like mutual consent. Neither pushed away far. They kneeled in front of one another, staring into each other's eyes, drawing in deep, ragged breaths.

"What's going on?" she asked, settling back on her heels, touching her fingers to her lips. She looked small and vulnerable and altogether desirable, something he hated like the devil to admit.

He kept his voice low. "I didn't want you talking. Someone might overhear."

"You were doing more than just keeping me quiet."

He started to deny it, then settled on, "That's the way it started out."

She studied her hands, which were twisting in her lap. "Maybe we're just excited about what lies ahead."

Reed wasn't in the least excited. He was running for his life. But he didn't see the purpose in pointing out what she already knew.

"That must be it." He lifted her chin. "I'll try not to do it again, but I'm not making any promises."

"You never know when you'll have to hush me."

"Kissing's all I will do. That I can say for sure."

"It's more than I usually want." She caught her breath. "I shouldn't be saying that to you."

For the first time he began to wonder what her married life had been like. It must not have been a loving relationship, and yet he sensed the possibilities of passion within her. Too bad he would never discover exactly what those possibilities were.

He growled and shook himself. What the devil was he thinking?

Outside the wagon, the noise of preparation grew louder, and he did not bother to keep his voice low.

"Look," he said. "We've got a problem here. In front of the world we have to show affection, or at least pretend we know each other pretty well."

The warmth in her eyes cooled. "I think I've done my part of that all right."

"You didn't respond when the sheriff called you Mrs. Porter."

"That was the first time I heard it. He surprised me. I won't be surprised again."

"And don't flinch when I touch you."

"I didn't. Well, maybe I did, but just a little."

"Where you should have been flinching was in here."

"Don't blame me for that. You started the kiss."

"And you joined right in."

She glanced toward the front of the wagon, through the opening to the yoke of oxen waiting patiently to begin the long journey.

"Does it seem we've had this conversation before?"

In profile, she looked more vulnerable, more delicate than ever. At that moment he wished he had never met her, never come up with his absurd scheme. Still, touching the loose hairs at the back of her neck couldn't do any harm.

He reached out.

"Well, if it isn't the lovebirds," a voice trilled from the back.

The speaker was one of the Hudson girls, the blonde. He couldn't recall her name. The dark-haired sister stood grinning close beside her. Once again they were dressed in clothes a little too flamboyant for the day awaiting them. Their hair disheveled, their eyes heavy-lidded, they had a sleepy look about them, as if they had just crawled out of bed.

"If I had a handsome new husband like you," the second sister said, "I'd be staying in the wagon with him, too."

Reed watched as Celinda slowly turned her attention to the pair. "I'm sure you would. Perhaps someday, if you're very, very good, you can be as lucky as I am."

Was there sharpness in her voice? He grinned. Damned if she wasn't showing signs of jealousy.

"Mary Ellen. Lodisa. You girls come on now. Your uncle will be along any minute, and we need to be ready to leave."

He recognized the strong voice of the formidable, big-bosomed aunt.

"Oh, Aunt Dorothea," Mary Ellen, the blonde, said. "We're behaving ourselves."

The aunt hove into view. He struggled to remember her last name.

"Mrs. Clapp," Celinda said, "how nice to see you again. How is Mr. Clapp?"

"Fine, just fine." She looked past the girls. "Why, here he is now. I was worried about you, Fisher. Come on over and meet these fine folk."

A gray-haired man in a far-too-fine suit joined the women. Everything about him looked gray, from his slicked-back hair to his narrow eyes, his bushy brows, and his thick moustache. Even his skin had an ashen cast to it, as if he rarely went into the sun. He was a head shorter than his wife, his narrow shoulders at a level with those of his nieces. Something stirred in the back of Reed's mind, a vague memory that refused to come into focus. Whatever it was, Fisher Clapp was definitely involved.

Beside him he felt more than heard Celinda's sharp intake of breath.

Dorothea Clapp took care of the introductions. Fisher Clapp's initial glance at Reed was a little too shrewd, a little too calculating, to be softened by his too-big smile.

"Pleased to meet you," Clapp said with a formal little bow. "I am looking forward to this journey across this great land of ours. We will, of course, become better acquainted as the miles go by."

He looked as if he could go on, but his wife tugged at his sleeve.

"We need to be getting to our own wagon. The sheriff himself was here not fifteen minutes ago bidding us all good-bye. Wasn't that nice of him?"

"Most certainly. Have I missed him? What a shame. Except for the dreadful murdering scoundrel who unfortunately escaped the gallows, this has been a most friendly place, and I would have liked to tell him so. A man could do worse than settle here. But, for us all, the West calls."

Another bow, and he was gone, his wife and nieces trailing after him, their skirts swishing from side to side with each step. Both Reed and Celinda watched the parade.

"Something about Mr. Clapp bother you?" he asked.

"Didn't his nieces say he had been ill? Bedridden? I didn't care much for the color of him, but otherwise he looked healthy enough." She hesitated. "And there's something else. I saw him in town, staring at your horrible Wanted poster."

"I would appreciate your not describing my likeness quite that way."

"Sorry. Anyway, there he was, looking fit as a

horse, speaking out loud and clear, proclaiming that you—the scoundrel they were calling Killer Shark—ought to be shot on sight."

"Not a man much in favor of the accused's day in court, is he?"

"I don't like him."

Reed felt the same way, but he kept that fact to himself.

"Honeybear, I took you for a woman who reserved judgment on others. Any particular reason for this instant dislike?"

She glanced sideways at him. "You took me for no such thing. And I don't know why I dislike him."

"Could it be because he wanted to shoot the killer?"

Her brown eyes glinted. "That can't be it. I've wanted to do exactly that a time or two myself."

"But not lately."

He hadn't meant the tone of his voice to change, but it did, thickening and deepening.

She looked at his lips. "No, not lately. I've decided I need you too much to want you dead."

With that, she grabbed her bonnet and crawled away from him, toward the front of the wagon, over the boxes of supplies and the small trunk, onto the wagon seat. The going was slow, giving him a long time to study her backside. He liked the view very much.

"Okay, folks," the wagonmaster bellowed from close by, "let's get ready to move. Crack those whips, and fall into line when I signal it's your turn."

Reed settled his hat low on his forehead, giving it a slight tilt, and sat beside his wife. Damned if he didn't feel a tingle of something that could be called excitement. Dumb, really dumb. He was a man with a price on his head, a wife he had a legal but not a moral right to touch, and an itch that couldn't be explained in any way he wanted to contemplate.

When the wagonmaster rode by and barked out, "Porter," he knew it was time to head out. Already the dust was swirling around them, stirred by the movement of the animals and wagon wheels. Celinda coughed, but she did not complain.

She would be brave. He knew it instinctively. Remembering the look of her from various angles, he added bravery to the list of traits that bothered him very much.

He cracked the whip over the broad rumps of the oxen as they took their first grudging steps. To the rear the milk cow bawled. Celinda had the poor judgment to look up at him and smile.

He answered her with a scowl, and she quickly looked away. He licked his lips and thought of all the whiskey he was leaving behind, the decks of cards, the loose women who had from time to time beckoned him to their beds.

He also thought of iron bars and a hangman's noose.

Mostly, though, he thought about his wife. He was a man who with regularity and little conscience gave in to temptation. And here he was, with the biggest temptation of his life sitting right beside him. In ways he didn't understand, she frightened him far more than the noose.

Chapter Four

"I do not understand the man."

Swish was the only reply Celinda got—understandable, since she was talking to the rump of the closest left-side ox. It was a habit she had fallen into over the past two weeks, except that occasionally she addressed the ox on the right. Other than the swish of their tails—or sometimes the execution of a bodily function she had long grown used to—neither beast ever responded.

Still, it was more communication than she had gotten from Reed.

He slept under the wagon, rose early to tend to the stock, ate breakfast, and generally kept his distance from her all day—except when she needed help lifting something heavy, when miraculously he was there to lend a hand before disappearing once again. Each night he strolled in late for supper and crawled back under the wagon. She noticed that most of the other men did the same thing. She did not notice any disgruntlement on the part of the other women as they made their campfires close together for cooking, but then, they were married for real. Maybe communication did not mean so much.

Strengthening her grip on the reins, she thought back to her years with Charles. Communication had never been a problem with him; he liked to have her close so that he could tell her what to do.

So why was she concerned about Reed? He didn't talk, not the way he had during their brief, peculiar courtship. Neither did he look at her, not straight on, though she caught a sidelong glance every now and then. She saw him talking with others, men and women, and even the children who skipped along beside their wagons.

Twice she even saw him in conversation with the Hudson girls, who would lean out the back of their wagon whenever he came close and call to him in greeting, practically spilling their ample bosoms out of their low-cut dresses.

She knew the truth, but it galled her to admit it. She was jealous. She missed Reed's teasing, that was all. The way he was probably teasing the Hudson sisters. She certainly did not care if he liked being with them more than he liked being with her.

She sighed. She was more than jealous; she

was lonely, wanting Reed's company though she knew the wanting was foolish. Even at his most exasperating, he made her feel very much like a woman, made her realize what might be possible for her with a man. If she ever did marry again—for real—it would be to someone who teased like he did.

And, she thought, almost blushing, her number-three spouse would have to be someone who knew how to kiss like Reed . . . if such a creature existed.

She added one big restriction: He must definitely not be wanted by the law.

"I think that's reasonable, don't you?" she asked the rump.

Swish was the only reply.

As always, Buck Dalton did not halt the slow progress of the wagons until shortly before nightfall, after they had covered the minimum twenty-five miles in the tracks set by wagons that had traveled before them. For the next day, however, with more than two hundred miles of the long journey behind them, he planned on an earlier stop.

The announcement came around the evening campfires. "Fields are green; and we'll have water from a creek not far away. It's time to give the animals a rest."

No one argued.

An early day, for once. The first one. Celinda thought about how to spend the time—after the washing was done and extra bread was baked to ease her workload over the next few weeks.

Reed came to mind. She found him a dozen

yards beyond the wagon, away from the fires and the people, staring at the fading rays of sunlight in the west. He looked tall and lean and very still, as if he were carved out of wood, his barely discernible shadow longer and leaner as it fell across the hard, flat ground behind him.

She hesitated to interrupt whatever it was he was thinking. But she was his wife—legally, at least. She had the right. Too, something was building inside her, something insistent that would not allow her peace. Talk might settle her disquiet. Simple talk.

"You heard Dalton?" she asked. "All that extra time. I was thinking we could—" She stopped herself, feeling foolish. "Never mind. I guess you'll be taking care of the stock as usual. Or maybe getting in some hunting."

He did not reply. He just looked at her, then looked away. In the dim light she could not see his eyes, but she could imagine the cool, distant expression in them.

"They must be temperamental animals, to need so much attention."

Again no answer.

"You must be doing a lot of thinking about going back."

His shrug was so slight, she almost missed it.

She studied the strong lines of his profile and realized anew what a handsome man he was. She wanted very much to trace those lines with her fingers and to rest her hand against his strong arm. The urge was so strong, it left her hollow inside.

She couldn't touch him, but neither could she go away.

"Your hair's growing. It's almost to your shoulders. I can trim it if you'd like."

"No need."

She swallowed her disappointment. "It was just a thought."

A cool breeze ruffled her hair, and she rubbed her arms. "I thought we were supposed to show affection for one another. You act as if you hardly know me."

"I don't."

He spoke the truth, but still it hurt.

"The others don't know that," she snapped.

"Hang the others."

"Under the circumstances, isn't that a peculiar thing to say?"

She could have sworn he grinned.

The breeze quickened, and she shivered.

"You don't have a wrap," he said. "Get on back to the fire, Celinda, where it's warm."

Her temper flared. "Show affection," she said, putting little of the tender emotion into her own voice. "Put your arm around me. I'll pretend I like it."

She surprised herself as much as she must have him.

He turned to face her. "You won't go away, will you." His voice was low, insistent, like the beat of a drum. "Even when you're not with me, you won't go away."

"I don't under—"

He did not let her finish. "You want affection? You got it, honeybear."

He pulled her into his embrace, holding her against him with one arm, cradling her face with his free hand. Solid and hard though he was, she sensed tension in him. She took it for the same longing that was pulsing through her.

And he was warm, thrillingly, deliciously warm, far more so than any roaring campfire.

When he kissed her, she was ready, parting her lips, opening herself to him in what he should have realized was complete abandon. But, of course, he did not know her very well.

His tongue knew what to do. It danced against hers in motions of such intimacy and hunger that she almost exploded from the heat building inside her. Wrapping her arms around his neck, she held on tight, pressing her breasts against his broad chest, thrilling to the throbs in her belly, their cadence powerful enough to obliterate everything but her desire for Reed.

For desire was what she felt—pure, raw desire that swept over her like a raging storm, blocking out the world. Never had she felt like this. The power of her emotions frightened her as much as it made her bold.

Like her, Reed wanted more than a kiss. His hands pressed against her back, lowered to her waist, and at last cupped her bottom, holding her hard against him.

He drove her wild. Crazily she thrust her tongue into his mouth, tasting him for the first time, truly understanding the savage sweetness of such a complete kiss. She would do anything for him as long as he did not go away.

He broke the kiss brusquely, his hands digging into her shoulders, holding her close and yet apart. She felt as if he had slapped her.

She studied his heaving chest and tried to slow her own breathing, tried to still her raging thoughts. The sudden, unexpected death of passion brought tiny pinpricks of pain skittering across the surface of her skin, and she felt an unwanted flush creep up her neck and across her cheeks.

Mostly, she felt humiliated. He must think she had come out here to taunt him into exactly what he had done. Much to her shame, he was right.

Miraculously, she found her voice. "I guess we showed anyone who might be looking that we're really man and wife." She spoke to the top button of his shirt. It was, she decided, the safest place to look.

"But we're not," he said. "Not the way they'll be thinking."

"I know that." Much to her added shame, she sounded wounded.

He hesitated, and his grip eased to a gentle touch on her arms.

"I apologize. I went too far."

But not far enough.

She dared to look up at him, grateful he could not see into her mind. "Why did you?"

"I couldn't stop."

"Why couldn't you?"

He dropped his hands and stepped away. She could feel him withdraw into himself. It was as if he were building a wall between them, quickly, before she could break through and do him some kind of harm.

"That's a question I don't want to think about. You're a woman. It's lonely out here. Besides, I've got worries. With a rabble-rouser like Fisher Clapp around, any misstep I make might give me away, and someone will shoot me down for sure."

She shivered. "Don't say such a thing."

"It's the truth. Maybe I just thought you could keep me from worrying so much. You should know a man has needs. And, as I said, you're a woman. Figure it out for yourself."

He threw the words at her, then left fast, his long legs carrying him past the wagons until the darkness completely swallowed him, leaving her to hold herself, to stare at the setting sun, and finally to walk slowly toward the circle of dying fires. She still felt the moist pressure of his lips; she felt the touch of his hands. She did not want the feelings to go away.

Much later, when she was lying in a cocoon of blankets inside the wagon, she heard him crawl underneath into the bedroll she had left for him, atop a waterproof canvas to protect him from the cold ground.

Listening to his restless movements, she thought about what he had said and what he had done.

"Even when you're not with me, you won't go away."

He hadn't made sense then; hours later, she still couldn't figure out what he had been trying to tell her.

But she understood what he had been doing. He had been drawing pleasure from her—selfishly, no doubt—little caring that he was giving far more pleasure to her. She tried to understand what was happening to her. She couldn't possibly love him. He was a rover, a gambler, and, when he had whiskey, far too heavy a drinker for any woman's peace of mind. She had seen Charles try to care for such drinkers. They rarely changed.

Celinda Cheney Ward Porter's marriage existed on borrowed time. So why were tears staining her cheeks? She most definitely could not possibly care for Reed Bayard Porter.

But, of course, she could. Just how much, she did not want to know.

When dawn came, she crawled, stiff and tired, from the wagon and began to prepare breakfast while Reed yoked the oxen in place. This morning he milked the cow, usually Celinda's chore, before leading the creature back to her place with the trailing stock. As soon as he returned, they ate their bacon and biscuits in silence, avoiding each other's eyes. Celinda poured the remaining milk into a churn and hung it from the back of the wagon, where the rocking motion of travel would turn the liquid into precious butter.

Later, after a six-hour ride, after they had made their early camp, she went with the women to the creek to do the wash.

"When we're done, how about joining my daughter and me in some berry picking?"

Celinda smiled at the woman addressing her. Mattie Biles was a friendly woman whose conversations during the wagon train's rare stops helped Celinda feel not so much alone. Her daughter, Elizabeth, along with one or two other children, sometimes rode in the Porter wagon, listening to the stories Celinda would make up, all about families who found happy homes in the West.

"I'd love to go with you."

"You need to tell that handsome husband of yours where you'll be?"

"No. He won't worry. Besides, I think he's out looking for game."

Celinda wasn't sure about the hunting, but she was positive about the worry. She sighed. He probably would not even realize she had gone until long after she had returned and served him a bowl of berries topped with whatever cream she could rescue from the churn.

"She went where?"

Reed did not bother to keep his voice low.

Geoffrey Biles gestured vaguely toward the creek. "Out there somewhere. Berry picking." He looked as worried as Reed felt. "It's time for Mattie to be fixing supper. Time for Elizabeth to get back here and see to her evening chores."

Reed glanced around the camp. Celinda had hung their damp clothes on a line strung between two of the wagons, as the other women had done. Shirts, underclothes, socks—all his, except for a couple of her dresses. Just like the other women, she had done her man's wash.

He did not want her taking care of him. She was not truly his wife. Mostly he wanted her here in front of him now so he could tell her to leave his belongings alone.

He admitted the truth. He wanted her here so he would know she was all right.

Strapping on his gun, settling the hat she had bought him low on his forehead, he said, "I'm going looking for them. They don't know this land. It's cloudy. They won't have the sun to tell them east from west."

"You go one way, I'll go the other. Fire your pistol if you find 'em. I'll do the same."

Several of the men volunteered to join in the search—not that they were calling it a search yet, but the meaning was there. All the other women were back with the wagons. It was, they agreed, time for supper to be cooked.

Buck Dalton put their fears into words.

"Indians haven't been much of a problem around here, not lately, but that ain't to say they couldn't be. Best be safe and ride armed."

Reed resaddled his horse and headed north, while Biles and a half dozen others scattered in different directions. Reed hadn't gone fifty yards when he came upon Fisher Clapp standing alone and smoking a cigar, away from the wagons.

Again, vague memories stirred. He had seen Clapp before the wagon train. One of these days he would remember where and when.

Celinda had been right to dislike Clapp. Reed's own, similar feelings, however, had little to do with any danger the man presented, and his reasons weren't in the least vague. Clapp wouldn't help with the herd, wouldn't help with the hunting, wouldn't help with much of anything. He always had a slick excuse why not— his wife was feeling poorly, he had a bum leg—but the pair of them looked healthy enough to Reed.

No one on the train looked healthier than Mary Ellen and Lodisa Hudson. The way they leaned out the back of the wagon whenever he rode by, exposing themselves in a way he had not seen outside a saloon, he decided they were not so innocent as they pretended.

But he was not worried about them right now. Celinda needed to be found. He had not thought her a foolish woman, but he was thinking it now.

Thunder rumbled in the distance. He remembered the way she had looked up at him last night, before and after he had kissed her. Forgetting Clapp, he slapped leather and took off across the plain.

Figuring the outermost point the women could have walked during the time allowed, he confined his search to a wide, half-mile circle, then proceeded to ride in concentric circles, each one narrower than the one before. Most of the land was treeless, but there were a few copses where he paused to shout Celinda's name. The thunder continued to rumble, and the clouds were laced with flashes of lightning in the distance. Night fell, and on he rode.

The first time he heard a woman's call, he thought it was the wail of the wind, but it came again, high-pitched and broken. It emerged from a stand of trees at the top of a rise, barely visible in the dark.

"Celinda!"

The woman's voice cried out in answer. He rode like fury toward the sound.

He found her standing in the midst of the trees, looking more beautiful than he had ever seen her, the wind whipping her dress and hair wildly. On the ground, another woman crouched beside a small, still figure he took to be the daughter, Elizabeth.

No sooner had he dropped to the ground than his wife was throwing herself against him, holding on tight, as if the wind would drag her from his arms.

"Thank God you're here," she whispered hoarsely. "Thank God. And thank you for coming."

Holding her in the same tight way came naturally. She felt soft and strong at the same time, and she felt needy. He shouldn't like her need for him, but he did.

With a sob, she pushed away. "Elizabeth's hurt," she said, turning toward the child.

Mattie Biles stroked her daughter's forehead, then stared up at him. "She fell. Her leg's broke, but I think that's all. She's resting now. I don't know what we would have done without your wife."

Reed knelt beside the child, whom he had seen riding on the wagon seat beside Celinda. She was lying on a makeshift bed fashioned from the women's cloaks, her eyes closed. He glanced down to where her skirt was covering what appeared to be a splint on her left leg. Easing the skirt up carefully, he inspected the straight, smooth branches and the strips of petticoat binding them in their supportive place.

He glanced up at Celinda. "You did this?"

"I saw Charles do something similar once. This is all my fault."

"It's not your fault, I told you," the mother said. "Now hush up about that. Lizzie got rambunctious, that's all."

Hugging herself, Celinda turned and walked to the edge of the trees. Reed joined her.

"I need to signal where we are," he said loudly enough for both women to hear. Stepping several paces down the hill, he fired three pistol shots, pausing between each one. He waited a minute, then fired them again, taking time to reload before rejoining the women under the trees.

"Mattie's wrong," Celinda said as the roar of the shots died in the windy air. "I made up stories for the child, one about a young girl who had helped her family find their way by climbing high in a tree to scout their location. We weren't really lost—we just went farther than we'd intended—but I guess she thought we were."

"So she climbed a tree and fell."

"It happened so fast, we couldn't stop her."

Celinda buried her face in her hands. "What a mess I've made. How will we ever get her back to her wagon?"

"Help will come. Or we'll all spend the night here."

He rested an arm around her shoulder, trying to block the wind, as they waited to see which outcome it would be.

Help came in the form of Geoffrey Biles and three searchers. After much hugging and a little lecturing to his wife, Biles insisted on carrying his daughter across his lap for the slow journey back to the wagon train. Horse blankets were donated to make her ride as comfortable as possible. Mattie Biles rode with one of the other men. Celinda rode with Reed.

She huddled against his chest, his arms around her, his hands on the reins. She did not speak, not even when the rain came.

When they reached camp, Buck Dalton and a few of the other men who had stayed behind to watch over the women and children volunteered to care for the horses. Celinda watched as the wives and mothers flocked around the Bileses' wagon, even in the rain, offering suggestions, mostly expressing their sympathy. They scattered back to their respective wagons only when lightning and thunder struck the camp.

Reed helped Celinda into their wagon.

"S-someone gathered in the wash," she said, her teeth chattering. "I must remember to thank them."

He leaned inside far enough to set down a lantern one of the men had passed to him. Celinda stared at him in the flickering light. Water still streamed from her hair, and her gown was plastered against her body. He looked at her—all of her—and knew she watched his eyes.

"You're not sleeping on the ground," she said in a breathy way he had not heard before. "Not tonight."

"No. I'm not sleeping on the ground."

Crawling in beside her, he lowered the back flap of the canvas, giving them privacy, and began to unbutton his shirt.

"You're freezing," he said. "Get under the blanket. But first, take off your clothes."

Chapter Five

Celinda went from cold to hot in an instant.

"Take off your clothes."

Coming from a man like Reed, it was an order no woman could resist. Except he was taking off his clothes at the same time, which made concentration on the task next to impossible.

She brushed the wet hair from her eyes. As long as she was watching him, she wanted an unimpaired view. He reached inside one of the pockets she had sewn inside the canvas and tossed her a dry cloth. She squeezed it around her hair, tossed it aside, and kept watching.

His lips twitched, and her heart took a fast trip to her stomach and back. Outside, the storm intensified, shaking the wagon until it creaked, making the canvas snap. She barely noticed, not with a wilder storm raging inside her. Reed had unbuttoned his shirt. Short dark hairs covered his chest. There must have been an acre of them. The hollow at his throat looked especially enticing, offering a woman a place to put her tongue.

Just looking at a portion of his bare skin was enough to send her fingers flying to her own buttons. But she had suddenly turned clumsy, and her fingers refused to work. The cold or the heat—she didn't know which to blame.

He helped her, unfastening the front of her gown, pulling the fabric aside to expose her sodden undergarment. He held still. She glanced down. The thin, damp cloth revealed the hard, dark tips of her swollen breasts, as if she, too, had bared a naked chest.

She shivered.

"You're cold," he said.

He was wrong.

He made quick work of the rest of her clothes. He was not in the least bit clumsy. How many times had he done this for other women? She did not care. She would never ask.

But she did grow shy. Scrambling under the blanket, she watched him finish his own undressing. She wasn't so shy that she could not look at everything. She certainly was not a maiden—she knew the way a man was put together—but she was not prepared for the particulars of Reed. He was magnificent. Desire jolted through her. She did not breathe.

He joined her under the cover just as thunder rumbled through the night. Seconds later, lightning followed, but she was too busy pressing her flesh against his to pay any mind.

I love you.

The thought came unbidden to her mind and most certainly would remain unspoken. Reed did not know her well enough to understand that she could never give herself to him like this unless love was in her heart. She was crazy, wild in love with him, a man she barely knew, yet she felt as if she had known him all her life.

He kissed her eyes, her cheeks, her lips, and stroked her damp hair.

"Are you warm enough?" he asked, rubbing one hand down her arm.

"I'm warm enough."

"Do you want the lantern out?"

"Leave it on." This might be the only time they would do what they were doing. She wanted to see all that she could see.

"You surprise me. You like light."

"I hope that's not your only surprise."

"I get the idea I'm going to like them all."

"If you like the light, you will."

She was talking boldly. He was an inspiration.

His hand shifted to the side of her breast, and he ran his thumb across its tip. Folding the blanket back, he leaned down to replace the thumb with his tongue. She caught her fingers in his hair and held him in place, fearful he would abandon her breast too soon.

But Reed clearly had no such intention. He kissed her thoroughly, and she allowed him access to her other breast. Bending her head close to his, she managed to kiss his hair, his forehead, to run her tongue around his ear.

He came up fast and covered her lips with his, rough hands roaming wildly over her body, a long, strong leg wrapped over her hip to hold her nakedness against his. She felt his erection against her belly and gasped.

"Are you all right?" he asked.

"I'm fine." She tried to laugh and sounded foolish. "More than fine. Don't stop, Reed. Don't stop."

For once, he did as she asked.

He held her so tightly, kissed her so thoroughly, she did not know where his body ended and hers began. They were one, legally, and now in a way that mattered just as much. Any other consideration would be for the daylight, when sanity would return. Tonight she was insane. And her insanity filled her with joy.

He made her feel beautiful; he made her feel like the most desirable woman on earth. For him she would be exactly that. With her hands and her body she told him how she felt. Every place he touched, wherever he kissed, she returned the favor, and it brought her sensations a thousandfold more pleasurable.

It was the most natural thing in the world to open herself to him, to allow the penetration of her body, to wrap her legs around him and answer his thrusts with her own. The wagon rocked, but not from the wind, fierce though it was. This was a new kind of lovemaking for her, an abandoned giving and taking of rapture that made her want to laugh and cry all at once. When he spilled his seed inside her, for the first time she experienced what men did, the ultimate pleasure that was the natural culmination of all the touching and kissing that had gone before.

She exploded. She clung tightly to him. She wanted never to let go.

She would love him forever because of what he did in the next few minutes: He held her just as tightly, he stroked her hair, he kissed her cheeks, he made soft, soothing sounds to show he was as moved as she. He did not speak. He did not tease. He offered no recriminations or speculation about what the outcome of tonight would be.

He simply held her while she brought herself back into the real world.

Incredibly, she felt herself growing sleepy, in the most satisfied way she had ever experienced. She had no business being at peace, but that was exactly how she felt. Kissing his furry chest, she snuggled against him and gave in to the sleepiness. She did not waken until she heard the early-morning sounds of breaking camp around the wagon.

She was alone.

And the embarrassment came. Not regret— never that—but the sense that she had done something Reed would view as foolish on her part. He did not want a permanent marriage. He wanted only the one night.

So did she. One night, and a million more

like it. Sadly, she knew he was the one who would get what he wanted.

Dressing hurriedly, binding her hair and thrusting on her bonnet, she dropped to the muddy ground. The sky was cloudless, and she could still see the last of the stars. The few people who had managed to start a fire on the damp ground offered coffee to the rest. She accepted a steaming mug from one of the women and rummaged at the back of the wagon for cold bread and bacon. She waited for Reed, but he did not appear until it was time to yoke the oxen and be under way.

"Are you all right?" he asked as she joined him.

"Of course." She couldn't resist adding, "How about you? Are you all right?"

His dark eyes shifted to her for only a moment. "Of course," he said and turned back to the yoke.

His brusqueness bruised her heart, but she could not say much to him, not with so many eager ears close by. One thing she had learned early on was that gossip thrived on a wagon train.

She went back to check on Elizabeth. The girl had spent a restless night, but her mother, sitting high on the wagon seat, ready for the day's journey, said confidently that she would be all right. Celinda could do nothing but believe her and offer her help whenever it was needed.

When she returned, Reed was gone. This time she was not content to be abandoned. Geoffrey Biles, the worried father, was staying by the wagons this morning. She asked him if he could take over the reins for her for a short while, and he agreed.

Hurrying past the other wagons as they fell into line, she found her husband astride his horse twenty yards away from the other men and the stock. He sat still, his hat obscuring his eyes, as she approached.

"Have you come to shoot me?" he asked.

"Don't make light of me, Reed. Not this morning."

He nodded, threw a long leg over the saddle, and dropped to the ground beside her, his motions smooth and fluid, the way they had been last night.

She caught the cry in her throat before he could hear it. Behind her, she could hear the snap of whips and the creak of wagons and leather as the day officially began.

She held her ground. "What happened last night?"

"If you don't remember, then I must not have done a very good job."

Her vision blurred. "A job?"

He shrugged. "Don't push this, Celinda."

"I have no choice. We weren't supposed to . . . do what we did, so I don't know the rules anymore."

"I can tell you the first one. I took advantage of you. It won't happen again."

"You're not very good at making predictions. I don't believe you."

And you certainly did not take advantage of

278

me. You will never have a more willing partner than your short-term wife.

He did not respond right away, and she thought for a moment he was going to take her into his arms.

Instead, he broke her heart.

"I'm not a marrying kind of man. I figured that out a long time ago. But if I were, you shouldn't want me anyway. You already had one bad marriage. Don't ask how I know; I just do. You sure as the devil don't want another."

If that was supposed to soothe her, he was proving himself as big a fool as she. What he did was drive nails into her already damaged heart.

"In a day or so I'll be heading back to Independence," he said. "Don't worry. I've talked to a couple of the men about helping you out. Dalton won't object at this late date."

"I'll go with you."

She had no idea where the offer came from, but she meant what she said.

"To witness the hanging?" he asked.

"That's a terrible thing to say."

"Sometimes I'm a terrible man."

"But you're not. The trouble is, you just don't know it."

Thumbing his hat away from his eyes, he settled a gaze on her that chilled her soul.

"Pay very close attention to what I'm going to tell you. Last night was special. It was the best night I have ever spent, and if we could always stay in bed like that, we could get by. Since that's impossible, we've both got to look at the situation realistically. You've got plans. I've got plans. You're forgetting you are a borrowed bride."

This time she let the cry out.

He looked past her, as if the sight of her was too bothersome or too painful for him. He took a moment to speak. "The wagons are moving. Let me take you to ours."

"I've got legs, in case you haven't noticed."

"I noticed."

She ignored him. "I can catch up without your help." She brushed tears from her cheeks. "But you're wrong about one thing. You're a better man than you think you are. The problem is, I don't know if you'll realize it before you make the biggest mistake of your life."

Not once during the long day's ride did Reed ride by to help Celinda, to talk to her, to make sure she was all right after the scene she had made. He gave her ample time to think—to remember everything that had passed between them since he'd first put his hands on her in her hotel room. She could see now that fate had drawn them together, putting them both at the livery stable at a time when she was arguing with the wagon master about needing a husband and he was searching desperately for a place to hide.

Yes, fate had brought them together. But it would take more than fate to keep them that way. It would take a miracle. And she was beginning to believe that miracles did not exist—not for her, not in this life.

When they stopped for the evening, one of the men came to unhitch the oxen. She wanted to ask about her husband, but she could not humiliate herself in such a way. She had pushed Reed into considerations he did not wish to make, and he simply did not want her to do it again.

He worried needlessly. Outside of confessing outright how much she loved him, she had said all that she could, opening herself to him in a way she could scarcely believe. She would not do so again.

When he did not return to the wagon for the evening meal, she began to wonder if he had already gone back to Independence. The thought panicked her. Unable to sit still by the fire, to listen to the chatter, even to hear a report on how Elizabeth had fared during the day, she took to the hill beside which the wagons had halted. The night was cloudless, and moonlight showed her the way.

She did not hear voices until she was at the top of the rise. Angry voices. She recognized the speakers as Fisher and Dorothea Clapp. It was obvious they had not heard her approach and thought they were talking in privacy. She turned to leave when the woman's furious words stopped her.

"You need to do something about those two bitches."

"What am I supposed to do?" her husband

replied. "Beat them? I don't want them bruised. I have a use for those luscious white bodies."

"They're lazy, Clapp. They're no good. They're going to seduce one of the men on the wagon train some night, use those luscious bodies you're so proud of, and then demand money. Next thing you know, we'll be ordered to leave. Is that what you want?"

"California is what I want. It's damned certain I can't go back to New Orleans."

"You can't go back to Independence, either. You shouldn't have killed that marshal. He wasn't even sure who you were. I thought you were smarter than that, or I never would have agreed to ride with you."

Celinda gasped and slapped a hand over her mouth. Fisher Clapp had killed the marshal, then loudly demanded that Reed be shot on sight. As bad as she had thought the man, never had she imagined anything like this. She had to get back to Reed and let him know.

"Gawddamn," Clapp growled, "keep your voice down. Someone might hear."

"Those fools are busy clanging pots around the fire, staying as close as if they were tied to one another."

"Yeah, well, sometimes they wander. We can't be too careful. I'd hate to have to deal with an eavesdropper."

Sudden fear washed over Celinda. She was out here alone, knowing something she wasn't supposed to know, and there was a killer only a few yards away. She ducked low to the ground, in case he looked toward the hill, and took a step backward. A twig snapped. It sounded like a gunshot.

Terrified, she began to run, but suddenly a body slammed against hers and knocked her to the ground. She struggled wildly, but the breath had been taken from her, and she had no leverage for the fight.

Clapp had her hopelessly pinned down. He covered her nose and mouth with one hand, almost smothering her, and jerked backward until she thought her neck would break.

"Shut up or I'll kill you here and now," he growled in her ear.

She believed him. She held still.

Pulling her to her feet, he pressed a gun to her side and gestured for her to walk down the far side of the hill toward the woman who was supposed to be his wife. If she had not been thoroughly terrified, she would have appreciated the irony of their similar situations.

The woman she knew as Dorothea Clapp stood silently and watched as she drew near.

"Damned nosy fool," the woman snarled.

"If you hadn't been talking so loud, she wouldn't have heard anything."

"You can't hurt me," Celinda said shakily. "We're with an entire wagon train in the middle of nowhere. You'll never get away."

Clapp dug the end of the gun into Celinda's side. "If I take you as hostage, they'll have to let me go."

"Reed would never allow it. He'd come after me."

"Maybe we don't have to leave," Dorothea

said. "I've got an idea. Our newlyweds had a big argument this morning—must have been a dozen men who saw them. Couldn't hear, but they watched Mrs. Porter crying as she ran away from Mr. Porter. I listened to 'em talk afterward. What if we say we saw her wandering off, the way she did yesterday? We make her death look like an accident. Whoever finds the body will blame *her* for being such a fool."

In the moonlight Celinda could see Clapp's evil smile. "I knew there was a reason I brought you along, my dear," he said to Dorothea.

Celinda's blood ran cold. She started to scream, but Clapp backhanded her before she could do more than get out an ineffectual squeal. She stumbled and fell. He turned the pistol on her. In the moonlight he projected a silvery madness. She heard the click of the trigger, and—

"Drop the gun, Clapp."

Celinda stared beyond the killer to where Reed stood at the top of the hill. She blinked once, to make sure he was really there. Her spirit soared, but then fear cut off the joy. He was strong and towering, but he also presented a target no one could miss, especially one who had killed before.

"Drop it," he snapped.

Clapp straightened, his back to Reed. "Looks like you got me." He held out the gun as if to release it, but instead he whirled fast and fired.

Reed was faster, getting off a shot that threw Clapp backward, lifting him off his feet, sending his bullet whizzing harmlessly into the air over the hill. Clapp crumpled to the ground and did not move.

With a cry, Dorothea headed out at a run across the valley. In an instant, Celinda sprang after her, tackling her before she had covered a dozen yards, and they both tumbled to the ground. The other woman outweighed Celinda by fifty pounds, but Celinda had righteous fury on her side. Without thinking, she socked Dorothea in the jaw.

Her strategy worked. The woman gave a loud moan and lay still.

Celinda pulled herself shakily to her feet and watched Reed standing over the fallen man. Slowly he raised his eyes to hers.

"He missed you," she said.

"He missed me."

"I suppose he's dead."

"Yep." He started down the hill toward her. "That's quite a right hook you have."

She rubbed her stinging fist. "She made me angry."

"I'll have to remember that."

Celinda could not bring herself to speculate what he meant by that.

"Fisher Clapp killed the marshal."

"I know."

"You were listening when he talked about it?"

"No, but I finally remembered where I had seen him before. It was at a poker table a few hours before the shooting. I lost my two-headed coin to him. It was not my most successful night."

"And what was?"

"There are two of them. When I decided to sleep it off in the stable. And last night."

Her heart was pounding so hard, she wondered if he could hear it.

"You think that was successful?" she asked.

"Oh, yeah. When you're up to it, I'll see if I can do it again."

She wanted to ask him a hundred more questions, to hold him, to cover his face with kisses, but by now the gunshots were drawing a crowd. She gave up on the asking, but the holding and the kissing were two things he could not avoid.

He didn't seem to mind, not even when the men were gathering noisily around them and inspecting the fallen Clapps.

"See here," Buck Dalton growled, "what's going on here? You've got some explaining to do, Porter."

Reed ignored him, instead directing his attention to Celinda, as if they were all alone in the world.

"I love you," he told her. "When you walked away from me this morning, I was more miserable than ever before in my life."

"You were miserable?" The news made her giddy.

"I decided that maybe I was the marrying kind after all. As long as you're my bride."

"I love you, too," she said.

"Will you marry me?"

"We're already married."

"I want to do it right. I know you've already

had one wedding, but I want us to do it right, in front of a preacher with people we know as witnesses."

Dalton cleared his throat. "Folks, I don't want to break up this happy little time for you two newlyweds, but we got a woman moaning on the ground and a man with a bullet clean through his heart and more questions than you can believe."

Reed gave Celinda a chaste peck on the cheek, but his dark eyes, no longer unreadable, told her his kisses wouldn't be chaste for long.

"We've got answers for you, Buck—even more than you've got questions for. And we've got a question of our own. How far is it to the next church? My wife and I have business to take care of. I'd like it seen to as quickly as possible."

Chapter Six

The body of Fisher Clapp was wrapped in cloth, there being no wood to spare for a coffin, and buried on the hill near where he had been shot.

Under harsh questioning by Buck Dalton, his supposed wife confessed to being Dorothea Rudd, madame of Clapp's New Orleans brothel, who had planned to fulfill the same role at a similar establishment in Sacramento. The "nieces," Mary Ellen Colby and Lodisa Belshaw, were to be the main attractions.

"Fisher had got himself in trouble back in Louisiana," Dorothea Rudd told Dalton and the half dozen men with him. "He was wanted for a barroom shooting. There was a reward out. He thought that U.S. marshal back in Independence recognized him."

After a brief discussion among the men, it was decided to turn the three women over to the first authorities they came upon. They also offered sympathy in advance to any lawmen who had to deal with Mary Ellen and Lodisa, who seemed more irritated than anything else over the inconvenience of their employer's demise.

Celinda stayed as far away from the questioning as she could, relying on camp gossip for the news. Reed stayed close by her side. He didn't seem inclined to stray too far, which was fine with her.

When the wagon train finally got under way once again, after a half day's delay, he took the reins and sat beside her on the wagon seat. At night he slept beside her, and they made love. She couldn't get enough of him, and, from everything he said and did, it seemed he felt the same way about her.

Their second wedding ceremony was held at Fort Kearney, just south of the Platte River, in a small chapel on base, with a visiting Methodist minister presiding. Everyone from the wagon train crowded inside, including Elizabeth Biles, who was carried in by her father. There was even a small organ to provide music for the bride's processional into the chapel. Mattie Biles stood up for Celinda as her attendant; Buck Dalton served as Reed's best man.

Celinda was as proud of Reed as she had ever been of anyone or anything in her life. He was going with her to California, to make his fortune off the rich land, his gambling and drinking days a thing of the past.

More to her immediate satisfaction, she found he couldn't keep his hands off her.

She was second proudest of her wedding dress, because it came from her newfound friends on the train. Finery of any kind was a rare and treasured commodity among the women. Because she had torn up her petticoat to secure the splint for Elizabeth's broken leg, her mother, Mattie, had collected undergarments from the other women and sewn them into a beautiful gown, the full skirt formed by soft cotton panels of white and ecru, lace trimming the rounded neck and puffed sleeves.

To Celinda, no pearl-trimmed gown of silk could be finer. When she walked down the aisle to her waiting groom, she caught the approval in his eyes, and she almost burst into joyous laughter.

A captain at the fort offered them his quarters for the wedding night, but they declined, choosing instead the wagon bed.

"For sentiment's sake," they told him.

He looked at them in puzzlement but did not ask what they meant.

Later, after a wedding feast on the grounds of the fort, after the emigrants were settled down for the night in their respective wagons, Celinda showed Reed once again how much she loved him.

"I'm not always easy to live with," she said, when the showing was done.

"Your temper does tend to get you into trouble. It's something I've already noticed about you."

"I can be stubborn," she added. "And I walk fast, not daintily. Sometimes too fast."

"Keeping up might be a real problem for a short guy like me."

"You're making fun of me."

He kissed her cheek. "A little."

She fell silent. There was something she had to tell him, and she was not sure she knew exactly how. But procrastinating was not the answer.

"Reed . . ." She took a deep breath and plunged ahead. "We've talked about land and about maybe opening a store the way your father did back East. Maybe we could even start a partnership with my brother. But there's one subject that hasn't come up yet." She needed another deep breath. "A family."

He took a long time to respond. "Do you want one?"

"Do you?"

"I want what you want."

"That's not fair. You're usually more honest than that. At least you're blunter."

"All right, then, here's the truth. I never thought about it. Since I never planned to get married, it wasn't a subject for consideration. And then I figured since you and Charles Ward had no children, maybe you had a problem."

"I did. Being a physician, Charles diagnosed it as my fault we were childless."

"Then that's it. You're about all I can handle, anyway."

"Charles was wrong," she said softly.

She waited for the implication of what she had said to sink in. She did not have to wait long.

"You're sure?"

"No. But there are definite signs. I probably should have told you before today, but I was too cowardly."

He held her, and he kissed her, and he stroked her long hair.

"You could have told me. I was already your husband."

"A borrowed one, remember?"

He chuckled. "Do you think we'll tell her how the first ceremony came to be? About your being a borrowed bride?"

"Who are you talking about?"

"Our daughter."

She let the words thrill her for a moment and fill her already warm heart.

"What if we have a son?"

"We can tell him, too."

"Then you're not disappointed? Not upset?"

"Celinda Porter, I am not in the least disappointed in anything about you. I know I borrowed you temporarily, but one thing I know for sure: I am never going to give you back."

SOMETHING BLUE

Bobbi Smith

To Elaine Barbieri, Constance O'Banyon, and Evelyn Rogers—the three best friends a girl could ever have.

Chapter One

"You ready for another drink, General?" Mattie asked the military man as she stopped before his table in a back corner of the Palace Saloon. She'd waited on him when he'd first come into the bar and thought him quite handsome in his blue cavalry officer's uniform. Tall and blond, he had an air of quiet authority about him. She'd been watching him while he'd sat alone, downing the drink she'd served him, and he looked so serious that she'd thought he might be in need of some cheering up.

"It's *Captain,*" Philip Long corrected as he glanced up, surprised by her presence. He had been so deep in thought that he hadn't noticed her approach. Not that she wasn't worth notic-

295

ing. He supposed for a bar girl she was pretty enough, with her dark hair and green eyes, but she was definitely not his type. He hadn't met his dream woman yet, but he was certain she wouldn't be wearing a skin-tight, low-cut, red silk dress and heavy face paint.

"Well, you look like a general to me," Mattie countered with a wink.

"I appreciate the promotion, but I don't think my superiors would approve."

"Pity. I'd follow any orders you'd want to give me," she told him, grinning.

Philip shoved his glass across the table to her. "Then I'll take a double whiskey."

"Right away, sir." She moved off toward the bar.

Philip watched her go and distractedly tried to guess her age. Not too young; judging by the ample display of bosom her dress provided. He didn't consider the possibility of any kind of encounter with her, though. He had too much else to think about, too much else to worry about.

"Thanks," he said when she returned to place the drink before him.

"You're welcome, and my name's Mattie if you want anything else tonight."

Philip paid her and gave her a good tip.

"Thanks, General," she said, her eyes widening at the generous amount. "Just let me know when you need me."

Philip nodded but didn't respond as he lifted the tumbler and took a deep drink. It wasn't good whiskey, but it was strong enough to do the trick. Right now, he needed something that would ease his dark mood and help him see things a bit more clearly. Rotgut would do.

The last month had been a hard one for him. His father had passed away back home in Boston, and, as his only son and heir, Philip had had to take a leave from his post at Fort McDowell in Arizona Territory and head east to settle the estate.

In life, wealthy Charles Long had been domineering, controlling, with firm ideas about his sole heir's brilliant future. Father and son had not had a close relationship since Philip had chosen to serve in the cavalry on the frontier. Charles had wanted Philip to remain in Boston, marry a rich, well-connected girl like Dwylah Carpenter, and become influential in political circles. But Philip would have none of it. He had been drawn to the adventure of the untamed West. Though the senior Long had argued vehemently against such a notion, Philip had stood his ground and had become his own man. Now, however, even from the grave, his father was once again attempting to control him.

Philip gave a cynical laugh and took another drink as he remembered meeting with his father's lawyer back in Boston. The attorney had read the will aloud, and Philip had been shocked by the unusual clause his father had inserted into the document—that his only son had to be wed within six months of the reading of the will, and remain married for over a year, or lose every cent of his inheritance. Clearly, Charles Long had wagered that such a requirement would make Philip quit his remote frontier outpost for genteel Boston, where he'd find suitable females in far greater supply.

Philip had been furious. He'd wanted to contest the will, but the lawyer had told him it was ironclad. Unless he fulfilled his father's matrimonial requirement, the entire estate would be divided among several of his distant cousins—cousins neither he nor his father had had any use for. His father had been shrewd to add that Philip had to stay married for a year; Charles had thereby sealed up his son's only escape route from the clause. Unless he chose to walk away from his fortune without a backward glance, Philip was trapped.

The thought of abandoning the money had occurred to him. He made a decent living in the military and was basically content with his life. Busy with the demands of his command, he had always believed there would be time later for getting married, settling down, and starting his own family. Evidently, however, his father wanted that time to be now. And Charles had wagered—correctly—that Philip would not stand for his obnoxious cousins to inherit. Conspicuously greedy for Charles's wealth, the relatives had offended Philip by kowtowing in Charles's presence but belittling him behind his back. Philip despised them for their hypocrisy. He could not step aside and let them claim his father's legacy.

"I said *no*, mister!"

The sound of a woman's frantic protest interrupted Philip's troubled thoughts. He looked up to see the pretty barmaid struggling to free herself from another customer's grip. The man had hauled her onto his lap and was attempting to take liberties with her person.

"Easy there, Mattie girl," the man said in a slurred, drunken voice as he all but salivated down the front of her gown. "You know you love ol' Micah. That's why you're working here, just so you can spend time with me. Now, quit fighting me so hard, and—"

"No!" Mattie twisted with all her might to avoid his groping hands. "I'm here only to serve drinks!"

"Well, darlin', I know something else you can serve me right now," he growled, laughing evilly and trying to reach up her skirt.

The girl's desperation was real, and Philip rose from his table to go to her aid. No one else, not even the bartender, had made a move to help her.

"The young lady said she isn't interested in your attentions," Philip told the man named Micah.

"Sure she is," the lecher sneered, grabbing at her curves.

"Let her go," Philip commanded.

Silence fell over the saloon.

Micah looked up, clearly irritated at being interrupted. "I ain't in the cavalry, soldier, so your orders don't mean a damned thing to me. Go on back to your table, and leave us alone. Little Mattie here is just playin' hard to get. I know she's selling, and tonight I'm buying." He slipped a hand inside her bodice and squeezed her tender flesh.

"Don't!" The girl shoved violently against his chest, hitting out at him blindly, trying to escape his vile hands upon her.

Philip saw the panic and horror on the girl's face and didn't waste any more time trying to reason with the drunk. He simply took charge. In one commanding move, he gripped the lecher by the throat and squeezed until the man released Mattie.

"Why, you—" Furious and red in the face, Micah reeled to his feet and reached for his gun.

Philip was ready for him. He laid the hulking Micah low with one blow to the jaw. "A gentleman doesn't treat a lady that way," Philip pointed out, looking down at the prone figure.

"Mattie ain't no lady!" Micah whined, rubbing his aching jaw. "She ain't nothing but a whore! Everybody knows that!"

"I am not!" Mattie cried, backing away from the table, frightened and humiliated.

All eyes were on her as she turned and ran into the back room. Cal, the bartender, went after her.

Micah stood up slowly and spit blood on the floor. "I'm getting the hell out of this lousy joint," he snarled. He snatched up what was left of his drink, downed it, then slammed the glass onto the table and stomped out of the saloon.

The two men he'd been boozing with, who'd

been watching what had transpired, followed him from the bar.

Philip didn't relax his vigilance until they were out of sight. Then he turned to go after the bartender and the girl. He wanted to make sure Mattie hadn't been hurt.

"I know what I told you when I hired you, Mattie, but—" Cal was ranting. He stopped when Philip appeared in the doorway. "What do you want?"

"I came to check on Miss Mattie," he answered, his gaze settling on her as she stood glaring up at the man who was her boss.

"She's fine," Cal said dismissively.

"I'd like to hear that from her, if you don't mind," Philip said calmly but firmly.

Cal glowered at Mattie as she glanced at Philip.

"I'm all right." She quickly dropped her gaze from his.

"You're sure?" Something didn't feel right to him.

"Yes. Thanks." Her voice was flat.

Philip looked at the two of them yet had little recourse but to leave the room. He returned to his table to finish his drink. He'd come into the Palace to relax a bit, but it hadn't turned out that way. Of course, lately nothing was turning out the way it was supposed to.

Philip drained what was left of his liquor as he reconsidered his future. Marrying as his father had ordered, receiving his inheritance in full, and staying on in the military wasn't, he supposed, a bad idea. Except that there wasn't a woman around he'd even consider marrying right now. He wasn't in love; he never even had been.

His thoughts drifted on. He could resign his commission, return to Boston, marry, and collect the money, but he didn't like that idea at all. He was dedicated to his command and didn't want to leave it. And, of course, there was still the problem of the missing bride.

Last but not least, Philip mused darkly, he could turn down the money and continue as he was, allowing the fortune to go to his greedy cousins. That wasn't an option.

Philip frowned and glanced up just in time to see Mattie rush out of the back room, her head down, her manner tense. She fled the saloon without a word. Cal emerged to watch her go, his expression angry.

As much as Philip told himself it was none of his business, he wondered what had transpired in the back room. It was still early in the evening, and yet the girl had left her post. Curious, he got up and made his way from the Palace.

Outside, the night was dark, moonless. Philip looked around to see where she had gone, and it surprised him to find no sign of her anywhere. And then he heard it—one brief, desperate cry for help that came from the alley alongside the saloon. He headed that way at a run.

Chapter Two

"You shoulda just given me what I wanted inside, girlie!" Micah Johnson leered down at Mattie. He had thrown her to the ground and covered her mouth with one hand to stifle her screams. "You wouldn't have gotten yourself hurt then."

Mattie was fighting for all she was worth, desperate to defend herself. Micah and the other two men had been lurking outside, waiting for her. She'd always known that Micah was a low-life bastard, but until tonight she'd never had to deal firsthand with his ugliness. Now, however, she was really frightened. If she could get one hand free, she might be able to reach the small derringer she kept hidden in her garter. But even if she did manage to get the gun, it was only a single-shot, and there were three men.

Trembling, Mattie made her move. Micah was too busy tearing at her clothing to notice. She offered up a silent prayer as she tugged the weapon free. She dug the gun into her assailant's side as she bit his hand.

"Why, you—!" Micah yanked his hand away from her mouth, swearing violently.

"Get off me, or I'll shoot!" Mattie ordered, pressing the gun even harder against him, wanting to make sure he knew she was serious.

For an instant, Micah was stunned, but then he reacted. He slapped her and managed to knock the gun from her hand in one vicious blow. He drew back, ready to hit her again, when he felt the sting of cold metal against the back of his neck. He went still, his upraised hand frozen in midair.

"I think I already told you once tonight how to treat a lady. I don't like having my orders ignored," Philip said in a soft yet dangerous voice. He glanced over at Micah's two friends, his deadly expression warning them to stay out of the fight.

Cowards that they were, they turned tail and ran.

"Get up," Philip ordered Johnson.

Micah stood and turned to face him, keeping his movements slow and steady. He didn't want to give the soldier any reason to shoot.

"If you ever go anywhere near this woman again, I'll hunt you down. Do you understand me?"

Micah nodded, a cold sweat beading his brow.

"Now get out of here." Philip spoke slowly and quietly, but there was no doubt of the threat behind his words.

Micah didn't have to be told twice. He fled into the night.

Philip slowly holstered his sidearm, then held a hand out to the barmaid to help her up.

Mattie couldn't believe what had just happened. One moment she was facing her worst nightmare, and the next her "general" had come out of nowhere to save her again. She didn't immediately take his hand but merely stared up at him, thinking him some wonderful, avenging guardian angel in blue. He was tall and strong and brave and handsome. And in that instant, Mattie fell in love.

"Are you all right?" Philip asked when she didn't immediately respond to his gesture of help.

"Oh—yes—" Mattie stammered nervously, summoned back to reality.

She put her hand in his, and a thrill coursed through her. His touch was strong yet gentle as he helped her to her feet. She almost didn't want to let go, but she knew she had to. She wasn't the clinging type—or at least she never had been until now. But somehow the thought of a little clinging with her general seemed suddenly quite wonderful.

"Thank you," she breathed, lifting her gaze to his.

The emotions stirring within her were confusing. One moment she'd been fighting for her very life, and the next she'd been rescued by her knight in shining armor. The fantasy was real, only instead of armor, her knight wore a blue cavalry uniform. She felt him drawing his hand away and abruptly released her grip on him. Certain she was blushing, she was grateful for the darkness to hide her disquiet.

"I'm glad I found you in time," Philip told her, peering at her, trying to determine if the drunk's blow had injured her. "Are you sure you're not hurt?"

Mattie lifted one hand nervously to her cheek. She winced at the tenderness there. "I'll be fine," she said.

Philip looked around the deserted area. He couldn't leave her out there to fend for herself. "May I escort you home?" he asked.

"Well, I—" She wasn't sure what to say. In all her eighteen years, she'd never had a man so politely offer to escort her anywhere.

Philip thought he understood the reason for her hesitation—that she believed he was just like the other men and would try to take advantage of her. He spoke up quickly, wanting to put her mind at ease. "Miss Mattie, I only want to see you home safely. I wouldn't feel right leaving you here to your own devices after what you've been through tonight." He crouched to pick up her derringer from the ground, then straightened and offered it back to her. "Would you really have shot him?"

She took the gun and stared down at it.

When she looked up at her general again, she answered simply and honestly, "I don't know."

"You shouldn't carry a gun unless you're willing to use it," he told her. "Otherwise it could be used against you. Do you know how to fire it?"

"Yes."

Philip nodded his approval. "That's a start. If you ever find yourself in a situation like this again, don't hesitate to shoot to defend yourself."

"Don't worry. It's never going to happen again."

Given her profession he had no idea how she could be so sure, but he was glad to hear it. "May I see you home now?"

"Thank you."

Mattie started to walk from the alleyway but found herself a bit unsteady from the trauma of all that had happened. Philip gallantly offered her his arm. For a moment, she stopped and stared at him, once again surprised by his courtly manner. Then, grateful for the offer, she accepted his help. Mattie told him where she lived, and they moved slowly but steadily toward the run-down boardinghouse.

Mattie didn't say much during the walk. She wasn't sure what she could say to him. Lord knows, she didn't have anything in common with her general—him being so important and all. She simply held on to his arm, feeling the power there, knowing he was a brave man. She was certain there would never be another moment in her life as special as this one. She almost didn't want the walk to end. If they could have kept going forever, she would have, for she felt safe and protected by his side. They reached the boardinghouse all too soon, and it was time for them to part.

"This is it," she said simply, sorry they were there.

"Oh." Philip looked up at the decrepit building and struggled to keep his dismay from showing. The place was hardly suitable for a young woman. "Do you have family here to take care of you?"

"No, I live alone."

"Shall I escort you in?"

"No," she answered quickly, not wanting him to see the squalor of her pitiful room. It wasn't much, but everything she owned was in that room—some clothes and the few family keepsakes she'd managed to save. Her general, being the gentleman he was, wouldn't understand her way of life. She was certain he came from a moneyed background, for he had that kind of self-assurance about him; he was calm, collected, and certain that everything was going to turn out the way he wanted it to. She wished she had his kind of confidence, but things seldom turned out well for her. Just look at what had happened tonight. "But thank you for bringing me home."

"Do you need any help?" he offered.

"No." Mattie didn't dare look up at him again. She feared that too much of what she was feeling would show in her expression. *Do you need any help?* The thought almost made her hysterical. She needed help all right, but she would do what she always did. She would survive on her own. She'd been taking care of herself for the last ten months since her parents had died and left her alone and penniless, and she would keep on doing so. She had no alternative.

Mattie hurried toward the door, hating that the moment was over yet knowing there was no way to linger and make it last any longer. Her general was a stranger, and he would remain that way. She would never see him again after tonight. He was just passing through her life on his way to better things.

It suddenly occurred to her that she didn't even know his name. Stopping, she turned back, and she found that he was still there, keeping watch.

"What's your name?" she called out softly, just a hint of longing in her voice.

Philip gave her a half smile. "My name is Philip. Philip Long."

"Good-bye, Philip Long," she said quietly as she stared at him, committing to memory the vision of him standing guard over her.

Something about her good-bye bothered Philip, but he wasn't sure why. "Go on inside. I'll wait here until I'm sure you're safe."

"Yes, General."

Only when Mattie had disappeared inside and shut the door did Philip walk away. He considered returning to the saloon for another drink, then thought better of it. He'd go straight to his hotel and bed down. He was due to head out of town tomorrow and needed to get a good night's rest. The stage ride would be rough on this last part of his return journey to the fort. He wasn't looking forward to the long days of travel, but he was anticipating getting back to his command at McDowell. The cavalry was his life.

As Philip strode through the night, thinking about returning to the fort, thoughts of his dilemma interfered. He suddenly wondered where in the world he was going to find a suitable wife on such short notice. There were few available women at McDowell. His commander did have a daughter of marriageable age, but Philip knew that nothing could ever come of a relationship with her. She was passably fair but incredibly dull. Any attempts he'd had at intelligent conversation with her when they'd danced together at various functions had fallen terribly short. One thing Philip knew for certain: he couldn't marry a dullard. He needed a woman who was smart and quick-witted. He needed someone like his friend Sheridan St. John, or her cousin Maureen. The trouble was, they were both already married— Sheri to a scout from the fort and Maureen to a newspaperman in town.

Thinking back, Philip understood now why his father had tried to force him to get serious about Dwylah. He'd been too restless to think about marriage then, but his father had thought her the perfect match for him. Young, pretty, smart, and the daughter of a congress-man from their home state, she'd have done well as an officer's wife. But Philip knew there was no point in dwelling on Dwylah Carpenter. She had long since married someone else and had several children.

Philip had to find someone, though, and try to make a go of a marriage he didn't really want. Where he was going to find his bride in the middle of Arizona Territory, he had no idea, but he was going to be on the lookout from now on. According to the will, he had only a lit-tle over five months left.

Chapter Three

Dawn found Mattie huddled on her bed, clutching her blanket to her breast, trying not to cry. She'd passed a miserable night.

Last night, Cal had fired her.

The realization that she was in serious trouble had haunted her through the long hours of darkness. It had been bad enough that she'd had to fight off Micah Johnson, but knowing that in just a few days she would be completely out of money and officially destitute scared her. She tried to comfort herself with the knowledge that she'd suffered through bad times before and survived. She told herself she could do it again. But, somehow, she knew it wouldn't be in this town.

After her parents' deaths, she had come here,

believing an aunt and uncle still lived in the area. Once she'd arrived, though, she'd found that they had moved on. She'd been out of money and had no one to help her. She'd tried to find a job, but the only work she could get was at the Palace Saloon. She'd balked at being a barmaid, but desperation and hunger had forced her to take what Cal had offered. Now, after months of working in the saloon, she was certain no one else would hire her. Despite her attempts at chaste behavior, her reputation was ruined. She had no family or friends, and certainly no marriage prospects. She was in dire straits, and she had to think of something fast.

The idea of packing up and leaving sounded wonderful, but she didn't have enough money to pay for a stage ticket anywhere and keep eating, too. Her choices were severely limited—unless she decided to put her morals aside in favor of survival and go back to work at the Palace, doing the things that Cal and Micah both wanted her to do.

Mattie shuddered at the thought. If there was one thing she wouldn't do, it was sell herself to men.

She finally gave up and let her tears flow. Crying wouldn't solve anything, but she hoped it would make her feel better. Still, she had little time to feel sorry for herself. She had to figure out a way to survive.

An image of her general shone in her thoughts, and she smiled a watery smile. He had been wonderful. She sighed deeply. She would never see him again, but she would always remember his kindness.

Philip Long

She sighed again as tears streaked down her cheeks.

Morning couldn't come soon enough for Philip. He awoke just before dawn, as was his usual schedule, and lay in bed, enjoying the peace of the moment. But then thoughts of his father's demands returned with a vengeance and seemed all the more infuriating in the quiet of the predawn darkness.

Marriage.

To please his father.

Thinking that way irritated him. Why did he have to marry someone who would please his father? He should marry a woman *he* wanted, not one his father wanted.

A vision of Mattie floated before him. He grinned as he imagined what his father would have said if he'd ever taken Mattie home to meet him. His father would have judged her immediately and found her wanting. Philip had to admit that he'd judged her immediately, too, but he had been proven wrong. Mattie was no prostitute. Why she was working in the Palace Saloon, though, was a mystery to him.

As he lay there, thinking about the night before, he found he wanted to see Mattie one more time. He wanted to make sure she had suffered no lasting ill effects from Micah Johnson's attack. His stage wasn't due to leave until early that afternoon, so there was plenty of time to stop by the Palace. He would feel better knowing she was all right.

"Mattie Jackson ain't here," Cal said, looking disgusted. "She's been nothing but trouble for me from the first night I hired her, so I fired her last night after that scene she made with Micah."

"You fired her?" Philip repeated, frowning.

"What's it to you?"

His pointed question made Philip think. What was it to him? Why did he care? Mattie hadn't said a word about being fired when he'd walked her home. He wondered why. She could have taken him up on his offer of help. He would have given her some money. Certainly, judging from the boardinghouse where she lived, she didn't have much.

He realized then that Mattie was too proud to ask for help. She did carry a gun and seemed determined to be self-sufficient.

"It's nothing to me. I just wanted to make sure she was all right."

"Who cares?" Cal shrugged, then snarled, "Women are all alike, whether they sell it or give it away. Hell, when you think about it, even brides are selling it for a price. A man's got to vow to take care of them for the rest of their days just so they put out a little." He moved off to wait on another customer.

Philip suddenly felt the need to get out of there. He walked outside into the sunshine and strode down the street. Getting fired from the Palace was probably the best thing that had ever happened to Mattie Jackson, whether she realized it or not. But Philip knew she would need some way to support herself, since she'd mentioned that she didn't have anyone to help her. He found himself heading for her boardinghouse.

Mattie was surprised by the knock at her door. She'd gathered her wits and had been trying to come up with a plan for the future. Things looked bleak right now, but she would find a way—somehow. She went to the door and opened it, expecting to find Mrs. Harper there. Her landlady was the only person who ever bothered to check on her.

"Oh!" The sight of her general standing there left Mattie momentarily speechless.

"Miss Mattie, I'm glad you're here. I wanted to talk to you. May I come in?" Philip asked, remaining just outside her door. He was staring down at her, amazed by the difference in her this morning. Last night, in her low-cut red dress she'd looked older and wiser and . . . somehow used—jaded, almost. Today, her face was washed clear of paint, and she was wearing a demure if slightly shabby day gown. Her hair was tied with a simple ribbon and tumbled about her shoulders in a dark, lustrous cascade, giving her an almost—well—wholesome look.

Mattie knew she should never let an unrelated man into her room, but this was her general, and he'd already proven himself a true gentleman. She opened the door wider to allow him to enter. "I'm surprised to see you again."

"I went by the Palace to talk to you. The bartender told me he'd fired you last night. Why didn't you tell me that when we were together?"

"What difference would it have made?"

"You had already suffered enough abuse last night without losing your job, too."

"Cal thought I should be more than just a barmaid. He told me I should keep men like Micah happy. I refused."

"You did the right thing," Philip stated firmly, proud of her determination.

She gestured for him to sit down in the one and only chair in the room while she sat on the side of her bed. "Maybe, but I won't be able to pay the bills for long."

"Surely there are other jobs you could take."

Mattie's laugh was derisive. "Not in this town. I may not have done anything bad while I was working at the Palace, but the good townsfolk won't believe that. They'll think the worst about me, no matter what."

"What are you going to do?"

"I don't know. I barely have enough money to buy a ticket on the stage, let alone feed myself for the next few weeks."

"It's that bad?" His desire to help her grew even stronger.

"Yes," she answered without hesitation.

There was no point in lying to him. "So why are you here?"

"I wanted to see if I could help you," Philip began.

As he spoke, Cal's harsh, demeaning words echoed in his thoughts. *"Hell, even brides are selling it for a price."*

An idea came to Philip—one that would cause Mattie no dishonor yet would solve both their problems. She was poor and in desperate need of a job. He was wealthy—or at least soon would be, once he claimed his inheritance—and in desperate need of a wife. He could *hire* Mattie to be his wife! He smiled at the brilliance of the idea. The marriage would be in name only, of course, and they could get an annulment as soon as his year was over. Such an arrangement would suit them both perfectly!

"You want to help me?" she said cautiously, wondering at his smile.

"Yes, and I think I just figured out how."

"You did?"

"Yes, I have the perfect solution—for both of us."

"Both of us? I didn't know you were in trouble."

"I'm not in trouble exactly," he began. "I'm going to be honest with you. I can offer you a position that will pay handsomely and get you out of this town."

"Why would you?"

"Because, right now, I need your help as badly as you need mine."

"I don't understand." She was confused and

growing a bit nervous. Why would a man like her general need her?

"It seems, Mattie, that I am in dire, immediate need of a wife." He met her gaze forthrightly as he spoke, and he would remember forever the change in her expression at his words. She was stunned and staring at him in total disbelief.

"You need a wife?" Mattie repeated, unable to believe what she was hearing. What female in her right mind wouldn't want to marry him? Her general was perfect. He could have any woman he wanted. Why did he feel the need to make a bargain with her?

Philip quickly explained the stipulation—and its deadline—in his father's will. As he talked he realized just how perfect his plan was. If he married Mattie, he would not be surrendering completely to his father's order. He would be marrying someone his father would think was totally unsuitable. The will didn't dictate whom he had to marry; it just said that he had to marry.

"So," he concluded, "I'm making you an offer I hope you will accept. Today. Right now. Before I have to leave. I would like you to marry me as soon as possible and come with me to Fort McDowell. We must make the relationship convincing, even to legal skeptics, and we must remain married for one year, but you and I will know it is a marriage in name only. When the year is over, we can get an annulment and go our separate ways. I will pay you handsomely for your time. You'll never have to work again."

Mattie wasn't sure whether to laugh or cry. It seemed like a fairy tale, a dream come true. The man she thought of as a true hero, her general, her Philip Long, had come to rescue her. He was going to save her from her terrible fate. He was going to marry her and take her away from all this. Her spirits soared.

But then, their marriage would be in name only, and they would part after a year.

The realization that her fantasies were just that—fantasies—hurt. This was no love match for Philip, and it never would be. He'd made it clear that it would be a business arrangement, nothing more. And she had to decide right now what she was going to do.

"Miss Mattie?" Philip said questioningly, for she hadn't responded to his offer, and he couldn't read her expression. "Will you accept my proposal?"

Mattie took a deep breath. "Yes, Philip Long, I accept your proposal. I'll marry you."

Philip smiled, "Good. This will work out well for both of us."

"Yes, it will," she answered, still stunned by what had transpired. *She was going to marry her general!*

Philip suddenly felt a bit awkward. He'd just asked this woman to marry him, and she'd said yes. What was he supposed to do next? He told himself to focus on one thing at a time. "Would you like to get married here?"

"No!" Her answer came quickly. "The sooner I get out of this town, the better."

"All right. I planned on leaving on the two-o'clock stage. Can you be ready by then?"

"Yes. I don't have much to pack." She glanced around the room at her paltry possessions.

"There's an overnight stop at a way station, and then we can be married in the next town."

"That'll be fine."

"I'll check out of my hotel and come back for you." He stood.

"I'll be waiting for you."

Mattie lifted her gaze to Philip's, and for an instant she was lost in the depths of his eyes. She saw kindness and gentleness there. She wondered what it would be like to kiss him, then realized how silly the thought was. Her general had offered her a job. Nothing more. Still, a glimmer of hope burned within her heart. Philip had said they'd have to stay married a year to claim his inheritance. That meant she would have twelve whole months to try to win his love.

Chapter Four

Mattie stared out the stagecoach window but gave no thought to the passing scenery. She couldn't. Every fiber of her being was focused on Philip as he sat so close beside her. They had been traveling for several hours now, and with each bump of the stage, his thigh pressed against hers. Mattie found that simple physical contact most distracting, but Philip appeared completely unaffected. Several times she'd cast surreptitious glances his way to see if he'd even noticed, but his expression remained inscrutable.

Mattie realized she shouldn't have been surprised by Philip's lack of reaction to her nearness. He'd made it perfectly clear from the start that their relationship was a business arrangement. He would marry her, but that didn't mean he cared about her. What he cared about was his inheritance.

She told herself that the deal they'd made was a blessing for her. Philip had shown up just in time to save her from a terrible fate, and she would forever be grateful. She would repay him by doing exactly what he wanted her to do. She would play the role of his wife until such time as he was ready to part from her; then she would leave him and never look back. There would be no emotional scenes, no heartbreak, no despair in their parting. It was strictly business. They meant nothing to each other.

On a logical level, Mattie accepted that she had no real future with Philip. But in truth, her heart ached with the knowledge that for the next year they would act married, but they would never be anything more than strangers to each other.

That was the way Philip wanted it, and Mattie was certain she knew why. She was, after all, just a saloon girl.

Self-consciously, she smoothed the skirts of her simple day gown. She wanted to make Philip proud of her, and it bothered her that this was her best dress. It was old and far from stylish. Since Philip had paid for her ticket, though, she did have a few dollars left to her name, so she intended to buy a new dress for her wedding once they reached town. Even though theirs wasn't going to be a "real" wedding, she wanted to look her best for him.

Mattie closed her eyes and imagined herself standing at an altar in a beautiful white lace gown and veil. It was an image she'd cherished since she was a little girl. She'd always dreamed of walking down the aisle and marrying a handsome prince, and very soon she would be. Only her "prince" was actually her general.

Philip was having second thoughts about his situation. He rarely acted impulsively, but he had done it this time. Not that he'd been without motivation. He had to get married, and he was doing what needed to be done to accomplish that end.

At the time, proposing to Mattie had seemed a brilliant strategy. Now, though, he wondered if he'd done the right thing. Helping her out of a desperate situation was one thing; throwing her into an even more difficult one was another.

Mattie was about to enter a world completely foreign to her. As an officer's wife, much would be expected of her, and it was up to him to make sure she'd know what to do. He wanted everything to go smoothly for her. He wanted her to be happy.

He glanced over at her to find her staring out the stagecoach window, completely unaware of the challenges she would be facing shortly. Philip vowed to himself then and there that he would make sure everything went as easily as possible for her. After an obviously hard life, she would be his wife, even if in name only, and he wanted to take care of her.

Of course, if she was going to be Mrs. Philip Long, she would have to look the part. His gaze went over her critically, assessingly. The first thing he was going to do was make sure she had a suitable wardrobe. Officers' wives could be gossipy and sometimes judgmental, and he wanted to protect Mattie as much as he could. When they reached town tomorrow, one of the first things he would do was look for a dress shop and provide Mattie with a new wardrobe with which to begin her new life at Fort McDowell.

The stage hit a jarring bump, and Mattie was thrown hard against him. Philip instinctively slipped an arm around her shoulders to steady her.

"That was a rough one," he told her with a smile.

"Yes, it was," she agreed.

As he looked down at her, he was lost for a moment in the depths of her green eyes. He suddenly became aware of how fragile she felt beneath his touch. Mattie had acted so strong and brave that he hadn't really thought of her as delicate. The realization surprised him. When she shifted away from him, he quickly withdrew his arm and let her go.

"This is one helluva trip," the grouchy-looking old man sitting across from them complained. He was the only other passenger, and he'd been sleeping most of the way. The last bump, however, had jarred him awake. He was scowling and looking irritated with the world. "I'll be damned glad when it's over. Oh, pardon me, ma'am. I forgot there was a lady on board."

After her long months at the Palace, Mattie was amazed that the man apologized for cursing in front of her, and even more amazed that he thought she was a lady. It pleased her so, she had to fight to keep from laughing aloud. "I understand," she told him. "These roads are rough."

"That's putting it politely. I'll be glad when we finally make our destination."

Mattie hid a smile at his complaining, considering that he'd been asleep for most of the trek so far. She had to admit, though, that she couldn't have agreed with him more. Sitting this close to Philip was proving to be both heaven and hell. She shifted her position to put a little more space between them. It wouldn't last long, but it was a bit of a reprieve for now. "How much farther is it to the way station?"

"Another hour or two," the codger answered. "By the way, I'm Gene Gibson."

"It's nice to meet you. I'm Mattie Jackson, and this is my fiancé, Philip Long," she said.

Philip nodded his greeting.

"It's nice to meet you both. Where you heading?" Gibson asked.

"To Fort McDowell," Mattie told him. "I'm really excited. This is quite an adventure for me."

"I don't know if I'd call it an adventure. I hear there've been a lot of Indian raids going on thereabouts lately. I hope you have a safe trip out."

"Oh, we will," Mattie insisted. "No Indian would dare attack us with my general along."

Philip almost groaned.

Gibson snorted a laugh as he looked at Philip. "General? Pardon me, ma'am, but in case he ain't told you yet, he ain't a general. He's a captain."

"He's a general to me." She smiled brightly as she gazed up at Philip. "We'll be getting married once we reach Crawford's Gulch."

"Well, congratulations. You're a lucky man," he told Philip.

"Yes, I am," Philip responded.

"So where are you heading, Mr. Gibson?" Mattie asked engagingly.

Philip listened to their conversation, joining in only when asked a direct question. He was amazed at how easily Mattie had charmed the old man. He'd expected Gene Gibson to be surly for the rest of the trip, but Mattie had the man relaxed and smiling and telling her all about his family waiting for him in Crawford's Gulch.

The next several hours passed quickly, and when they pulled to a stop at the way station, Gibson looked surprised.

"I can't believe we're here already," he said to Mattie as the driver opened the door for them to climb down. "It was a pleasure having you to talk to. You certainly made the time go faster. If your officer there hadn't claimed you already, I'd be tempted to see about courting you myself."

Mattie actually found herself blushing at his kind words, while Philip merely smiled slightly.

Through the evening at the station Philip stayed attentively by Mattie's side, playing his role of fiancé perfectly. After they'd eaten the hot meal that was provided, everyone bedded down for the night. The men slept in a bunkhouse out back, while Mattie was given the small room in the main house that was reserved for female travelers.

She appreciated the privacy. She was exhausted and needed some rest. But as she started to undress, she realized that by this time the following night she would be Mrs. Philip Long! She would be beginning a whole new life. A life with Philip. Although, she acknowledged sadly, they would be sharing nothing meaningful, no matter how she looked at it, she knew things would never be the same again. And sleep was long in coming.

They were up at dawn and soon on the road again. They didn't reach their destination of Crawford's Gulch until late in the afternoon.

Philip climbed out of the stage first and put his hands at her waist to help Mattie descend. He thought her light as a feather as he set her before him, then went to retrieve their bags.

Gene Gibson started to climb out next, and it was then that excited shouts and squeals erupted.

"There's Grampa!"

Philip and Mattie both saw three young boys no older than ten running at full speed toward

Gene, who was soon enveloped in enthusiastic embraces.

"It was nice to meet you two," he called out to Mattie and Philip as he was surrounded by loved ones and hustled away.

"You, too!" Mattie responded.

The driver climbed back up to his seat and drove the stage off to the stable area, leaving Mattie and Philip alone.

"Well, here we are," Philip announced as he looked around the town. Crawford's Gulch wasn't very big, but Philip was certain it had to have a justice of the peace somewhere, not to mention a shop where he could find Mattie at least one or two new dresses. "Let's find the hotel and check in. The desk clerk should be able to tell us what we need to know about getting hitched in Crawford's Gulch."

Mattie accompanied him without a word, not quite sure what to say. In a very short time, they would be married. She was excited and a bit frightened too. She leashed both emotions and tried to appear calm.

When they entered the hotel, Philip registered and then asked the clerk for directions to the justice of the peace.

"His name is Russell Bailey, and his office is just down the street about three blocks."

"Thanks." Philip escorted Mattie upstairs to their chamber and held the door for her as she entered.

Mattie stepped inside and found herself staring at a large double bed. She knew a moment of nervousness as she realized that this very night she would be sharing this room with Philip.

"Do you want to freshen up a bit before we go to the justice of the peace?" Philip asked casually as he carried their bags in.

"Yes, please." She was amazed at how calm he seemed about the whole situation.

"I'll leave you alone then and be back in a little while."

"Thanks."

Once Philip had gone, Mattie took a look at herself in the mirror over the bureau, and she knew what she had to do. She had to go buy the new dress for their wedding. On the ride into town, she had noticed a small ladies' shop next to the general store. She would make a quick trip there to see if she could find something suitable.

Mattie knew she was romanticizing the ceremony—this wasn't a real love match—but she did want to look her best for Philip. She wanted him to be proud of her. After freshening up a bit, she got out her small purse and counted all the money she had in the world. It wasn't much, but she hoped she could find something she could afford. She did so want to please him.

Philip found a saloon down the street from the hotel and went in for a quick drink. He stood by himself at the end of the bar, thinking about the changes the next few hours would bring. He was about to marry Mattie Jackson. The prospect of marriage had never before excited him, but somehow he knew that this coming year with Mattie would not be dull. He hadn't told her yet that he wanted to take her shopping for new clothes. He wanted to surprise her when he went back to the room.

After stalling a reasonable amount of time, Philip quit the bar and headed back to claim his bride to be. He knocked at the hotel-room door before opening it, for he didn't want to startle her. But when he received no answer, he stepped inside the room, and he was shocked to find it empty.

"Mattie?"

He searched for her, but the room was too small to offer anyplace to hide. It was then that he noticed her purse was gone, too, and the reality of what had happened hit him.

She had fled. She'd changed her mind about the marriage and had not had enough nerve to tell him to his face.

She was gone.

Chapter Five

Philip pivoted and strode from the hotel room, swearing under his breath. He'd sensed that Mattie had been a bit uncomfortable when they'd entered the room together. That was why he'd excused himself; he'd wanted to give her some time to compose herself before they went to the justice of the peace. But now it seemed his attempt at being solicitous had failed. Mattie had walked away, and she hadn't even said good-bye.

Philip's expression was thunderous as he made his way to the lobby. Wherever Mattie had gone, she couldn't have gotten far. The town wasn't that big. He was going to find her. He couldn't let her just disappear this way.

"Did you notice my fiancée leaving the hotel?" Philip demanded of the desk clerk.

"Why, yes, sir. She left right after you did."

"Did she mention where she was going?"

"No, but I did notice that she headed down the street toward the general store."

Still frowning, Philip started off in the direction the clerk had indicated. He kept careful watch as he made his way down the street. His confidence in his ability to find Mattie was rock solid. He'd been successfully tracking renegade Indians for years, so finding one woman in a town the size of Crawford's Gulch didn't seem too challenging.

Twenty minutes later, Philip was beginning to have his doubts. He'd covered most of the town and had yet to catch sight of Mattie anywhere. Why would she feel the need to flee him this way? Had he completely misjudged her character? He didn't think he had. She hadn't stolen anything out of their room. She had simply vanished without a word.

Philip was heading back toward the hotel when he walked by the ladies' shop he'd passed earlier. He took a quick glance inside and came to a halt. Mattie was there. She was standing on a riser wearing a pale blue gown while a seamstress was working on the hem. He entered the shop abruptly, standing just inside the door.

"Mattie?"

Mattie gasped, surprised that Philip had found her. She'd known the fitting was taking a little longer than she'd expected, but she hadn't thought she'd been gone so long that he would come looking for her. She had so wanted to surprise him. But it wasn't to be. Looking over her shoulder, she saw the dark look on his face and wondered what had angered him so. "Philip, I'm sorry this has taken so long. I didn't realize it would be so complicated."

"What would be so complicated?" he demanded, remaining where he was, standing stiffly, as if prepared for trouble.

"You must be Mattie's 'general,'" the seamstress said, smiling at him as she stopped working and stood up to greet him.

"Yes, he is, Dora," Mattie affirmed. Stepping down from the riser, she went to him. "Philip, I wanted to have a new dress for the wedding, so I came here to see what I could find." When she saw his expression grow even darker, she thought he was angry because she was spending money. She hastened to calm him. "I'm paying for it, so you don't have to worry. I've just enough money left of my savings to buy it."

If Philip hadn't been an officer and a gentleman, he would have sworn out loud right then. He forced himself to calm down a bit. "I'm not worried about the cost of a dress. I was worried about you. When I got back to the room, I didn't know where you'd gone, and I feared something had happened to you."

"Oh." Mattie was completely taken by surprise by his concern.

The seamstress sighed dreamily, clearly thinking her new client a very lucky woman to have such a handsome, caring man in love with her.

"In fact," Philip continued, "I'd planned to see about getting you a few new dresses myself."

"You did?" Mattie was shocked.

"I was going to surprise you."

"But that wouldn't be right for—"

"It would be very right," he cut her off. "You're going to be my wife." Then, looking at the seamstress, he asked, "Do you have any other gowns already made up that will fit my fiancée?"

"I have two more that might do," She offered.

"We leave tomorrow at noon. Could you have any alterations that are needed done by then?"

"Absolutely."

"Fine. Then we'll take the three gowns. Do whatever needs to be done. We'll pick them up tomorrow before we leave."

"Philip, are you sure?" Mattie asked as Dora hurried to get the other two garments to show them. She knew the gowns would be expensive.

"I'm very sure," he told her, finally relaxing enough to really look at her for the first time.

The pale blue dress highlighted her flawless complexion and brought out the beauty of her dark hair. The neckline of the gown wasn't low cut but slightly scooped, and he knew exactly what it needed.

When the seamstress returned, Philip asked, "Will it take much longer to finish hemming the blue gown?"

"About twenty minutes," Dora answered.

"I'll be back for you then, Mattie. There's one thing I forgot to do."

The two women watched him leave the shop and disappear down the street.

"Your fiancé is one handsome officer. You're a very lucky woman," Dora told her as she worked on the hem.

"I know. I'm very lucky," Mattie answered.

Dora had just helped Mattie down from the riser when Philip returned and paid Dora for all three gowns. The price didn't seem to bother him at all. When he'd finished taking care of business, he turned to Mattie.

"Are you ready?" he asked, his gaze meeting hers.

"If you are." She was suddenly feeling a bit timid.

"You look lovely," Dora told her.

Philip took a small box out of his pocket. "I thought the gown was missing something," he said softly. He lifted the lid of the box and took out a golden heart-shaped locket. "And I thought this just might be it."

"Oh!" Mattie said softly. She had never seen anything so pretty. "This is for me?"

"It's my wedding present," Philip said as he came to stand behind her and fasten the necklace at her throat.

Mattie closed her eyes at the warmth of his touch, then lifted one hand to caress the necklace reverently after he'd stepped away. She'd never owned any jewelry before. She stared in the mirror in awe. "It's beautiful."

"You're beautiful," Philip said on impulse, surprising himself.

"Yes, you are," Dora agreed.

Mattie gazed at her reflection, finding a sophisticated young woman staring back at her. She could see no trace of the Mattie Jackson who'd worked at the Palace Saloon and had to wear gaudy red dresses and face paint. The woman in pale blue gown appeared genteel, ladylike, someone who might be accepted by polite society. Mattie smiled, amazed at her own transformation.

"Are you ready?" Philip asked.

His question broke through her reverie, and she turned to face the man who would soon be her husband.

"I'm as ready as I'll ever be," she said in a soft voice.

"Shall we go?"

Philip offered her his arm in a courtly manner. Mattie accepted it, and they left the store.

"Do you, Philip Long, take this woman, Matilda Jackson, to be your lawfully wedded wife, for better or worse, for richer or poorer, in sickness and in health, until death do you part?" Ben Strickland, the justice of the peace, asked.

"I do," Philip responded.

"Do you, Matilda Jackson, take this man, Philip Long, to be your lawfully wedded husband, for better or worse, for richer or poorer, in sickness and in health, until death do you part?"

"I do," Mattie answered breathlessly. She looked up at Philip and managed to smile. A part of her yearned for this to be a real ceremony, one that meant something to Philip, but in her heart she knew better. She fought down her own betraying thoughts and emotions. There was no love between them, and she had to remember that.

Philip took Mattie's left hand and slipped a simple gold band onto her ring finger, marking her as his wife.

"By the power invested in me, I now pronounce you man and wife. Captain Long, you may kiss your bride," the justice told Philip with a grin.

Philip turned to take Mattie in his arms. He felt her tense at the contact, and with utmost care, he bent and captured her lips in a simple kiss. He'd meant it to be a chaste, innocent exchange, and it was. Yet something in it stirred him, and suddenly he needed more. He deepened the kiss, tasting of her sweetness. He was shocked to find he wanted even more, and he forced himself to draw back from her, keeping himself in check. He saw Mattie's wide-eyed look and realized she'd been just as surprised as he had by the power of their kiss. He turned to the justice of the peace.

"Thank you, Mr. Strickland," he said, keeping a possessive arm around Mattie's waist.

"My pleasure. I always enjoy weddings. You two be happy together, now."

"We appreciate your help," Philip said cordially as he paid him for performing the ceremony.

They left the justice of the peace's office and didn't speak until they were almost back to the hotel.

"I guess this means we're married," Mattie said quietly.

"Yes, we are," Philip said. "I thought we should have dinner and celebrate a little before we call it a night. What do you say?"

"All right," she agreed, still stunned by all that had happened in the past few days. She was now married.

She was Mrs. Philip Long.

They made small talk as they dined at a small restaurant near the hotel.

Mattie found herself growing more and more nervous with each passing moment. Soon they would finish eating and return to the hotel. Soon she would be alone with him in their room. Though she had worked at the Palace, she was still an innocent in many ways. She'd had no brothers and no gentleman callers to speak of. She wasn't quite sure how to behave alone with a man.

Reminding herself that this was a marriage in name only, Mattie told herself she had nothing to worry about. Philip had made it plain he had no intention of making love to her, so she was getting nervous for no good reason. Besides, she concluded logically, what did it matter if they shared the same room? They *were* married.

But Mattie's mood was still unsettled when they started back to the hotel. She walked in silence by Philip's side, trying to anticipate what the night would bring.

As Philip escorted Mattie back to their hotel room, he was feeling quite pleased with the way everything had gone. Their marriage had taken place without any difficulties. Now all he had to do was send notice and proof to his father's lawyer that the ceremony had taken place and then stay married to Mattie for one year to claim his inheritance.

Philip still resented his father for forcing him to wed, but he was satisfied with his own choice for a wife. In fact, he was finding himself drawn to Mattie in ways he'd never thought possible. There was a refreshing air of innocence about her—surprising, since she'd worked at the saloon, but nevertheless real. He found, too, that he quite liked her. She was bright and witty and open with her opinions. She said what she was really thinking, and in his experience he'd found that a true rarity among females.

"Tired?" he asked her as they neared the hotel.

"A little," she answered, looking up at him. "What about you?"

"Very. I'm looking forward to getting into bed."

His statement sounded innocent enough, but Mattie swallowed nervously. He was looking forward to getting into bed. If he planned on using the bed, she wondered where she was going to be sleeping.

Mattie pictured herself trying to sleep in the small chair in their room. That would likely be torture. Probably she'd end up on a pallet on the floor. She convinced herself it wouldn't be that bad. She'd certainly slept in worse places since her parents died.

When they reached their room, Philip unlocked the door and held it open for her to enter ahead of him. "You might as well go ahead and get comfortable," he said as he closed and locked the door behind them.

The sound made her all the more jittery. "Well, I didn't know . . . I mean, I was wondering . . ."

He turned to look at her and frowned when he saw how stiffly she was holding herself, staring at the bed. "Mattie? What's wrong?"

Girding herself, she turned to face him. "I'll need an extra blanket."

"Why? It's not that cold."

"For a pallet," she answered simply.

Chapter Six

Mattie was surprised by the sudden change in Philip's expression. She was certain that the look he gave her could cow even the bravest of his enlisted men. But she wasn't a soldier under his command. She refused to flinch.

"What are you talking about?" he demanded.

"I'm talking about where I'm to sleep tonight. We had an agreement about this 'marriage' of ours. Should we be sharing the same bed, do you think?"

For a moment, Philip was silent. He had to admit to himself that he had enjoyed their wedding kiss, but he had not thought much beyond that point. His ego, however, was a bit bruised by Mattie's brusque treatment of the subject.

"You're right," he agreed. "We shouldn't be

sharing a bed. But you won't be the one sleeping on a pallet. I will." Philip eyed the chair, wondering if he could find any rest there. The floor certainly didn't seem any more inviting, but he had made a deal with Mattie, and he had to uphold his end of it.

"Are you sure?" Mattie couldn't believe that he would give up his comfort for her. No one else had ever put her needs first.

"I'm sure. Let me give you some privacy to undress. We won't be able to avoid close quarters for an entire year, especially after we're at McDowell, but I can leave now for a while," he offered.

"No, it's not necessary," Mattie answered not wanting to put him out even further. "But would you mind turning your back for a few minutes while I do change?"

He smiled at her. "Not at all, ma'am."

"You won't look?"

"I give you my word as an officer and a gentleman."

"Thank you," she said, smiling back.

Philip walked to the window and looked out, keeping his back to Mattie. "Would you like me to speak with the clerk and see if it's possible to get a bath brought up for you in the morning? Our stage doesn't leave until noon."

"That would be wonderful!" She was delighted at the prospect. Certainly she'd washed up before the wedding, but getting the chance to soak in a real bath would be heavenly.

Philip smiled to himself. He remembered how much his mother had enjoyed her baths and was glad that he'd pleased Mattie. He heard the rustle of her clothing as she started to undress, but he kept his gaze directed at the street below.

"Philip?" Mattie finally gave up trying to unfasten her gown by herself. "I need your help."

He turned, and she presented him with her back, lifting the thick mane of her hair out of his way.

"I thought I could do it myself, but I can't." Mattie stood perfectly still before him.

Philip stared down at the tantalizing line of her neck and shoulders and found he wanted to press a kiss there. Or maybe several kisses, right along the line of the locket's fine gold chain. Jerking his wayward thoughts away from the dangerous direction they were taking, he quickly unhooked Mattie's gown. It gaped open, but she was holding the bodice close, so he was treated to only a glimpse of her back as she moved away from him.

"Thank you," she said a bit nervously. The warmth of Philip's nearness and the touch of his hands had aroused new feelings deep within her, and she knew she had to get into her nightclothes and under the covers before she'd feel safe. Though what it was she needed to feel safe from, she wasn't quite sure.

"Do you want me to unfasten the locket, too?"

"No. No, I'd like to keep it on." She lifted one hand to her throat to touch the necklace. She never wanted to take it off again.

Philip returned to his vigil at the window. He was tempted to lift his gaze just a little to watch Mattie's reflection in the glass as she finished undressing, but he didn't. He'd given her his word, and he stood by it.

"You can turn around now," Mattie told him as she lay down and pulled the covers up to her chin.

Philip turned toward her but stopped at the sight of her in bed. Her eyes were wide, and her expression was wary and a little frightened. It troubled him that she might be afraid of him. He knew this was the first time they were alone together in such intimate confines, but he wanted her to trust him and to be able to be comfortable in his presence.

"Mattie," he began seriously, "I want to make you a promise tonight."

"About what?"

"I want you to know that I will never do anything to hurt you and that I will never try to take advantage of you in any way."

Relief rushed through her, and she nodded, only a bit embarrassed that Philip had seemed able to read her thoughts so easily.

"I'll just get undressed myself. You go ahead to sleep."

Philip moved to the dresser, and, after turning the lamp down low, looked through the drawers and found an extra blanket he could use. He tossed it onto the chair and started to get ready for bed. He shed his jacket, then unbuttoned his shirt and stripped it off.

Mattie had closed her eyes and curled up, trying to sleep. But then for some reason she had to open her eyes to take a look. She saw Philip standing near the dresser, naked to the waist and getting ready to shed his pants. He looked so handsome, all she could do was stare. His shoulders were broad, and his chest was heavily muscled and powerful. A hot blush stained her cheeks at the sight, and she quickly shut her eyes lest she see even more of him than she had intended to.

Philip was unaware of Mattie's gaze upon him. He took off his boots, then started to doff his pants. But he thought the better of it. Mattie was uncomfortable with their current situation, so he would bow to her delicate sensibilities.

Gathering up his blanket, he turned the lamp all the way down and sought what ease he could in the rooms one chair. He discovered quickly that there was little rest to be had there. The chair was definitely not meant for someone his size to relax in. Even so, he was determined to get some sleep.

Mattie had thought, as tired as she was, that she would immediately fall asleep once her head hit the pillow. But it didn't happen. The knowledge that Philip was so close at hand disturbed her—though not necessarily in a bad way. She was just very, very aware of his nearness. Long minutes passed as she lay, unmoving, seeking the peace and forgetfulness of slumber. But still it didn't come.

Philip was miserable. It was bad enough that he couldn't forget how beautiful Mattie had looked tonight, but he could not find any rest at all in the cramped chair. After almost an hour of suffering, he finally gave it up. He stood and spread the blanket out on the floor. He'd been out on patrol and had slept by campfires many a time. He was certain the hotel floor had to be more welcoming than some of the terrain he'd slept on in the wilds.

He lay down. The floor was hard, and thoughts of Mattie and how she'd looked when she swept her hair up out of his way to bare her back to him haunted him. It had been a purely innocent gesture on her part, but he had found it a very sensual one. He rolled over with a disgusted growl, telling himself he was the lowest of the low to even be thinking about her that way.

"Philip? Are you all right?" Mattie had heard him make a strange sound and realized that he'd moved from the chair to the floor.

"I'm fine," he ground out.

He did not sound "fine."

"Are you sure? Was the chair that bad?"

"The floor will be all right. Go to sleep."

Mattie was quiet for a second, then offered, "Do you want to share the bed? I promise I'll stay on my half. I won't touch you or move around too much and disturb you or anything."

Philip almost groaned out loud at her offer. Trying to be logical, he asked himself why he was so miserable but couldn't really find an answer.

347

"You don't want to?" Mattie asked when he didn't respond.

Philip got up slowly. The softness of the mattress was inviting, and with Mattie lying there, it was even more so. "I'll take you up on your offer, but I'll sleep on top of the covers."

"Oh."

He grabbed up his blanket and stretched out next to her. He took care to stay as far from her as he possibly could, and he lay very still.

"Good night." She was smiling in the darkness, glad he would be more comfortable now.

"Good night," he responded.

But for some reason, he didn't really think it was.

Mattie had thought she might have trouble sleeping with Philip lying so close beside her. She quickly fell asleep, though, and slept soundly through the rest of the night.

Philip lay on his marriage bed, pondering the irony of his situation. If anyone had ever told him that when he finally got married he would spend his wedding night like this, he would have laughed. But he wasn't laughing now.

When the quiet, even sound of Mattie's breathing came to him, he realized she'd fallen asleep. He shifted his position slightly so he could look at her as she slumbered beside him. In the semidarkness, he took the time to study her, and he realized she was quite lovely. He realized, too, that she was his wife.

Philip did not sleep well all night.

* * *

In the morning, when he awoke, Philip slipped carefully from the bed, taking care not to disturb Mattie. He wanted to wash up and dress before she awoke so he wouldn't embarrass her. It surprised him that she still wasn't stirring when he'd finished, but he realized how very tired she must be. He quietly let himself out of the room.

He returned some time later, quite pleased with himself. "Mattie?" he called to her once he'd let himself back into their room.

She awoke quickly but was still groggy from the depth of her slumber. "Is something wrong?"

"No, but your bath will be up here in a few minutes, and I wanted to give you time to get ready."

"My bath? Oh, thank you!" It took her a moment to remember, and she was thrilled with what he had accomplished for her.

"Will you need any help?"

"No, I'll be fine," she told him quickly.

"Then I'll go on to the dress shop and pick up your other gowns. That should give you enough time to bathe."

Before he could leave, a knock came at the door, and he opened it to admit the maids with the bath. Mattie pulled the covers up high as they hurried into the room to set up the tub.

"My wife is most appreciative of your help," Philip told them when they were leaving. He looked back at Mattie. "I'll leave you to your privacy now. I'll be back in about half an hour."

Mattie nodded, and he quit the room. When

he'd gone, she got up and undressed quickly. She couldn't wait to take full advantage of the hot water.

Philip made his way to the dress shop and was pleased to find it was just opening as he got there. The dresses were ready. He headed back to the hotel, trying to strike the vision of Mattie bathing from his thoughts. It wasn't easy. He was half relieved that she was already dressed and ready to go to breakfast when he returned.

"So, what is it going to be like when we get to your fort?" she asked once they were in the restaurant.

Philip's expression turned serious as he looked at her. He had been anticipating this conversation but was not looking forward to it. "I'm afraid it's going to be different from anything you've likely experienced before," he told her.

"It is? Why?"

"Being an officer's wife may not prove easy for you. Much will be expected of you, and the other women . . ." He hesitated.

"What are they like?" she asked cautiously.

"It's been my experience that the other officers' wives can make life difficult for a newcomer if they choose to. Don't be surprised if they seem a bit close-minded or judgmental at first."

"They sound like a warm, wonderful bunch," she said drolly to cover her nerves. Would she end up embarrassing Philip instead of doing him proud?

"Sometimes they can be quite nice. I've seen them at their best and at their worst. I'd be lying to you if I said they were going to immediately accept you into their midst."

"What do I need to do to make them like me?" she asked, determined to do her best by her new husband.

"First, just be yourself," he began.

Mattie smiled at him. He almost sounded as if he liked her himself and wasn't the least ashamed of her less than glamorous circumstances.

Then he went on. "There are a few things, though, that are important to remember." His gaze held hers as he spoke. "You'll have to watch your language and your appearance. Don't ever cuss in front of them, and don't wear any kind of face paint or . . . gaudy attire."

"You don't think they'd approve of my red dress from the Palace?" Mattie asked. When she saw his stricken expression, she grinned at him. "Don't worry, General. I was only teasing. I didn't even bring that red dress with me."

"Good," Philip said. "Probably most important, though, is that you'd better not call me 'General' in front of them—especially not in front of the general's wife." He could just imagine the outrage that would ensue. "When you're with them, always be on your best manners. They will be judging both of us, you and me, by your behavior, so you have a standard to uphold. An officer's wife is to be an asset to his career."

"I am?" She suddenly felt a bit alarmed by all that he'd told her. "I thought we were just doing this so you could claim your inheritance at the end of the year. I didn't know I was going to affect your career when I agreed to marry you."

"Don't be afraid," he tried to reassure her. "It won't be that difficult. You'll do fine."

"But I really won't know anybody to seek guidance from but you, and I'm sure you'll be very busy most of the time."

"You'll have one ready-made female friend— I can guarantee that."

"Who?"

"Sheri," he answered, smiling as he thought of his novelist friend. He had once been rather smitten with Sheridan; she'd been the first real writer he'd ever met. He had hoped she might feature him in one of the dime novels she was writing, but she'd fallen in love with Brand, a scout at the fort, and had used him as the hero in a series of books. The books featuring Brand had sold well, the couple had married, and they were now ranching in the area. Philip was proud to call both her and Brand his friends.

"Who's Sheri?" Mattie asked suspiciously, suddenly wondering, judging by his expression, if there was another woman Philip was truly in love with.

"Sheridan is married to my friend Brand. He was a scout for McDowell. She's a writer."

Finding out that the other woman was married eased Mattie's fears. Hearing that she was a writer amazed her. "You know a real writer? I love to read."

"You can read?" Every day it seemed he was learning something new about Mattie that pleased him.

"Oh, yes. My mother insisted that I learn how when I was young. What does Sheri write?"

"Dime novels. I've got one with me, if you'd like to read it."

"I'd love to."

"Once Sheri learns you've read her books, you'll have a friend for life."

Mattie couldn't wait to get back to the room to start reading. "Will she be at the fort often?"

"She and Brand visit regularly. I think you'll like them both."

"From what you've been telling me, I'm not sure how comfortable I'm going to be living at the fort, but I am going to enjoy meeting this Sheri."

"I'm sure she'll be glad to help you if you have any trouble with the other officers' wives."

"I've got the feeling I'm going to need all the help I can get."

"Well, let me tell you about the people you're going to be meeting." Philip took the time to describe all the women, their husbands, and their places in the hierarchy at the fort.

"I hope I can remember everybody," Mattie said when he finally finished.

"It may take you a few days, but I'm sure you will."

"I hope I can do you proud," she said, wanting to please him.

Philip's gaze met hers across the table. He saw the earnestness in her expression, and something tugged at his heart. "You will," he told her.

Chapter Seven

"We're here," Philip said as the coach slowed to a stop in front of the stage office in Phoenix.

"Already?" Mattie glanced up, surprised. The last few days of travel had passed quickly because Philip had given her one of Sheridan St. John's books to read. The hours and the miles had flown by while she'd been absorbed in the exciting tale. She was delighted, though, to learn that they were finally nearing the end of their long trip.

Closing the book, she prepared to descend from the stage.

Philip climbed out first and reached up to help her down. "I'll see about transportation out to McDowell," he told her as he stacked their baggage near the stage-office door.

"What should I—"

"Philip?"

When heard a man call his name, they looked up.

Philip broke into a smile at the sight of a tall, dark, broad-shouldered man coming toward him. "Brand! I can't believe you're in town!"

The two men shook hands.

"How did it go back East? I'm sorry about your father. Sheri and I didn't hear about his death until after you'd gone."

"It wasn't easy, but I've taken care of everything," he said, a sadness in his tone. Then he brightened. "I have someone I'd like you to meet."

Brand looked to Mattie.

"This is my wife, Mattie. Mattie, this is Brand. I was telling you about him and his wife, Sheri."

"You got married?" Brand glanced at Philip in surprise. "You, the career officer, always too caught up in military life to even think about starting a family?" Then he smiled warmly at Mattie. "I can see why it finally happened." He shot Philip an approving look. "Mattie, it's a pleasure to meet you."

Mattie looked up at the dark-haired man and smiled, realizing this was the real "Brand, the Half-Breed Scout" she'd been reading about in the book Philip had given her. "It's good to meet you, too. I've heard wonderful things about you and your wife from Philip, and I'm really enjoying your wife's writing." She showed him the dime novel she was holding.

"Sheri is going to love you, I'm sure." Brand laughed.

"Is she here in town, too?" Philip asked.

"Yes, and she'll want to meet Mattie and see you before you head back out. I'll go see if I can find her."

"I'm going to arrange our transportation to McDowell; then we'd like to get something to eat."

"Why don't we meet you at the hotel restaurant?"

Brand left to find his wife, while Philip took care of their business. A short time later they were seated in the restaurant, and Sheri came in with Brand.

"Philip, I am so sorry about your father," Sheri said as she approached him.

"Thank you." He stood to greet the pair. "Where's the baby?"

"With Maureen right now. But what's this Brand just told me about your getting married?" She smiled at Mattie.

Philip quickly introduced them.

"I love your writing," Mattie told Sheri without hesitation as the couple joined them at their table.

The two women launched into a discussion of the book Mattie had been reading, while Philip and Brand looked on in good humor. The meal was served, and the conversation never lagged. When it was time for Philip and Mattie to leave for the fort, Sheri and Brand walked out with them to see them off.

"I'll come to the fort with Brand the next time he makes the trip," Sheri promised.

"I'll be looking forward to it," Mattie told her, and she meant it. "I'm a little intimidated by everything Philip's told me about the officers' wives."

"Don't be. You'll do just fine."

Sheri's words bolstered her confidence, and Mattie was feeling much better as they began the last leg of their journey to the fort.

Mattie had never been at a military fort before, and she was impressed by what she saw when they arrived at McDowell. The parade grounds were spacious, and the buildings looked clean and well kept. Philip ushered her toward his quarters, and she noticed as they made their way that she was given many curious looks by the soldiers they passed.

"Welcome home," Philip said as he held open the door for her.

Mattie stepped inside. *Home*. She wondered if she would ever come to think of this place that way and immediately told herself it would be better if she didn't. Theirs was a temporary arrangement. It wouldn't do for her to get too attached.

"This is lovely, Philip" she told him.

"It's not very big, but I never needed much room before."

"This will be fine," Mattie assured him. The three rooms were larger than anything she'd lived in lately.

She roamed around, peeking into the bedroom and exploring the small kitchen.

"While you're unpacking, I'm going to report in to General Mason and let him know I'm back, although word has probably reached him already," he told her with a grin.

"Talk travels fast here?"

"Very, and I'm sure there's a lot of speculation about who you are." He started for the door.

"Philip?"

He looked back.

"There is one thing. The bedroom—there's only the single bed in there."

"I'll check and see about a double."

With that he was gone, and Mattie was left staring after him. She had thought he might reassure her that he would be sleeping elsewhere. Or at least that he would get a second mattress. But it didn't look that way. Then again, she supposed, how would it look for newlyweds to be sleeping apart?

"How did everything go? Did you get your father's estate settled?" General Mason asked as Philip sat across his desk from him.

"Yes, sir. Everything's been taken care of."

"And what's this I hear that you've brought a young woman back with you?" he questioned in his usual blunt style.

Philip smiled. "I warned Mattie that news traveled fast here."

"This is my command. It's my job to know everything that happens here."

"Well, sir, I got married while I was away. My wife's name is Mattie."

The general rarely showed surprise, but Philip's statement did evoke a raised eyebrow. The general's daughter, Caroline, had had hopes of winning Captain Long's affections. She would likely be distressed by the news that he'd wed. "Married? This is quite a surprise."

"I know, sir. I met Mattie, and, well, it seemed we were meant to be together."

"Congratulations, Captain."

"Thank you, sir."

"We'll arrange a celebration of sorts to welcome your bride to the fort."

"Thank you again, sir."

"But there is something serious going on, so I am glad you're back. There have been numerous Apache raids to the north and east of us. I need you to take a patrol and ride out at first light. Make a sweep of the entire area."

"Tomorrow, sir?" Philip had hoped to have some time with Mattie to help her get oriented.

"First light. That's an order, Captain." He was unyielding.

Philip saluted. "Yes, sir." He was a military man.

General Mason watched him go. In her pique, his daughter might just be glad that he'd sent Philip on such a dangerous mission.

"You have to leave tomorrow?" Mattie was staring at him, shocked. "Why?"

"Orders, Mattie," he answered.

Usually Philip accepted such orders willingly; he'd always enjoyed the adventure. But the prospect of leaving Mattie alone, in a place where she knew absolutely no one, didn't sit well with him.

"I knew you'd have to perform your duties, but I didn't think you would be leaving so soon."

"Neither did I."

"How long will you be gone?"

"It's hard to say. Likely several weeks."

"What will you be doing?" she asked, curious.

"Tracking some Apache renegades."

Her eyes grew round. "Won't that be dangerous?"

He saw her concern and hastened to ease her fears. "We'll be fine. My men are the best. We'll find the raiders doing the killing and get back here as fast as we can."

"But you could be attacked yourselves," she said worriedly, considering his dangerous profession.

"We're always careful, Mattie."

"Couldn't someone else go in your place?"

"No. It's what I do. I'm a cavalry officer, and I'm very good at my job," he told her without false modesty. "Now, since I'm leaving so soon, there's a lot we have to do before tomorrow. I'll show you around the fort, so you'll know where everything is."

"This is where it's important we make sure everyone believes we're really married, right?"

"Right."

They left his quarters, and he introduced her to everyone they met as they walked the grounds. Philip watched Mattie with the others and was impressed by how well she handled herself. They stopped at the store and purchased the supplies she would need while he was away.

"Why, Philip, I didn't know you were back!"

Caroline Mason's call stopped Philip in his tracks, and, gentleman that he was, he was forced to greet her with Mattie on his arm. Caroline was a pretty enough girl, with her blond hair and blue eyes, but Philip had never been attracted to her. Especially not after he'd found out how dull she was.

"Hello, Caroline. It's good to see you."

"It's good to see you, too," she said flirtatiously, then turned a curious but slightly cold, assessing look on Mattie. "Who's this?"

"Caroline, may I present my wife, Mattie. Mattie, this is Caroline Mason, the general's daughter."

"It's a pleasure to meet you," Mattie said, smiling. Her smile faded, though, as she watched the other woman's expression turn even colder.

"Your wife?" Caroline bit out. Then she quickly recovered her composure. "Welcome to Fort McDowell. Well, I must be on my way."

Philip immediately steered Mattie toward the items they were after. Mattie glanced back to see the other woman striding from the shop, her back straight, her manner tense. She wondered at her response to Philip's announcement.

"Does Caroline care for you?" Mattie asked once they'd returned to his quarters.

"We've danced a few times at various social functions, but she never meant anything to me."

Mattie nodded, believing him. Certainly Philip could easily have married Caroline if he'd wanted to. It lifted her spirits a bit to know that he'd chosen her, when he could have had someone like Caroline Mason—a general's daughter and clearly a lady born and bred.

"I didn't have time to find out about getting another bed for us, but since I'm leaving first thing in the morning, I'll just sleep on the sofa tonight," he told her.

"I can take the sofa, if you'd like the bed. I don't want you to lose any sleep."

He gazed at her, knowing she meant it and wondering if she had any idea just how much sleep he had lost since their marriage. It would probably be a relief to lie alone on the sofa. At least he wouldn't have the temptation of her curled up so closely and so trustingly beside him.

"The sofa will be fine."

Later that night, as Mattie lay alone in bed, she found she was actually missing Philip. Though they'd shared only a few nights together on the trip, she'd become accustomed to his nearness, to the warmth of him and the clean, manly scent of him.

Mattie sighed and plumped up her pillow, seeking a comfort that was proving elusive. The painful reality that Philip would be riding out into danger in the morning haunted her.

Through the long, dark hours of the night she worried about his safety and silently prayed that he would be safe while he was away from her.

The depth of her concern for Philip proved to Mattie all the more that she loved him. She had never let on, for she hadn't wanted to complicate things for him, but there could be no denying the truth of her feelings. She had never known a man like Philip, and she wanted him to come back home to her—even if their marriage was a sham.

The night passed, but Mattie got little rest. When she heard Philip moving around, she got up, donned her wrapper, and sought him out. She was surprised to find him already up and dressed. She thought he had never looked more handsome, so tall and proud in his blue uniform. He was a fine commander, she could tell. He had an air of authority and control about him.

"Philip?"

He looked up from where he stood, buckling on his gunbelt. "I'm sorry, Mattie. I didn't mean to wake you."

"Do you have to leave already?"

He nodded. "We have to head out at dawn. We can say good-bye now, and you can go on back to bed if you want."

"Would it be all right if I got dressed and went with you to watch you leave?" she asked, not ready to say good-bye to him just yet.

"If you'd like to, you can, but you'll have to

hurry." He was strangely touched by her sentiment.

"I won't be but a minute," she promised, and she hurried back into the bedroom to dress.

Philip had just gathered his saddlebags when she appeared in the doorway.

"I'm ready whenever you are," Mattie told him, smiling to hide the truth of what she was feeling. She wanted to grab him and hold on to him and never let him leave, but instead she acted the demure young lady.

"We'd better go," Philip said, thinking she looked quite pretty and realizing for the first time that he just might miss her while he was away. "Will you be all right here alone?"

"I'll be fine. Don't worry about me. You just be careful."

"We will be," he assured her confidently. As deadly as the renegades could prove to be, the scouts who rode with the troops were very good. He believed all would go well.

They left the house and made their way to the staging area. Most of his men were already there, waiting for the order to move out. Philip left Mattie alone for a moment as he spoke to Sergeant O'Toole, then he returned to say his final good-bye.

"I hope everything will be all right for you here while I'm gone," he told her, feeling a bit awkward. He'd never had to say good-bye to his wife before, and certainly not with an audience watching.

"I'll be waiting for you," Mattie said, gazing up at him in the first glow of the morning light.

Philip wondered whether he should make a show of kissing her or not. It was the perfect opportunity, so he decided to take full advantage of it. It wasn't that often that he got the chance. "I'll see you when I get back."

With that, he drew her to him and pressed a tender kiss to her lips. He wanted to do more—so much more—but he couldn't. Not now. Not ever.

Mattie's heartbeat quickened as Philip's lips moved over hers. It felt so right to be in his arms, so right to be kissing him this way. But all too soon the kiss was over.

"Good-bye, Mattie," Philip said. He ended the kiss yet seemed almost reluctant to let her go. He stood staring down at her for a long moment.

"Captain? We're ready to ride, sir!" Came the call.

Mattie noticed for the first time that the soldiers had all mounted up and were watching them with bemused expressions. She'd been so caught up in Philip's kiss that she hadn't even noticed that they were the center of attention. His kiss had touched her very heart and soul.

"I have to go," Philip said almost regretfully as he let his arms fall away from her. He stepped back and started off.

Mattie didn't know what made her do it, but, impulsively, she ran after him. "Philip!"

He stopped, frowning, and turned back to

her. In a bold move, she wrapped her arms around him and kissed him soundly. A fire of desire ignited within Philip, and he crushed her against him, returning the kiss full measure.

A cheer went up from Philip's men. They knew their captain and his wife were newly wed, and they were pleased to see the display of affection.

Philip realized what he was doing then, and with iron-willed self-control, he broke off the kiss and set Mattie from him. "Take care."

"You, too," she whispered, blushing at the men's cheers.

Mattie watched as Philip mounted his impressive black stallion. When he reined the powerful horse in so he could glance her way one last time, Mattie saluted him smartly and called out, "I'll miss you, my general."

Philip smiled in spite of himself as he led his troops from the fort.

Chapter Eight

Mattie was crying as she sat alone and miserable in the parlor of Philip's quarters. She wondered, as feelings of unworthiness overwhelmed her, why she had ever agreed to be a part of Philip's deception. She should have known that she wouldn't fit in here. She should have known she wouldn't fool anybody with her act of being a lady.

Forlorn tears trailed down her cheeks as she thought about what she'd just overheard at the sutler's store. She'd wanted to get out of the house for a while, so she had gone to the store to look around. While she'd been wandering up and down the aisles, Caroline Mason had come in with her mother, Gloria. It was obvious they hadn't known she was there, for they had been talking about her.

"I don't know why Philip married that Mattie, Mother. She's nothing but a slut!" Caroline had said.

"Maybe that was exactly why," her mother had commented cattily.

"Do you mean you think she forced him to marry her?"

"Who knows? She certainly acts like a loose woman. Just yesterday, I saw her walking across the parade ground with Lieutenant Roberts. I wonder what they've been up to while her husband's away?"

Their conversation had continued, but Mattie had been so aghast at their cruel insinuations that she'd fled the store. Lieutenant Roberts had been helping her carry the groceries she'd bought. He had seen her struggling with them and had come to her aid. He had left her at her door, never venturing inside. He'd been a perfect gentleman, but Gloria had made the innocent encounter sound so dirty, so vulgar.

Her confidence had been shattered by the two women's remarks, and she wished with all her heart that Philip would hurry back. She wanted him there. She missed him.

A knock came at the door, surprising her. Now that she realized how the women at the fort felt about her, she really didn't want to talk to or see anyone. Reluctantly, she wiped her eyes and went to answer the door. She was surprised to find Sheri standing there, holding her baby.

"Would you like some company? Brand had to come to the fort today, so Becky and I came with him." She had been smiling when she started to talk, but her gaiety faded when she realized Mattie had been crying. "Mattie? What's wrong? Are you all right? Has something happened to Philip?"

Sheri didn't wait any longer for an invitation. She stepped inside and closed the door. Mattie still hadn't spoken, so Sheri went on. "What's the matter? Can I do anything to help?"

Mattie sniffed loudly as she tried to pull herself together. "I'm fine, and so is Philip, as far as I know."

"As far as you know?"

"He had to ride out on patrol the first morning after we arrived here."

"If he's safe, then why are you crying?"

"It's nothing really." Mattie had a great desire to confide in someone, but she had to keep their secret.

"I don't believe that for a moment. You wouldn't be this upset if it was nothing." The baby began to get restless and fuss. "Can we sit down and talk for a while?"

"Oh, yes. I'm sorry."

They went to sit in the parlor, and Becky quieted immediately, content to play near her mother's side.

"She's a beautiful baby," Mattie managed.

"Thank you. She's our pride and joy. She already has her father wrapped around her little finger," Sheri told her with a grin.

They made small talk for a few moments, and Sheri spied the book Mattie had been reading.

"You really were serious about liking my writing."

"Very much," Mattie responded, glad to direct the conversation away from her tears. "Your books are fun. They keep me from being too lonely while Philip's away."

"It must be difficult for you, left here all alone like this. It's terrible that he had to ride out so soon. After all, you're newlyweds!"

"He had to go. He said some renegade Apaches had been raiding, and he had to go after them."

Sheri nodded, knowing how dangerous the Apaches could be. "We'll just pray that everything goes well for him and that he gets back to you real soon. Did he know how long he'd be gone?"

"He thought at least a few weeks. It's only been one week now, and I'm already missing him." She paused and smiled a teary smile. "Actually, I was missing my general as soon as he rode away."

"Your general?" Sheri laughed.

"That's my nickname for him. Philip can be quite impressive, you know."

Sheri thought back to her first encounter with him. "Yes, he can be. When I first met him, he was a lieutenant. He's proven himself to be a strong leader and an excellent cavalryman. Maybe one day soon he really will be a general."

Both women laughed.

"You're laughing now. That's good," Sheri told her.

Mattie smiled. "I'm glad you came by. It's been a rough morning."

"Do you want to talk about it?"

Mattie supposed it wouldn't hurt to confide a little, so she told Sheri about overhearing the general's wife and daughter talking about her at the sutler's store.

"Oh, Mattie." Sheri sounded stricken. "That's terrible. I am so sorry."

"Lieutenant Roberts was just being a gentleman yesterday," Mattie said, her eyes welling up with tears again. "He carried some groceries for me, and he left me at the door. He didn't even come inside."

"Don't worry. I'm sure that even if Philip heard any such gossip, he wouldn't believe a word."

"I hope you're right. It's just that—" Mattie stopped when she realized how close she'd come to blurting out the whole truth.

"Philip loves you, Mattie. He wouldn't have married you if he didn't," Sheri said in reassurance.

A great sorrow filled Mattie. "If you only knew," she said with a sad laugh.

"I know about love. Don't forget I do a lot of research for my books, and I know a love story when I see one. That man loves you, Mattie."

"This time I'm afraid you're wrong, Sheri," she said in a choked voice.

"Mattie, what are you talking about?"

"Can I trust you, Sheri?" Mattie felt in her heart that she could, but she needed her word on it.

"Of course you can," Sheri said sympathetically, clearly eager to help in any way she could.

Mattie drew a ragged breath and started at the beginning. She told Sheri of her parents' death, of her desperation to get a job to support herself, and of ending up at the Palace Saloon. She expected disapproval when she told Sheri she'd been a barmaid and was amazed when she found the other woman smiling at her.

"I'm proud of you, Mattie. You're a survivor. Not many women could do what you did."

"I wish there had been some other way. But then again, if I had been working somewhere else, I never would have met Philip."

"How exactly did you meet?" Sheri asked, urging her on.

Mattie told her about that night at the saloon, how a drunken Micah Johnson had harassed her and how Philip had come to her defense.

"He is a gentleman," Sheri agreed.

She went on to explain how Cal had fired her.

"He fired you because you wouldn't prostitute yourself?" Sheri was shocked.

Mattie nodded. "It was terrible, and then, when I left, Micah and his friends were waiting for me. They grabbed me and—"

"They didn't—?" Sheri looked horrified.

"They tried, but Philip saved me—again. I think it was in that moment that I knew I loved him," she said simply.

"And he swept you off your feet and you were married?" Sheri guessed dreamily.

"In one of your books, it would have worked that way, but not in real life."

Sheri gave her a questioning look. "What happened?"

Mattie drew another ragged breath, meeting Sheri's gaze. "I didn't think I was ever going to see him again. But when he found out from the bartender the next morning that I'd been fired, he came to my room at the boardinghouse and made me an offer I couldn't refuse."

"An offer?" She sounded confused.

Mattie explained. "Philip's father's will stated that Philip had to marry within six months of the execution of the will, and stay married for twelve months, or he would forfeit his entire inheritance."

"No! What parent would do that to his child?"

Mattie shrugged. "So you see, Philip asked me to marry him, and stay married to him for a year, so he could claim his inheritance. It's to be a marriage in name only, and at the end of the year he'll pay me a generous amount and give me an annulment. The only trouble is, Sheri, I love him. I fell in love with him that night he saved me from those men. He's wonderful and—"

"And he doesn't realize what a treasure he has in you," Sheri finished with a conspiratorial grin. "How would you like to make this marriage a real one?"

"Oh, Sheri." Mattie looked at her hopefully for the first time. "Is there any way I can make Philip fall in love with me?"

"I think he's already well on his way."

"You do?"

"Yes. We just have to make him realize it."

" 'We'? You'd help me?"

"Absolutely," Sheri said with conviction. "I like Philip, and I think he'd be making the biggest mistake of his life if he let you go."

"Thank you." Mattie's words were heartfelt. "But—"

"But what?"

"I'm just afraid that everyone is going to think like Caroline and her mother. I'm not a slut, but I may not be good enough for Philip. He deserves someone who is—"

"Exactly like you," Sheri finished. "You are lovely and smart and kind and thoughtful."

"But Philip is an officer, and he deserves a real lady for his wife. I don't know how to be a real lady."

"You *are* a real lady. The general's wife and daughter may pretend to be ladies, but on the inside, they're mean and vicious. How dare they say those things about you?"

Mattie shrugged, feeling helpless.

"All we have to do is work on your self-confidence and polish you up a bit."

"And we can do that?"

"Yes, we can—starting right now," Sheri said. "When Philip gets back, he's going to be thrilled to see you."

Sheri gave Mattie a confident smile as she began to plot.

* * *

Philip and his men were tired as they made camp for the night. He ordered guards posted but allowed no fires to be built. They were closing in on the renegades, and he didn't want to reveal their own location. After making sure everything was secure, Philip bedded down himself. He kept his rifle and his sidearm close at hand. The renegades were ruthless, and he had to be ready for trouble at any moment.

They'd been trailing the Apaches for endless miles and days, and he believed they were close now. His scouts had told him that the band was hiding out at a canyon just up ahead, and he intended to attack with full force at first light. With any luck at all, they would trap the murderous Apaches there and end the reign of terror they'd been inflicting on the area.

Philip needed rest, but a vision of Mattie slipped into his thoughts: the image of her with her hair swept aside for him as he'd unfastened her gown. She was lovely. There was no denying it. And he missed her.

The realization shocked Philip. *Missed her?* Supposedly his "wife" meant nothing to him. They were friends, he supposed, but nothing more. True, they were married, but not really. Then the memory of the kiss she'd given him as he was leaving returned with a vengeance. It had been surprisingly sensual and definitely heavenly. He'd found that he'd hated to ride away from her that day. And then she'd jauntily saluted him!

Philip smiled in the darkness. Mattie had grit *and* wit. And he admitted to himself that he certainly would enjoy kissing her a whole lot more. No other woman had ever intrigued him the way she did. She'd faced rough times and places and people in her life, yet there was still an air of innocence about her that drew him to her. He wondered how she was doing back at the fort. He'd regretted leaving her alone there so abruptly, and he was eager to get back to her. He missed her.

Again Philip's smile turned to a puzzled frown.

He missed her? he questioned once more.

Damned right he did, he finally admitted to himself as he accepted the reality of what he was feeling. He loved her.

That thought left him stunned.

He loved her?

Was that why she seemed to be constantly in his thoughts? Was that why he found himself worrying so about her comfort and welfare? He had never been in love before. Was that why it had taken him so long to understand what it was he was feeling?

Mattie certainly was different from any other woman he'd ever known. She was brave and smart, thoughtful and kind. What more could he have been looking for in a wife? Mattie was perfect.

He grinned. The good news was, she was already his wife.

He scowled. The bad news was, she didn't want to be. Theirs was a business arrangement, nothing more. Money was the only reason she'd agreed to marry him. She didn't love him.

Then a flicker of hope shone in his dark thoughts. Just because she didn't love him now didn't mean she couldn't fall in love with him. He hadn't exactly courted her or tried to charm her in any way. They'd been married less than a month. He still had eleven more to go. Surely he could find a way to win her heart before the year was up.

As he lay there in the night, Philip made a battle plan. He would track down and defeat the renegade Apaches. Then he would lay siege to Mattie's heart. This was a war, and he intended to win it.

It might not be easy to win Mattie's love, considering how he'd treated her so far, but he wouldn't give up.

And after he'd won it—Philip wouldn't even allow himself to consider the alternative—he was going to spend the rest of his life proving to her just how much he really cared.

Chapter Nine

Early the next morning Mattie heard shouts coming from the parade ground. She hurried from the house to see what all the excitement was about. Her heart skipped a beat as she saw a column of soldiers riding in, and she hoped against hope that it was Philip and his men returning. They looked hot, dirty, and exhausted, yet their expressions were proud.

"Did you find them?" someone called out.

"We got 'em!" one of the cavalrymen replied as he rode by.

Mattie searched each man's face, looking for Philip. *Where was he?* When she finally saw him, she broke into a broad smile. He was riding tall and proud in the saddle and looked every bit the commander that he was.

Mattie ran toward him without a moment's

delay. She didn't care what the other wives were doing. She knew only a desire to go to her husband and assure herself that he was all right.

"Philip!" she called out to him.

Even with all the noise and clamor at their return, Philip heard Mattie's call. He looked her way, and across the distance his gaze locked with hers.

Philip had never known an emotion as fierce as the need he had right then to hold her. He wheeled his mount around and rode toward her. Sawing back on the reins, he all but threw himself from his horse's back and swept Mattie into his arms.

They stood in the middle of the parade ground, completely immersed in each other, unaware of the activity around them, as if they were the only two people in the world.

Philip looked down at Mattie. He wanted to tell her that he'd missed her and that he loved her and that he never wanted to leave her again, but "I'm back," was all he could manage.

"I'm glad," Mattie said in a soft voice.

Boldly she looped her arms around his neck and urged him down to kiss her. She felt him tense as their lips touched, and she hoped that was a good sign. Sheri had counseled her on ways to be enticing to a man, and she fully intended to use all her friend's advice on her husband. Mattie made sure her kiss was warm and welcoming, and when they broke apart, she smiled up at him sweetly.

"I missed you, my general," she whispered.

"I missed you, too," he admitted in a gruff voice.

"Captain Long!"

General Mason's shout interrupted the intimacy of the moment, and Philip stepped away from his bride. "I have to report in."

"Will you hurry back to me?"

"As quickly as I can," he promised. As a man who prided himself on his career above all else, it amazed him that he meant every word he'd just said to her.

An hour later Philip returned to his quarters. It was the first time he'd ever come home to anyone, and he found he liked the feeling as he let himself in to find Mattie waiting for him. He had, however, gotten his rampant desire for her back under some semblance of control. He'd realized as he'd listened to the general drone on about what had happened at the fort in Philip's absence that he had come very close to picking Mattie up in his arms and carrying her into the house and making love to her. The urgent need had been real, but logic now dictated that he woo her and win her love first. He had promised he wouldn't hurt her or take advantage, and he was going to keep that promise.

Mattie had been wondering what was taking Philip so long, and she was delighted when he returned. But he seemed a bit remote to her, so she kept her distance from him. She reminded herself that the kiss they'd shared on the parade ground had been merely an act for those watching them, nothing more.

"How did your meeting with General Mason go?" she asked.

"Fine. Routine. But he did announce one interesting thing," he answered as he started to strip off his shirt so he could get cleaned up. "There's going to be a reception for us tonight at seven o'clock."

"There is?" She couldn't believe it. "Why?"

"To officially welcome you," he told her. "If I hadn't had to ride out so quickly, it probably would have been held that first weekend we arrived."

"Oh." Mattie was not looking forward to the party. She didn't trust the general's wife or daughter and could just imagine what they might do or say tonight.

"You don't sound very excited about it," he said as he tossed his shirt aside and glanced at her.

"I'm not."

"Why? It'll be a good opportunity to meet everyone."

"I think I've met all the people I want to meet here," she said quietly.

"Did something happen while I was gone?"

"You said you wanted us to always be honest, right?"

"Yes." Philip turned serious.

"Then you need to hear this from me before you hear it from someone else," she began. And she went on to tell him about Gloria and Caroline Mason's remarks at the store. "Lieutenant Roberts did help me carry groceries, but he was a perfect gentleman."

Philip grinned at her. "That's good to know."

She frowned, wondering why he was smiling. "It is?"

"Yes," he told her. "I asked Roberts to keep an eye on you for me. I'm glad he did."

Mattie stared at him as tears burned in her eyes. He had cared enough to ask someone to watch over her. It was one more reason to love him. "But what about what the women were saying?"

"Mattie," he said patiently, coming to stand before her.

Mattie found herself gazing at the broad, powerful expanse of his chest. She wanted to reach out and touch him, to caress the hard-muscled ridges of his chest and shoulders, but that kind of familiarity was forbidden to her. She clasped her hands before her and lifted her gaze to his.

"I warned you on the way here that you might have trouble with some of the women. Just ignore them. I know how they are, and I also know that Caroline is probably more than a bit jealous of you."

"So she did love you then."

"No. There was no love between us. I might have seemed a good match for her, but I wasn't interested. You're the woman I married, Mattie." He made the statement firmly, wanting to put her fears to rest about any relationship he might have had with Caroline.

Mattie ached to believe that he'd said that to impress her with his devotion, but she knew better. She moved away, needing to distance herself from him, and busied herself laying out clean clothes for him while he bathed.

* * *

The day passed quickly. Philip had duties to attend to around the fort, so she was left to her own devices. She started getting ready for the party early, wanting to make sure she looked her best for Philip. She decided to wear the dress she'd gotten married in, for it was her most fashionable gown. Sheri had shown her how to style her hair up, and she worked on it for quite a while, artfully arranging it so she would look more sophisticated. She hoped Philip would approve. She had just put the finishing touches to her coiffure when she heard him return.

"Mattie?"

"I'm in here," she called out.

Philip was not looking forward to the reception tonight, but he knew there was no way out of it. He would do what was expected of him, but he would rather have had an evening alone with Mattie. He strode toward the bedroom door and stopped short at the sight of her. He blinked, finding it hard to believe that this was the same girl who'd served him drinks at the Palace Saloon. Any and all traces of that Mattie were gone. In her place was a sleek, gorgeous woman who took his breath away.

"You are beautiful," he said tightly. He forced himself to remain where he was, when all he wanted to do was sweep her up in his embrace and carry her to the bed that was oh, so near by.

"You like my hair this way?" she asked nervously. She wanted to look her best so he would be proud of her, but she was having trouble reading his expression.

"Very much. I guess I'd better get ready, too, if we're going to be on time for this reception."

Mattie quickly left the room so he would have privacy while he was changing. Philip watched her go, admiring the view.

A short time later, as Philip and Mattie drew near the general's home, they could hear music coming from inside. He glanced down at her, thinking she might be a bit nervous going into this reception. He was surprised and pleased to see that she seemed calm and sure of herself.

"Good evening, General Mason, Mrs. Mason, Caroline," Philip greeted them as he and Mattie entered the house.

"Good evening, Captain Long, Mrs. Long," the general and his wife replied.

Caroline stood with her parents in the receiving line but managed only a tight smile. The look she turned on Mattie was cold.

Mattie saw it and chose to ignore it. She smiled serenely at the other woman and held on to Philip's arm. She would do him proud tonight. After tonight, no one would ever say she wasn't a lady again.

There were many people at the reception when they arrived, and Philip drew Mattie around the room, making sure that she met all his friends. When the dancing began, he turned to her and asked, "Would you like to dance?"

She was so glad Sheri had drilled her on dancing, which she'd never done before. "I'd love to, my general," she told him, lightly resting her hand on his shoulder as he led her onto the dance floor.

"Keep it to a whisper tonight if you're going to call me general," he teased.

"Yes, sir."

Her expression was innocent enough, but there was a hint of devilishness in the curve of her lips. Philip was staring down at her, very, very tempted to kiss her. Instead, he concentrated on dancing, sweeping her around the floor. She moved gracefully with him, and he was delighted that she was so good at the steps.

"The locket looks wonderful with that dress," he told her. "My mother would be most pleased."

"Your mother?" The knowledge touched her heart.

"It was hers," he admitted. "The wedding ring, too."

Mattie looked down at the simple gold band that marked her as his. "I'm proud to wear them. She must have been a wonderful lady."

"She was," he confirmed.

The song ended, and Philip seemed sorry to let Mattie go.

The musicians almost immediately started up again, but before Philip could prevent it, Mattie was claimed for the dance by one of the single young officers. Philip smiled and bowed slightly to her as the man led her away.

Philip got himself a cup of punch and went to stand at the side of the dance floor. He noticed that Caroline was not dancing, but he made no move to go to her and invite her to dance. He wanted nothing to do with her, knowing what Mattie had told him. He remained where he was, watching his wife. When that dance ended and another started, Mattie was claimed by Lieutenant Roberts before Philip could get to her. She gave him an apologetic look, but he only smiled in approval. It wasn't often that a new woman came to the fort, and he understood how much the single men enjoyed dancing with a lady. He'd felt the same way—before Mattie.

"Your wife is most popular tonight, isn't she?" Caroline said as she came to stand at his side.

"Yes, she is," Philip agreed. He was certain that Caroline wanted to dance with him, but he was not going to ask her. He turned his attention back to Mattie's dancing.

Caroline was stung by the way he was ignoring her. "There are things you don't know about that precious wife of yours." Her tone was hateful.

"Really?" He did not even glance at her but kept his gaze warmly on his wife.

"Yes, really!" she said, growing angry. "While you were gone, she was acting like a slut. Why, she was flirting with the very man she's dancing with!"

Philip stiffened at her words. He turned on

Caroline, his temper barely under control. "I would be careful whom you say such things to Caroline," he ground out.

"That's why I'm telling you," she said, trying to sound sympathetic. "I thought it was important that you know your wife's a—"

"Don't say it," he snarled.

Caroline saw that his anger was real, and she realized, too late, that perhaps she'd handled this the wrong way. But it was too late to change course now. "Well, it's just that I saw them together, and I thought you should know when your wife is whoring around."

"For your information, Miss Mason, Lieutenant Roberts is my friend. Since Mattie didn't know anyone here at McDowell, I asked him to keep an eye on her. I had a feeling that you 'ladies' wouldn't be all that welcoming, and it looks as if I was right."

"But—" Her eyes were wide as she looked up at him, frightened by the anger she saw in his expression.

"I think you've said enough for one evening, Miss Mason. If you'll excuse me?" He turned his back and walked away from her.

Caroline watched him go, her expression pale and stricken.

The music ended, and Philip went straight to Mattie and took her in his arms as the next song began.

"You look angry," she said. "Is something wrong?"

Philip looked down at her and saw the openness and beauty that he loved. "No, nothing's wrong. In fact, everything is very right, Mrs. Long."

He had never called her that before. "I'm glad."

"So am I." He tightened his arms about her just a little to bring her even closer to him.

Mattie loved the feel of his arms around her. The other two men had been nice to dance with, but only Philip's touch sent shivers of awareness through her. The power of him, the scent of him, the warmth of him, all touched her. She loved him and never wanted to be away from him again. She wanted to tell him of her love, but she held back, fearful of his reaction.

And then their gazes met.

In that moment, somehow, they both knew the truth. Passion flared in the depths of Philip's eyes. Mattie instinctively responded, her pulse quickened, and she trembled before the power of his desire.

"I'm new at this military-wife thing. I don't know the protocol, but would it be rude if we left now?"

"You just read my mind, wife," Philip said in a husky voice. "Let's go."

He swung her around and maneuvered them closer to the door. Without speaking to anyone or saying any good-byes, they slipped away into the cool, dark night.

Chapter Ten

Outside, Philip took Mattie's hand and led her quickly away, seeking someplace where it would be just the two of them, alone and uninterrupted. As they passed a deserted walkway, he drew her into its shadowed privacy.

They stood together, neither speaking, just looking at each other. Then, ever so slowly, Philip drew Mattie to him and kissed her. His mouth claimed hers hungrily, telling her without words just how much he wanted her, how much he needed her. She responded without reserve, wrapping her arms around him and glorying in his nearness.

Philip gave a low growl as he ended the kiss. He knew that if he continued it there, they just might not make it back to his quarters. Mattie looked up at him, a bit confused by his abrupt ending to a wonderful embrace.

"Let's go home, Mattie," he said softly, and he took her hand as he started toward their house.

Neither spoke, as if each were fearful of breaking the magical spell of the moment.

Overhead, the moon was a silver sliver surrounded by twinkling stars. Mattie made a wish on the first one she saw.

Philip was tormented. He loved Mattie. He wanted to make love to her. He wanted to hold her and never let her go. But he still wasn't quite sure how she felt. True, her kiss was heavenly, and she seemed to be willing, but what if she wasn't? When they reached their quarters, he opened the door for her. He followed her inside and locked the door behind them.

Mattie went to light a lamp, but Philip stopped her. He took her in his arms again and held her close. She melted against him, reveling in the intimacy of the moment. She wondered, though, why he wanted to hold her. There was no one around now.

"Philip," she ventured, needing to know what he was thinking, "we're home. We don't have to pretend anymore."

"I'm not pretending," he finally admitted.

"You're not?" Mattie pulled away to look up at her general.

"No, Mattie. I love you," he said simply. He kissed her again, tenderly, softly. "I want you to be my wife in all ways."

She was stunned, and tears filled her eyes. She'd never dreamed he would fall in love with her, despite her planning with Sheri. Deep in her heart, she'd doubted he would ever love her. She was Mattie Jackson, barmaid from the Palace Saloon.

"Sweetheart, what's wrong?" he asked at her silence.

"You're my general, Philip. You deserve better than someone like me. You deserve a real lady," she told him, her voice choked with emotion.

"Ah, Mattie, how many times do I have to tell you? You're more of a lady than anyone I know."

He kissed her passionately this time, wanting to feel her response, wanting to know that she wanted him as much as he wanted her. Mattie needed no further encouragement. She surrendered to him, conquered by the power of his love.

Philip's lips left hers to trace a pattern of fire down her throat. She arched against him, wanting to know more. He lifted his hands to pull the pins from her hair, and the dark, glorious mane tumbled about her shoulders in a cascade of curls. He raked his fingers through the silken tresses, then sought the back of her gown and unfastened it. The dress slipped from her shoulders, but this time Mattie didn't try to stop it. She stood before him clad only in her petticoats and chemise.

"You're beautiful, Mattie," Philip said, reaching out to caress her.

She swayed weakly against him, over-whelmed by the emotions that filled her. He swept her up into his arms and carried her into the bedroom, laying her gently upon the single bed. After shedding all his clothing but his pants, for he didn't want to frighten her, he followed her down upon the bed, covering her body with his. He began to caress her, taking infinite care to arouse her and please her. He loosened her chemise and freed her breasts to his caresses and kisses.

Mattie gasped in shock at the exciting sensations his touch aroused but soon gave herself over completely to his ministrations. She had never been intimate with a man before, but this was Philip. This was her husband. This was the moment she'd been waiting for, longing for. He had told her that he loved her. But with the one shred of sanity she had left, she knew she had to make sure he really wanted this—really wanted her.

"Philip?"

He lifted his head to gaze down at her, all the love he felt for her shining in his eyes.

"You know that if we make love"—she blushed before she finished—"we won't be able to get an annulment."

He smiled at her and chuckled. "Good!"

"But—"

"Mattie, remember when you told me that I was your general and you'd follow any order I gave you?"

"Yes," she answered hesitantly.

"Then love me, Mattie," he told her softly, "and that's an order that stands for a lifetime."

"Yes, sir," she answered.

And she did.

They lived happily ever after.

Five Gold Rings

Constance O'Banyon,
Stobie Piel,
Lynsay Sands,
Flora Speer

In the Year of Our Lord, 1135, Menton Castle is the same as any other: It has nobles and minstrels, knights and servants. Yet from the great hall to the scullery there are signs that the house is in an uproar. This Yuletide season is to be one of passion and merriment. The master of the keep has returned. With him come several travelers, some weary with laughter, some tired of tears. But in all of their stories—whether lords a'leapin' or maids a'milkin'—there is one gift that their true loves give to them. And in the winter moonlight, each of the castle's inhabitants will soon see the magic of the season and the joy that can come from five gold rings.

___4612-1 $5.50 US/$6.50 CAN

Dorchester Publishing Co., Inc.
P.O. Box 6640
Wayne, PA 19087-8640

Seduction By CHOCOLATE

Nina Bangs, ♥ Lisa Cach, Thea Devine, ♥ Penelope Neri

Sweet Anticipation . . . More alluring than Aphrodite, more irresistible than Romeo, the power of this sensuous seductress is renowned. It teases the senses, tempting even the most staid; it inspires wantonness, demanding surrender. Whether savored or devoured, one languishes under its tantalizing spell. To sample it is to crave it. To taste it is to yearn for it. Habit-forming, mouth-watering, sinfully decadent, what promises to sate the hungers of the flesh more? Four couples whet their appetites to discover that seduction by chocolate feeds a growing desire and leads to only one conclusion: Nothing is more delectable than love.

___4667-9 $5.50 US/$6.50 CAN

Masquerade

Katherine Deauxpille, Elaine Fox, Linda Jones, & Sharon Pisacreta

In the whirling decadence of Carnival, all forms of desire are unveiled. Amidst the crush of those attending the balls, filling the waterways, and traveling in the gondolas of post-Napoleonic Venice, nothing is unavailable—should one know where to look. Amongst the throngs are artists and seducers, nobles and thieves, and not all of them are what they appear. But in that frantic congress of people lurks something more than animal passion, something more than a paradise of the flesh. Love, should one seek it out, can be found within this shadowy communion of people—and as four beauties learn, all one need do is unmask it.

___4577-X $5.99 US/$6.99 CAN

Winter Wonderland

**Emma Craig,
Leigh Greenwood,
Amanda Harte,
Linda O. Johnston**

Christmas is coming, and the streets are alive with the sounds of the season: "Silver Bells" and sleigh rides, jingle bells and carolers. Choruses of "Here Comes Santa Claus" float over the snow-covered landscape, bringing the joy of the holiday to revelers as they deck the halls and string the lights "Up on the Rooftop." And when the songs of the season touch four charmed couples, melody turns to romance and harmony turns to passion. For these "Merry Gentlemen" and their lovely ladies will learn that with the love they have found, not even a spring thaw will cool their desire or destroy their winter wonderland.

___52339-6 $5.99 US/$6.99 CAN

Midsummer Night's Magic

Four of Love Spell's hottest authors, four times the charm!

EMMA CRAIG
"MacBroom Sweeps Clean"

Stuck in an arranged marriage to a Scottish lord, Lily wonders if she'll ever find true love—until a wee Broonie decides to teach the couple a thing or two about Highland magic.

TESS MALLORY
"The Fairy Bride"

Visiting Ireland with her stuffy fiancé, Erin dreams she'll be swept into a handsome stranger's enchanted world—and soon long to be his fairy bride.

AMY ELIZABETH SAUNDERS
"Whatever You Wish"

A trip through time into the arms of an English lord might just be enough to convince Meredyth that maybe, just maybe, wishes do come true.

PAM McCUTCHEON
"The Trouble With Fairies"

Fun-loving Nick and straight-laced Kate have a marriage destined for trouble, until the fateful night Nick hires a family of Irish brownies to clean up his house—and his love life.

___52209-8 $5.50 US/$6.50 CAN

Dorchester Publishing Co., Inc.
P.O. Box 6640
Wayne, PA 19087-8640

Please add $1.75 for shipping and handling for the first book and $.50 for each book thereafter. NY, NYC, and PA residents, please add appropriate sales tax. No cash, stamps, or C.O.D.s. All orders shipped within 6 weeks via postal service book rate. Canadian orders require $2.00 extra postage and must be paid in U.S. dollars through a U.S. banking facility.

Name_____
Address_____
City_____State_____Zip_____
I have enclosed $_____ in payment for the checked book(s).
Payment <u>must</u> accompany all orders. ❑ Please send a free catalog.

ATTENTION ROMANCE CUSTOMERS!

SPECIAL TOLL-FREE NUMBER
1-800-481-9191

Call Monday through Friday
10 a.m. to 9 p.m.
Eastern Time
Get a free catalogue,
join the Romance Book Club,
and order books using your
Visa, MasterCard,
or Discover®

Leisure
Books

Love Spell

GO ONLINE WITH US AT DORCHESTERPUB.COM